KISS'D

D. C. Reep and E. A. Allen

1

I wonder if Aunt Connie will want me to join her weekly séances this summer. She always said sixteen was the best age to begin meeting ghosts.

Before I touch the antique brass door knocker, the door opens, and I'm enveloped in Aunt Connie's lavender scent, her arms tight around me. "Jenny, I'm so glad to see you." She pulls me and my suitcase into the dark paneled hallway. "When you called, I was so thrilled to have you visit for an entire summer. It's been four years since you were here." She steps back and looks me over. "How awful you got a concussion at a track meet of all things. I told your mother hurdle jumping was too dangerous."

I keep a reassuring smile on my face. "I'm all right. The doctor said I'd have headaches for a while and strange sensations while my brain heals, but the headaches should stop before too long." No point in telling her I've been hearing mysterious noises and seeing gauzy figures drifting around me since my fall on the track—I didn't even describe them to the doctor. "Can't fly though—Portugal with mom and dad was out. So you have me."

She shakes her head, silver earrings tinkling like wind chimes, and wild, red curls bobbing on the top of her head. "Portugal of all places. Last year it was Sicily. Why college professors want to spend the summer in musty archives I'll never understand." She peers through the window panel in the front door and frowns at the gray sedan parked in the gravel drive. "Did they let you drive all the way from Chicago by yourself with a concussion?"

"Sure." Her concern gives me a familiar warm feeling. My parents never worry about me—or notice me. Whenever I'm sick, I call Aunt Connie for love and sympathy.

Another hug. "Are you hungry? Wait, unpack first. I have your old room ready." She scoops up Snowball, her sixteen-year-old cat, and flips the light switch on the wall.

I follow her up the stairway to the second floor where frosted globes in bronze sconces cast faint light in the dark hallway. The bedroom hasn't changed. Pink roses cover the wallpaper, and the antique oak dresser is topped with a mirror, the glass so speckled with age, my face is wavy when I stare at myself. My short curly hair looks like a dark cloud around my head. The carved oak headboard towers over the double bed covered in the blue quilt embroidered with pink roses.

Socks and underwear go into dresser drawers. Jeans and shirts go into the closet while Aunt Connie sits on the bed and chatters about how wonderful it is to have me visit. She points to the battered wooden trunk at the foot of the bed. "There are extra pillows and blankets. It's June, but the air gets chilly at night." After she straightens a row of tiny porcelain figurines on the dresser, she sends a wide smile my way. "I'm so excited. I've told all the regulars you'll be here to help with my séances. We'll have such fun all summer."

She looks so happy I smother my impulse to tell her I don't believe in ghosts. "Great! When's the next one?"

"Friday. You'll have time to rest." She carefully moves a porcelain shepherdess closer to a porcelain lamb on the dresser top. "You'll bring us luck in reaching the spirits. I feel it."

Dinner is meat loaf and salad. I'm so tired I fall into bed by nine o'clock and adjust the pillows only once before my eyes close. Hours later, I jerk awake, my legs kick out, sending a pillow onto the floor. The house is old enough to have creaks and groans, but I hear nothing. Faint moonlight glows through the window and forms wispy shadows on the walls. I sit up, wrap my arms around my knees, and take in quiet shallow breaths.

Then I see them. Just fragile streams of protoplasm? No—phantoms—floating in the air—not clear enough for me to make out what kind of figures they are—or if they're figures at all. My concussion—I must be hallucinating. I squeeze my eyes shut, and when I open them, the ghostly swirling threads of light are gone. Lying back, I listen to the faint stirrings of the trees outside. I don't sleep again.

By Friday, I've been into nearby Fort Jefferson and reconnected with everyone who remembers me, including my old friend Dan Harris. We used to be the same height, but now he's taller with broad shoulders from swimming. His brown eyes are still friendly, and the birthmark on his wrist is still fiery red. His grandmother is Aunt Connie's best friend, and when Dan and I were kids, she gave us chocolate milk and oatmeal cookies every afternoon. She tells me she's excited about the next séance. Dan grins and winks at me over her head. I hold back a smile.

When I was younger, I ignored Aunt Connie's weekly séances, but now, as I help her arrange the dining room, she explains how reaching the dead is a formal process.

"I don't call on the spirits from Thanksgiving to April. Winter is so cold in northern Wisconsin. The spirits don't want to visit us then."

"Do ghosts really care about weather?" I pull the last chair into place at the dining table and pause to rub the back of my neck. A headache is starting—little pinpricks of pain.

"Of course spirits care about weather!" Aunt Connie played in community theaters for years, and she's very dramatic when she's excited. She makes a sweeping gesture and smoothes the fringe on her purple shawl. "Jenny, spirits may be on the other side, but they have preferences. They won't appear just because I call them. They do as they please. If they sense anything negative, they simply will not cooperate."

I nod to imply I'm listening, but a dark fuzzy spot dances in my vision, cutting off the edge of anything I look at. I blink a few times, looking around the room, testing the black spot, making sure it's really there.

Aunt Connie notices. "Is it a headache?"

"I'm not sure." A lie. I force a smile. "Should we set out the candles?"

"Oh yes, the spirits prefer candlelight. Electric lights frighten them away."

I take a box of lemon-scented candles from the glass cabinet, stepping carefully to avoid Snowball purring around my ankles. The distinct shades in the round wooden table create a pattern like twelve pie slices, and each slice gets its own candle. When Aunt Connie turns off the overhead chandelier, the candlelight puts wavering shadows on the walls. She sets a quartz crystal cut on twelve sides on a copper plate in the center of the table. I keep a serious expression on my face while she explains that the twelve sides represent the twelve astrological signs. Is all this séance stuff is written down somewhere? I don't ask because I might get a long, multi-part answer.

"And lovely fragrances," she adds. "Spirits like sweet smells."

I resist pointing out since ghosts are dead, they've already had a stretch of very bad smells. Her special mix of crushed flowers and leaves in little dishes on the table sends a heavy, sweet aroma around the room.

Aunt Connie's five "regulars," arrive for the séance at exactly five minutes to seven. Dan drops his grandmother off at the back door because she's on a walker, recovering from a hip replacement while the other women troop through the front door. Their excited voices fill the air, but when I pull the sliding doors to the dining room closed, they turn serious and silently take their places at the table. Candles flicker, but most of the room is dark and shadowy. The dark spot in my vision makes it impossible for me to see clearly, and when I stare directly at the candles, a rainbow halo surrounds each flame.

Aunt Connie rings a little brass bell. "Let us concentrate now as we reach for those beyond us." She rings the bell again. "Come Spirits, we await your presence. We have called you from the other side. Show us that you have returned. Spirits, we seek answers. Come to us now so we can meet." The ladies begin to chant softly, but I keep silent, the only nonbeliever at the table.

"Spirits, hear us. We call you from our time, but we know all the ages swirl around us, overlapping, bringing the past closer, letting us reach you, letting you visit us in our present."

The black spot in my eyesight disappears, and what looks like jagged lightning starts at the bottom of one side of my vision. The pain thumps in my head, matching the rhythm of my heartbeats.

Suddenly, Aunt Connie claps her hands. "Come Spirits, move among us." Her voice drops to a whisper. "Reach out, travel across shifting time and space, and return to your loved ones. We wait for a sign."

Silence. I draw in a long breath as the lightning in my vision moves upward, and I try to eliminate the pressure in my head through willpower. No luck.

Then a rush of air—a whisper—of what? The back of my neck tingles. A faint touch like fingers moves up my arm, over my lips, along the side of my face, so light I'm not entirely sure I feel it. I sense someone standing behind me, but when I glance around the room, the only people in it are the ladies sitting around the table, hands folded, eyes closed, faces calm. They haven't moved. Another puff of air touches me, spreading a prickly, icy shiver across my skin. I hold my breath, straining to concentrate on the sensation, but in a second, it's gone.

Aunt Connie lightly taps the crystal in the center of the table three times. "We must focus our energies on reaching those beyond us. Spirits, we call you." She repeats the call three times.

The ladies begin to hum again. I sit motionless. The odd sensation like fingers brushing over my skin is gone. We stay at the table until Aunt Connie heaves a long sigh and rings her bell. "I'm sorry. The spirits are not prepared to draw closer today. My friends, I have not sensed a visitation, but we must remain hopeful, so we'll be ready to meet the departed when they wish to return."

I expect someone to say she felt what I did, but instead the women whisper to each other, and little sighs of disappointment go around the table. By the time I help Aunt Connie serve tea and little sandwiches, they've lost their disappointed expressions, and they're chatting casually as if they'd never had a thought about contacting ghosts and didn't plan to come back next week to try again.

Leaving them in the dining room, I head for the kitchen where I gulp a pain pill from the bottle on the counter. A shiver goes through me, and I grip the edge of the kitchen sink. It's happening again. Cool air, then warm, sliding along my arms, winding around my neck, touching my cheek, eerie and soothing at the same time. The door to the basement is ajar, but when I fling it open, the stairs are empty. The kitchen window's open. Is it the night air? A moth? I swat at nothing.

Snowball hisses from under the kitchen table, shoots across the tile floor, pushes through his little exit door, and disappears into the back yard. Drawing a long shaky breath, I follow him outside. My headache must have caused another hallucination. The moonlight puts a silvery glow on pink and white flowers blooming along the flagstone path. Snowball pads delicately through the grass ahead of me and then circles my feet until I scoop him up, sit on the cast iron bench near the rose arbor, and run my fingers through his thick, white fur.

Snowball's deep purring stops, and he hunches his back. A light breeze like a long sigh whispers across the yard, wrapping around me, frigid at first, then fiery again. My headache disappears as scuffling noises sound along the side of the house. I squeeze Snowball, and he digs his claws into my shoulder.

My heart thumps so strongly I almost hear it. "Is someone there?"

2

Dan walks around the corner of the house and looms over me. "Did I scare you?"

I tug Snowball's claws one by one out of my shoulder. "Of course not. I knew you were coming to pick up your grandmother." I glance at the shadows near the arbor. "Were you in the garden before I came outside?"

"No, I parked in the driveway. Why are you out here? Gran said you were going to help bring up the spirits." He drops on the bench next to me.

"Séance is over, and they're having tea. I had a headache. I wanted some air."

"Did the chanting start your headache?" A low laugh gurgles in his throat.

I love Aunt Connie, but I can't help laughing with him. "I'm sure it was my concussion, but the chanting might have made it worse—or maybe it was the bell ringing. Anyway, my headache's gone."

He scratches Snowball's ear, and the cat immediately abandons me, jumps into his lap, and purrs a deep, steady rumble while Dan strokes his fingers through Snowball's fur. "Sorry about the concussion." His voice takes on that big brother tone he always used when we were kids although we're the same age.

"I'll be fine—just headaches for a while." I lean back against the bench and inhale the scent from the roses.

"Was Gran right? Did your presence bring ghosts to the séance? She was hoping you'd be a magic channel to the spirit world." He laughs as Snowball twists his head back and forth, making sure he gets scratched in the right places.

I glance sideways at him. "You know. . . Aunt Connie's never actually called up a ghost."

Another laugh. "Everybody knows that, but Gran has faith, and she says if reaching the spirits is possible, it will happen here."

"Who does she want to reach?"

"My great-great grandfather. He was a soldier in World War I, and she has his diary from the war. It's kind of interesting. I've read some pages. He was nineteen and fought in some rough battles, got caught behind the German lines, had to escape, and later in the war he drove an ambulance. Gran wants to print the diary, like a family history, but she says she needs more details from him so she can understand some of what he wrote." He shifts his legs, moving Snowball to a new position. "Crazy, huh?"

"How long has she been trying to reach him?"

"Years. My dad told her to print the diary the way it is, but she hopes a séance will call his spirit to answer her questions. He's been dead for decades, so he'll have to come as a ghostly presence."

A ghostly presence—the rush of air, my shivers, the breeze stroking my skin. I shake off the memory. Aunt Connie's theories, including all her oddities, are part of what I love about her, but believing in ghosts is too much for me.

Voices drift out of the house. A flurry of goodbyes. Car doors slam. Snowball scoots down Dan's outstretched legs, racing to the kitchen ahead of us. Aunt Connie and Mrs. Harris stand together near the back door.

"Any luck today, Gran?"

Clutching her walker, she shakes her head. "I felt nothing. It's so discouraging." A faint smile in my direction. "I hoped Jenny would bring us luck."

Aunt Connie frowns. "I'm still optimistic, Sarah. We can never be sure when the spirits will want to come to us."

"It's hard to be patient." Mrs. Harris reaches for her tote in the basket attached to her walker, fumbles in it, pulls out a small notebook with a tattered cover. "Listen, Jenny. My grandfather was trapped behind the German lines in Belgium, and someone—a young woman—helped him escape, but he doesn't write any details or give her name. It's so frustrating! I want to know what happened." She opens the notebook and reads, "*I owe my life to her, and I loved her, but I lost her in Roosendaal.* It's so mysterious."

"Very strange," I murmur.

Aunt Connie puts her arms around her. "We'll reach him, Sarah. Spirits sense negativity, so we must be positive."

"Oh, I'm entirely optimistic." Mrs. Harris closes the notebook and tucks it back into her tote. "He could come to me at any time."

Dan grins at me while the true believers discuss whether chanting or soothing music would be likely to call forth ghosts. I bite my lip and avoid looking at him while he holds the back door open for his grandmother.

While I help Aunt Connie put the dining room in order, the words *I loved her and lost her* run through my mind. "Does Mrs. Harris really believe she can reach her ancestor?"

"Of course. People who've gone before aren't gone. They're all around us, and they can take us back to our own past lives."

"Past lives?"

"We've all lived before—I do believe it. After George died in that highway pileup, I began to think that this life couldn't be the only one we'd shared. Time moves back and forth and gives us little glimpses of our past lives. I'm confident it's true because sometimes I remember bits of another life."

"What do you remember?"

She carefully slides the crystal into its velvet bag and places it next to the candles in the glass cabinet. "It's not clear. I'm not going to claim it is, but I do sometimes see myself living in another time." She turns to me, her eyes serious. "I think I lived during pioneer times. I can see myself in a wagon, and George is there with me. I know I'm right about this."

I can't think of a thing to say about Aunt Connie in a covered wagon, so I murmur "interesting" and concentrate on straightening the chairs.

After we put the dining room in order, Aunt Connie turns on the television for news, and I go upstairs to check email. One from Dad in Portugal with a single line asking how I am and three inches describing the documents he's reading about a seventeenth-century Portuguese pirate. Three emails from my friend Tess with the same message—she's tried to reach my cell but couldn't connect. I write back and explain cell phone reception outside Fort Jefferson is pretty hopeless most of the time because Aunt Connie's house is on the other side of some invisible line where all reception ends. I add what I hope is a funny description of the séance, but I don't mention any of my odd sensations.

After wandering around the Internet for an hour, I close my laptop and gaze out the window facing the back patio. The garden looks empty, but I can't shake the feeling that something's out there— something waiting for me. I kick off my sneakers, pull off my socks, and lie on top of the bedspread in my clothes, staring at the ceiling. Aunt Connie has gone to bed. The house is quiet—absolutely silent— no creaks from old boards, no humming from the kitchen appliances.

Sleep doesn't come, so I get up, kneel on the window seat, and gaze out the window again. The heavy aroma from the roses in the arbor seeps through the screen. The night air is misty now. A thin, white haze curls across the garden, wrapping around the cast iron bench and spreading across the flagstone path all the way to the back fence.

A shadow wavers near the arbor. Clouds cut across the moon dropping darker shadows over the lawn while the mist thickens and hovers motionless over the ground. The shadow drifts close to one of the birch trees near the fence. I blink hard and stare into the dark. A distinct shape—definitely male. I hesitate for a minute, but I can't resist investigating for myself. Tiptoeing down the stairs to avoid the squeaky step, I rush through the kitchen and grab Aunt Connie's big meat fork lying on the countertop. I don't know if I'd have the stomach to use it, but it's big enough to look like a weapon.

The mist curls around my bare feet while the figure drifts toward the rear of the garden, and the clouds split into thin hazy streaks across the moon, sending patches of light on the grass. The shadowy figure doesn't look entirely real because I can see through him—or it—and the face blurs as if I'm looking through water.

Heart pounding, I step forward. "Who are you?" My voice squeaks. Goose bumps race up my arms.

He stops, turns, and drifts closer to me, but his face isn't clear although the clouds have moved off, and the moonlight illuminates most of the garden. A sigh and an incomprehensible murmur. Maybe the concussion has truly messed up my brain, so I'll never be my ordinary, logical self again. Maybe they'll find me in Aunt Connie's yard, holding a meat fork, babbling insanely. Maybe I'm having another hallucination. I squeeze my eyes shut, but when I open them, the figure's still there. He's clearer now—a soldier in a uniform. He's young, not much older than me. My heart races as if it's going to explode.

"Who are you?" I want to sound fierce and dangerous, but my voice cracks. I swallow hard, working up some spit to coat my throat. My fingers tighten around the meat fork.

The edges of him break into pixels, but in a second the pixels slide back together. He's still transparent, but I can see him better now. Tall, dark eyes in a pale face, dark hair drooping in a wave across his forehead.

"Why are you here?" I whisper.

"You called me." His whisper is fainter than mine. "I need your help. Come with me."

"I didn't call you. I'm not going anywhere with you." My fingers are so tight around the meat fork, they're numb, and I'm a little dizzy. Having a conversation with a figure who looks like a bad television signal probably qualifies me for a hospital psychiatric ward.

He glides closer, not walking, more like floating over the surface of the grass. "Come with me."

I take a step back, raising the fork, which doesn't seem like a weapon any more, considering he's not solid enough to poke. "Who are you? Why are you here?"

"You called me."

"I told you—I didn't call, and I'm not going anywhere with you."

He reaches for me, fingers clear as glass. My body tenses, but I don't retreat. He seems sad, not dangerous. I keep the meat fork steady, pointing at his transparent chest. Closer. Closer. I hold my breath and shut my eyes.

A delicate puff of air slides across my cheek, drifts down my throat, my arms, the inside of my wrist and brushes my open palm. The sensation is so warm and comforting I take a slow, long breath and let my uneasiness dissolve in a delicious awareness of my own skin. Then the feeling vanishes as a chilly wind races through the trees, tearing at the vines in the arbor. When I open my eyes, he's fading, turning into a haze, lighter, lighter, and then nothing.

3

"**M**aybe you were asleep and dreamed you were in the garden and saw someone." Dan raises his eyebrows in a question.

One of his summer jobs is taking care of Aunt Connie's yard, and the minute I saw him kneeling in a flower bed, I dashed outside to tell him about my meeting with the strange night visitor.

"I couldn't sleep, and when I looked out the window, I saw a shadow—a figure out here in the garden." I pace back and forth in front of him.

He sits back on his heels and gestures toward the house. "Did you tell her?"

"Of course not. Aunt Connie loves mysterious events, but I don't know what I saw."

Dan snaps off a dead rose. "And he looked like a soldier?"

"He wore a uniform. I don't know what kind. He talked to me."

"What'd he say?"

"He said I'd called him, and he needed help, and I had to come with him. He didn't look quite real. I could see through his fingers and his face was pale—almost glassy."

"See through his fingers," Dan repeats. He turns his face away and snaps off another dead rose.

"Are you laughing at me?"

"Honest, I'm not laughing, but you must have been dreaming. You heard Gran's story, and you dreamed about a soldier. Dreams can seem real. I had a nightmare once about—"

"I'm sure it wasn't a dream! He touched me."

"What did it feel like when he touched you?"

"Not like skin on skin. Like a light breeze sliding over me—sort of."

"Maybe he was a ghost." This time Dan can't hold back his laugh although he tries to smother it with a cough. When I don't answer right away, he stops working and stares at me. "Do you believe you saw a ghost?"

"I don't know what I saw."

Dan gets to his feet, puts his hand on my elbow, steers me to the garden bench, and sits next to me. "Listen, I get that ghosts are important around here. Gran spends most of the week waiting for the séance, and she's always sure the next one is going to lead to some supernatural connection. But if you start telling this story, you're going to get those women all excited—for nothing. Other people will think you're crazy."

"Forget ghosts. Let's be scientific about this."

Dan runs his fingers through his hair. "Okay, I'll be scientific. You've had a concussion. You get headaches. The doc said you'd have strange feelings or sensations or whatever. Yesterday, you sat through one of those séances with all that mumble-jumble and chanting, not to mention that sickening aroma from the stuff in the dishes. Then you heard Gran's story. Last night you didn't realize it, but you did fall asleep and dreamed about seeing someone or something in the garden." He shakes his head. "I admit it sounds odd, but face it, you had a super, extra-real dream."

"I was standing out here. My toes were cold when I came inside."

"Maybe you were sleepwalking?"

I glare at him. "I was awake."

"You need to be careful." That big brother tone settles in his voice. "If you see a figure out here in the middle of the night, don't come out to talk to it. It could be a real criminal, not a transparent soldier. Don't get tangled up with a burglar or some kind of creep. Call the police. Promise?"

"Promise." It's a kid thing, but I take the precaution of crossing my fingers behind my back because even though I asked for his advice, following it is a whole other decision. The more I describe last night's experience, the more I wonder what really happened.

I switch the conversation to sports, setting Dan off on a monologue about the Fort Jefferson High School basketball team's near victory at the state regionals. Whenever he pauses, I nod to prove I'm paying attention, but I'm really scanning the yard and garden for signs of an intruder. Nothing. Dan must be right—I was dreaming.

I spend the next week helping Aunt Connie in her antique shop—*Time's Treasures*—and pretending I'm not waiting for the next séance. When Friday finally arrives, my nerves are a mess. As we settle around the table, I sit next to Dan's grandmother, my mind jumping from one ghostly possibility to another.

Aunt Connie rings the bell for silence. "We're going to try a new method. Place your hands on the table and spread your fingers so that your little finger touches the little finger of the person next to you. If a spirit visits anyone, the energy will flow to the others through our fingers." She claps her hands, silver bracelets clinking, while we carefully position our fingers.

Humming begins. The others close their eyes, but I keep mine open. Faces, lit by the flickering candles, look like floating pale masks in the darkness. The aroma from the crushed flowers almost overpowers the oxygen in the room, and I deliberately breathe through my mouth to keep from sneezing.

My fingertips pressed flat on the table are numb. Then I feel it—a whoosh of air slides along my arms, making my skin hot and cold at the same time. I search the faces around the table. Eyes closed. The candle flames are steady. Curtains don't move, but air whispers in my ears and skims over my throat and face. My hair stirs along my forehead. In spite of touching fingers, I'm completely disconnected from the others, alone with what Aunt Connie would call mystical sensitivity.

The séance ends with sighs and disappointed murmuring. After tea and sandwiches, Dan's waiting on the porch swing. He's popular with the ladies, holding the screen door open as they leave, making a little joke with each one. They giggle and pat his arm. He turns serious when he walks his grandmother to the kitchen door. "Did you have a good session, Gran?"

She shakes her head. "I'm getting discouraged again. I don't want to give up hope, but perhaps I should."

"We must keep trying, Sarah." Aunt Connie hugs her. "I thought I sensed a presence today, but I couldn't call it forward."

I want to be disappointed for them, but I'm relieved. If they had no special sensations during the séance, maybe my imagination is running in high gear. Dan's dream theory about the transparent soldier could be right. As he steers his grandmother toward his car in the driveway, he throws a backward glance at me. His eyes signal a warning—don't do anything risky. I shrug and put on my innocent look.

After dinner, I go to my room and start reading *A Special Year*, the summer reading book for juniors this year. The back cover says it's an inspiring story about a woman who taught school in rural Uganda, but I can't concentrate, so I open my laptop to check on summer courses at the Tri-Center Community College. I've got to fill the next two months with more than part-time work at *Time's Treasures*. A course on Caribbean history looks interesting. I check the book list and see the word *pirates* in three titles. Perfect.

I rearrange the porcelain figurines on the dresser and then shuffle my clothes in the closet so they're hanging in categories—jeans, shorts, tee shirts. No matter how much I'd like Dan's explanation about the figure in the garden to be right, I can't convince myself the see-through soldier wasn't real. I stretch out on the bed and stare at the ceiling until I hear Aunt Connie go to her room. Time barely moves. My hands curl into fists. I want to forget strange encounters and go to sleep, but I can't.

I don't even undress and get ready for sleep. Instead, I silently open my door and creep down the stairs. In the kitchen, Snowball circles my feet purring softly, while I hesitate in front of the meat fork. If the other night was a dream, I don't need a weapon. If I really saw a ghost, the meat fork won't protect me. Snowball follows me out into the garden.

The air's warm and humid, the moon half hidden under clouds. I forgot to turn out the lamp on my desk, so light from my bedroom window shines on the stone path. Walking slowly across the flagstones toward the arbor, I have to keep lifting my feet over and around Snowball who's twisting around my ankles, demanding attention. Near the arbor, I stop and stand in place, waiting—waiting for something. The clouds shift, and the moonlight breaks through, changing the shape of the shadows in the garden. The only sounds are Snowball's purring and the crickets. I feel alone, but then Snowball hisses and races back to the house.

"I know you're here," I whisper. I strain to see into the shadows cast by the rose arbor. "Why did you come?"

He seems to form out of the darkness, looking more substantial than before. Definitely a soldier. Brass buttons. Heavy boots.

My pulse jumps. "Why did you come?"

"You called me." His voice sounds like an echo.

"I already told you—you're wrong about that. Who are you?"

"I need your help."

I dig my fingernails in my arm. A jolt of pain. I must be awake. "Why do you need help?"

Edges of him break into pixels, but only for a second this time.

"Who are you?" I repeat.

"I'm looking for Jenny."

"I'm Jenny."

His eyes lock on mine, and he walks slowly toward me. "I know a poem about you." He smiles.

"Jenny kiss'd me when we met,
Jumping from the chair she sat in. . . ."

He holds out his hand, but I back up a step. While I try to decide whether to stay or run, he moves—he glides—close enough to touch me. Not transparent anymore.

"Jenny kiss'd me when we met," he repeats.

He's so close now I have to tilt my head to see his dark eyes. He puts his hands on the sides of my face, his fingertips slightly rough as a soldier's would be. I can't pull away. I can't resist. He bends his head toward me. My heart pounds. My blood whooshes through my body.

"Jenny, come with me now. You belong with me," he whispers.

Slowly, he leans down and presses cool, soft lips against mine. My head whirls, and thick darkness blots out everything.

4

Darkness breaks into cobwebs as I open my eyes. My mouth is so dry I can't swallow, and I'm face down on hard, uneven ground, my cheek pressed into a mound of tough, crackly grass. My fists are clenched, nails digging into palms.

Something happened to me. I strain to remember—I was in the garden, and the soldier, or ghost, or whatever he was, touched me. No, that's not right. He kissed me and everything went black.

The scratchy grass under me is nothing like Aunt Connie's well-kept lawn. Slowly, I uncurl my fingers, spread my hands flat on the ground and push myself up. Sitting there, I look around, close my eyes for a second, and then open them, fighting the panic bubbling inside me because I have to think clearly.

Where am I?

The grassy patch I'm sitting on is outside a short white picket fence surrounding a small, carefully tended cemetery. Neat, straight rows of large and small, white and gray tombstones. The grass and hedges inside the fence are trim, and the white fence looks freshly painted, but the gate hangs half off its hinges, and the ground is torn into ragged clumps of grass and soil. Flowers and cracked vases are scattered on the ground around the tombstones.

I press my fingers against my temples. No headache.

Loud pops crackle like fireworks. More pops. Faint shouts. Loose dirt near me sprays in the air.

Bullets!

I scramble across the grass on my hands and knees, through the half open gate, and drop behind a tall tombstone with a carved angel, wings spread on the top. Not sure which way to move, I fling my arms around the square base of the column inscribed "Marta Calvert, 1857-1906." Crouching low to the ground, I press my face hard against the cool gray stone. More shots. These sound farther away, but I can't tell and I don't raise my head to look. Panic has a firm grip on me now. I dig my fingers into the uneven spaces on the rough stone.

A sharp crack—bits of the tombstone explode above me. The angel's head blows apart, and a flash of pain streaks along my arm when a jagged piece slices a long scratch.

The thin trail of blood oozes along my arm, and fear turns my breathing into uneven pants. Where am I? I can't do anything but grip the stone base and wait. More sharp cracks. The rest of the angel shatters and pieces scatter over my head. I roll away from the tombstone, and slide into a slight hollow behind a big family stone—the Van Liews. Silence. All I hear is my own breathing as I lie flat, hugging the ground.

Be calm. Think. The scratch on my arm is drying already, so I'm not going to bleed to death. I wait in the silence, counting to sixty and then counting again to set the minutes. After three sixty-second counts, I peek around the edge of the tombstone. No one in sight.

A brick path leads directly to the back of a church where an arched wooden door is ajar, but it's not open enough for me to see inside. I'm not especially good at estimating distances, but I try to measure off the path in my head. At least a hundred and fifty feet. Being inside a building seems safer than being out in the open with only some tombstones between me and flying bullets, but to reach the church, I'll have to go out the side gate and around to the path or climb the fence to reach the path, and there's nothing to hide behind between the cemetery and the church door. Wait or run?

I run.

Bending over as far as I can, I dash out the side gate, around the front of the cemetery, and sprint over the brick path toward the church. As I reach the door, more shots are followed by screams, but they're distant. I slip inside the church, breathless and too scared to look back.

The church is empty, but it's a wreck. Huge brass candle holders have toppled onto the stone floor near the altar, and a statue of the Virgin Mary has fallen across the communion rail and crushed a section of the dark wood. Smaller statues along the side aisles lie on the stone floor, halos and arms broken off. Votive candles spread across the floor. A few are still burning, so I stamp out the last flames. One of the stained glass windows along a side wall has a gaping hole in it, and as I look up, more shots hit a stained glass window on the other side. It shatters, spraying pieces of glass in all directions. Ducking under a pew saves me from another cut or worse.

For long tense minutes, I kneel between the wooden pews, trapped again. Panic gets a stronger grip on me, but staying between these pews isn't necessarily safe. I have to move.

Slowly, I rise and peer around the church. I'm definitely alone. The shots must be strays from outside. Based on the condition of the candle holders and statues, the church has already been attacked. Deliberately, I take long, deep breaths to slow my racing pulse. If I don't know where I am, then no one knows I'm here. Moving carefully, I edge around the broken glass. Near the altar, on the right, another wooden door is ajar. No way to tell what's in there without getting closer.

Keeping my back against the side wall, I inch toward the door, then push it open with a piece of the broken communion rail. No noise. Nothing comes out, so I go in. It's a small room with hooks lining one wall and a chest in one corner. A priest's robe hangs on one hook, a plain black shirt hangs on another, and a pair of black pants is tossed over the back of a chair.

A door opposite the one I walked through is wide open, and I peek in, hoping I won't see anyone but at the same time wanting to find an explanation for where I am. The room looks like one in the old photos in Aunt Connie's antique shop—a small kitchen with dishes piled on the middle of a round, wooden table. An old wood-burning stove stands in a corner, but there's no refrigerator. The large rectangular porcelain sink is as high as my waist with an odd faucet rising a foot in the air and then extending another foot in an L-shape over the sink with one white porcelain handle. My mouth is so dry I can barely swallow. I have to balance on my toes, so I can get my face under the faucet. It's messy. Water splashes on the floor, but I gulp and drink until I'm almost water-logged.

Considering the destruction in the church, it's silly to feel guilty about spilled water, but I hunt around for a rag to mop up the floor. No rag. Instead, I find a crumpled newspaper pushed against the back of the wooden countertop.

It's in French.

As Miss Duprette so often pointed out when I was a freshman, I'm no good at languages. The front page says *Les Forums*. I've no hope of reading any articles, but I can read the date clearly enough—August 16, 1914.

The letters whirl on the page. My stomach starts to churn. I have to grip the edge of the sink and fight the urge to throw up. The newspaper isn't brand new, but it isn't a hundred years old. Where am I?

I struggle with the French. Something called *Liege* is important—seems to be a city. *Allemagne* is all over the page, but I don't know what it means, except that it's connected to *militaire* in every sentence. I can't understand enough to make sense of any of it, especially the date on the paper.

Now what?

A swinging door with a little window near the top leads to another room. I peer through the glass at a living room with a sofa, chairs, bookshelves, and cup and saucer on a side table. Clutching the newspaper to my chest, I try to decide what to do. The living area looks deserted, but staying here is too dangerous. Anyone could walk in and find me. The outside, full of random gunshots, seems even more dangerous. I need to figure out what's happened to me and hide while I do it. I need to think.

A door in the small cloakroom opens on a narrow side hallway leading to the church entrance. In the center of the hallway, a stairway goes up to the bell tower. I stop halfway up the stairs and listen. Nothing. In the tower, I crawl to the low railing and peer over it just far enough to see into the street below.

It's a wide cobblestone road with one- and two-story stone houses on either side. While I watch, four soldiers come out of one of the houses, dragging an old man with them. They're all yelling, but I can't understand any of the words. The soldiers push the man, still shouting, to his knees on the road, and one soldier yells at the others, gesturing with his rifle. An elderly woman, who followed them out of the house, screams and tries to haul the old man to his feet.

A priest in a long black robe runs into the street and argues with the soldiers, waving his arms and gesturing first at the woman and then at the man on the ground. He pushes past the woman to stand between her and the soldiers, continuing to yell and point at the church. The soldiers shake their heads, pushing him back with the barrels of their rifles. Two of them step around the priest, and shoot the elderly man. The woman screams again and drops to her knees in the street beside the old man while another soldier turns to the priest and shoots him twice. The priest spins backward and falls near the old man, his black robe fluttering around his ankles when the breeze catches the edges. The killings take only five seconds.

Terror streaks through me. The old man couldn't have done anything to deserve being shot in the street, and killing a priest is so horrifying I can't even imagine why it would happen. Shivers travel up and down my arms; my heart pounds as though it's going to jump out of my chest.

The soldiers are Germans. Their helmets with little pointy spikes on the top are the same helmets I'd seen in old war movies on television. Somehow I've ended up in a horrible time and place—in a war or something like one. What will the soldiers do to me if they find me?

More shots sound farther down the street. The old woman stays on her knees in the street wailing and rubbing the old man's shoulder. The soldiers ignore her. Two of them wander up and down the street, kicking open doors while the others rest on the ground in front of the houses across from the tower, their rifles across their knees. No one comes to carry away the bodies. I duck below the bell tower railing, holding my breath.

After a few minutes, my heart settles into something like a normal beat, and I risk another look at the street. The woman is still sobbing next to the old man's body. A soldier points at the church and shouts something to the others. He walks toward the main entrance, holding his rifle steady in a position to fire. If he enters the foyer, he can't miss seeing the passage leading to the bell tower, and if he gets that far, I know he'll check the bell tower.

My fingertips turn white while I grip the railing, my mind whirling. There's no time to find another hiding place in the church, and if the soldier comes to the top of the bell tower, he'll probably shoot me the minute he sees me. I can't speak German, and, even if I could, any explanation I gave would sound insane. Aside from the bell and the machinery to ring it, there's nothing else in the tower—nowhere for me to take cover.

More shouts from the street. Another soldier—maybe an officer because he wears a hat instead of a helmet—waves at the soldier with the rifle and shouts something that sounds like a command. The soldier with the rifle turns and answers, hesitates, then shrugs and walks away, heading down the road. A trickle of sweat rolls down my back, and I slump to the floor. I have to get out of here and back to Aunt Connie and my normal life—but how?

The sun slides toward the west while long shadows from the houses spread across the road. My stomach growls, but I'm afraid to move, afraid to do anything but pray I'm in a horrible dream, and when I open my eyes, I'll be back in Aunt Connie's garden. How stupid to rush outside like an idiot at midnight to find the soldier-ghost so I could bring him—it—to Aunt Connie. Why did I end up in this place?

I slump to the floor of the tower and lean against the wall, wrapping my arms around my knees. Crying won't help, but I can't stop the dribble of tears streaking down my cheeks. I don't dare leave the bell tower. I'm trapped.

5

I don't sleep—or maybe I do a little. Every time a gun goes off, I wake up with a jerk. When morning comes I'll have to decide what to do next, and that scares me more than hiding in the dark does. When the first glow of daylight breaks up the black sky, little brown birds arrive, perch on the open ledge, and chirp loudly.

I'm stiff and cold. Goose bumps run up my legs and arms. My khaki shorts and tee shirt are completely inadequate for a night outside—wherever I am. I tuck my hands in my armpits for warmth and try to plan. I can't stay in the bell tower forever. The priest is dead, but there's nothing to stop the soldiers from taking over the church whenever they want to.

Think.

I need someone to explain this mess I'm in. Does anyone miss me? Does Aunt Connie know I'm gone? I'd like to blame someone for my predicament, but no one forced me to run outside looking for a ghost in the middle of the night. If Dan knew what I'd gotten into, he'd shake his head and remind me that he warned me not to be reckless. Aunt Connie would be more understanding—she'd be excited about finding a ghost. I could tell her it was the kiss, the ghost's kiss took me away. She'd say it was romantic, and I must have known him in another life, but if I never get back, I'll never see her again. I put my head on my knees and whimper for a minute, my fear running wild. Shouts from the street bring me to the railing again.

Soldiers in orderly lines march down the road away from the church; others load wagons with squawking chickens and tie cows to the backs of the wagons. A few people in the street yell and wave their arms, but the soldiers ignore them. Far down the road, a house is on fire. While I watch, a soldier throws a torch through the window of another house. In a minute, flames shoot up. Some women run up and down the street, wailing and looking as helpless as I feel, but when the soldiers fire their rifles in the air, the women stop and collapse on the side of the road, hugging each other. No one tries to fight the fires.

I have to get out of the tower. If the town burns down, so will the church. I scramble down the steps and run through the cloakroom to the rectory, my heart thumping.

Back in the kitchen, I scrub my face in the sink, rub the dried blood off my arm with a few drops of water, and gulp a long drink from the faucet. The priest must brush his teeth at the kitchen sink because a stubby toothbrush sits next to a small box of salt. I grab the toothbrush and rinse it before I sprinkle the salt on it, shutting out thoughts about dental hygiene. Food has to be next. I search through the drawers and cabinets. A couple of mushy apples aren't any use, but I find a big chunk of pale yellow cheese, a thick summer sausage, and a loaf of dark bread in a marble-topped box near a window. Emptying a half-full wine bottle, I rinse it, fill it with water, and push the cork in tight. Everything goes into a canvas sack from another drawer.

Smoke drifts through the windows. More shouts from the street. The soldiers are leaving and taking the wagons. One soldier shouts something, and another one lights a torch and runs toward the church. He disappears around a corner, but the torch crashes through what's left of the broken window in the nave.

My breathing becomes a series of shallow pants, but I focus on thinking clearly. It's not hard to figure that the church will be in flames in a few minutes, and after that the rectory will burn. I don't have much time to get out.

While I watch from the window, the soldiers march down the road, disappearing around a bend. Some women and children drag what they can out of the burning houses before the roofs collapse. The street's noisy, filled with shouting and crying, and the only men helping the women are elderly, and the only boys are small children. Bands of people begin to leave, bundles over their shoulders, walk in the same direction as the soldiers ahead of them. Two women pull a children's cart filled with clothes they've saved from the fires, pots hanging from the rear clang against each other. I don't know where these people are going, but it makes sense to join them. There has to be a way out of this trap. Traces of smoke curl under the door leading to the church. I pick up my sack, take a step, and stop.

The women in the street are dressed in long, dark cotton skirts with big scarves covering their heads. I'll look like an alien in that crowd. My shorts and tee shirt are not even close to what they're wearing, and my shoes are even worse. My favorite rainbow-colored, iridescent sneakers look like flashing neon lights compared to the brown and black shoes on the women in the street. Panic takes hold again. Every time I have half a plan to save myself or at least live a while longer, a new problem stops me. I'm stuck in place until I remember the priest's clothes in the cloakroom between the church and the rectory.

The smoke from the fire in the church seeps under the door, so I concentrate on the fire drill advice we had at school and run my hands over the wooden panels. The door isn't hot yet. Stooping low, I slowly open the door. The air in the cloakroom is hazy with thin wisps of smoke, but no flames. I crawl across the floor, snatch the clothes, and scramble back to the kitchen.

In the kitchen I sort through what I have. The priest's robe is no help, but the sash can go around my head like a scarf. The black shirt and black pants will have to do. I pull them on over my clothes, but everything is too big, and the pants slip off my hips to the ground. Another desperate search of the kitchen, hoping for a belt or a rope, brings me nothing, and the smoke begins to slide under the kitchen door. I check the window again—people straggle down the street, carrying their bundles. As I step back from the window, I see what I need. The window slides up and down a rope on each side of the frame.

Bracing my feet against the wall, I pull hard on one of the ropes. One end comes free, but the other end is in tight. Smoke creeps under the door, getting thicker every second. I get a fresh grip on the rope and pull again. The wooden frame creaks, but the rope holds. I brace my feet against the wall again and throw my entire body against that rope. Part of the frame splinters, and the rope breaks free.

I slip the rope through the belt loops on the pants and tie it high around my waist so I don't trip over the pant legs. The shirt hangs loose over my waist and hides the rope, but my sneakers peek out from the bottom of the pants, one red toe and one blue toe. Someone's going to notice these peculiar shoes, but I can't go barefoot. I sling the canvas sack over my shoulder as I slip out the side door.

The air in the street is nearly as smoky as inside the burning church. I linger under a tree in the churchyard until a group of women pass me, and I shuffle into the road a few yards behind them, keeping my head down. The priest's sash wrapped around my head is my best imitation of the women's scarves, and the shirt collar pulled up around my face keeps me half concealed.

The refugees—including me—are silent. A few mumble to each other. Women cry. Babies scream. Feet shuffle along the road, and carts rumble and squeak. For an hour or so, no one notices me. Then a woman glances back and tugs at the arm of another woman, who turns to look at me. Panic again. I keep my head down, avoiding their gaze. The women murmur to each other, but finally they shrug and ignore me.

There are no clouds in the sky, and the day gets hotter. I want a drink of water, but I'm afraid to take out the wine bottle or show I have food. I'm afraid of everyone. Who can I trust? Who would help me? The road is rutted from wagons, and the people walking in front of me slow down as they steer their carts through the ruts. I cut my pace, so I don't catch up to the main group because staying behind seems like the safest idea. I don't want to stand out or let anyone get a better look at me. The dust from the road turns some of the wild colors in my sneakers into a blurry brown.

After we walk about two hours, the road dead ends into a broader paved road, clogged with refugees coming from another direction. They mix in with the people from the village, and we stumble on together, some groups faster, some slower, while people enter or leave the groups. More refugees crowd the road. They seem to have a clear destination, but I can't tell what it is because I can't ask, and I can't read the signs posted on the side of the road. Finally, I'm so thirsty, I have to take a chance and gulp some water from the wine bottle, putting it out of sight as fast as I can. We plod on. Some old people drop back, their feet dragging. One old woman near me stops at the edge of the road and sits on a rock, her feet sticking out from under her long black dress, her eyes closed. I wonder if she'll ever get up again

Shouts up ahead. A horrible stink lingers in the air as we get close to a grove of trees. When I get to the edge of the trees, my stomach churns, and I swallow hard, trying not to throw up. Four bodies on the ground under the trees are sprawled in a tangle of arms and legs, dark and decayed, thousands of flies crawling over them. I hold the ends of the scarf tight over my nose and mouth to shut out the smell and smother the nausea building in my stomach. I expect something to happen, someone to do something, but people take a quick glance and then go on—no one stops. I stumble after them.

"*Atroce*," someone says close to me.

She looks older than me, eighteen or nineteen. Her long blonde braids swing down her back. She smiles—friendly—and says at least three or four sentences in French.

My nerves go on alert, but all I can do is smile and nod, and hope that my nod will be the right answer to whatever she said. My guess doesn't work. The girl smiles again, but she looks me over, up and down at my clothes, the priest's sash over my hair, and especially at my shoes. Then she says something again in French and waits for an answer. Her gray eyes are still friendly, but her voice carries a ring of suspicion.

My weak smile and nod aren't enough to fool her. She twists one of her braids around her finger and studies me for another long minute. "English?"

I have to take a chance. I nod. "Yes. No, not English—American." "American? Here?"

Lying is the only safe response. "Visiting."

She puts her hand over her heart. "I am Elise Martane."

I put my hand over my heart. "Jenny Tyler." I'm so grateful to find someone who speaks English I want to hug her. I point to the people ahead of us on the road. "Where are we going?"

She looks surprised at my ignorance. "Brussels."

Brussels is in Belgium. I'm in Belgium. A dizzy sense of relief takes over—I finally know where I am.

Elise points at my shoes. "American?"

"Yes. All Americans wear these shoes."

She accepts my fashion lie. "Where did you visit?"

I start to construct a history I can keep track of—lies mixed in with truths. "I was visiting my aunt." The priest's newspaper flashes in my mind. "In Liege," I add.

Elise frowns. "Much fighting in Liege. Germans captured the forts." She thinks for a minute. "You are far from Liege."

I have no idea where Liege is or what happened there. Lying is tricky. If you make it too elaborate, you forget the details, so simple is best. I wave my hands in a helpless gesture. "I got lost. I wandered. My aunt stayed behind."

Gunfire ahead brings everyone to a standstill. In the distance, on a low hill, houses are in flames. The afternoon sun shines in our eyes, but the dark smoke rising from the fires filters the light. The soldiers ahead of us must have slowed down to burn a village, no one in the crowd wants to meet the soldiers again. People scatter into the brush, dragging their belongings, heading in all directions away from what-ever's ahead.

Elise sprints between bushes. I follow her into a meadow sloping downhill. We race across the grass, stumbling along, gasping, cough-ing, and collapse against a low stone wall near the bottom of the hill.

"We must stay far from the soldiers," Elise says. "There is no rain in the sky, and we can rest here tonight. There is a stream." She points to a line of trees. "I hear it."

I don't hear anything that sounds like water, but I have to trust her instincts. Other refugees drift down the hillside and settle on the ground. A mother tries to keep her two children quiet by singing a soft lullaby to them.

I'm ferociously hungry. When I open my sack and take out the bread, Elise sucks in her breath and fixes her eyes on the loaf. She's hungry too, and I need a friend, so I tear the bread into chunks and divide my sausage and cheese between us. We eat like starving refu-gees, which is what we are, chewing thoroughly, and washing the food down with water from my wine bottle. The others in the meadow are eating whatever they have with them, but tomorrow we'll all be out of food.

The crowd consists mostly of women and children, but one man sits alone under a tree. He's in his forties or fifties, shirtsleeves rolled up showing his heavy muscles. He's wearing brown work pants and a thick gray shirt like the other men I saw in the village, but he also wears a flashy green silk scarf with gold fringe and tiny gold tassels at the ends. He's facing us, and when I look directly at him, he pulls his cap down to shade his eyes and leans back against the tree.

He's probably curious like some of the women who stare at me. My head isn't covered because the sash fell off when we ran down the hill, and I'm afraid to walk up the hill to look for it in case the soldiers are on the road. My legs stretch out in front of me with my dusty but colorful sneakers exposed. I should cover my shoes, but I'm too tired to care what people notice.

Elise is talkative. "In Charleroi, I work for an English family."

Lucky for me. That explains her good English. "Was there fighting?"

"Mon Dieu!" She rolls her eyes and spreads her arms. "The Germans attack for three days. Our Belgian soldiers are very brave. They fight from house to house, but the Germans are too many. Many people die. My poor English family. . . ." She shakes her head and twists her hands. "They are shot in the house, and I run away. I run all night."

By the time we finish the last of the bread and cheese, the sunlight has faded into red streaks across the sky, and shadows from the trees stretch across the grass.

"I'll go for water before it's too dark." I hang my sack with the empty wine bottle over my shoulder. "Which way is the stream?"

Elise points. "Beyond those trees. You will hear it."

I don't hear it until I'm nearly in it. The water rushes between low banks. In biology class, Mr. Jeffords said running streams were safe to drink. Kneeling on the moist ground at the edge of the stream, I dip the bottle into the water.

Crunching twigs sound behind me, and I look over my shoulder. The man with the green scarf is standing only a few feet away, watching me.

6

All my senses jump to attention and my adrenaline surges. I know danger when I see it. I shift slightly, enough to put my heels on the ground and bend my knees, so I'm ready to jump. He doesn't move. Standing half in the shadows spreading across the open ground, he stares at me, big hands loose at his sides. I know he hasn't come to the stream to offer me help. My fingers tighten on the wine bottle. I can't believe I'm in this mess, can't believe the ghost's kiss or the séance or some mix-up of the stars dropped me into danger. All I want is to be back in my real life.

I suck in a long shivery breath, clutch the wine bottle, and come up from the ground fast, aiming for an opening in the trees, but he moves at the same time, fast for a big man; his hands grab at my waist and pull me back. Screaming is probably useless, but I do anyway before he clamps his fingers over my mouth, grinding my lips against my teeth. I jab my elbow backward as hard as I can and hit his ribs. He grunts. His hand slips a little away from my mouth, giving me the chance to bite hard on two dirty fingers tasting like stale tobacco. He yelps, jerking his hand away, but at the same time, he shifts his feet to keep his balance and tightens his arm around my waist. Pulling and twisting in his grip, I kick his knee, making him grunt again just as he yanks me off my feet.

Holding me off the ground with one arm, he fumbles with the window rope I've tied through the belt loops on my pants. His arm is so tight across my ribs, I have to gasp for air, but I kick out, twisting, touching only empty space. I struggle to punch him, but I'm crushed against his chest at an awkward angle. I can't reach him with my feet, but I manage to turn my head and look into his face. Little beads of sweat shine in a row over his upper lip, eyes like flat black stones.

Desperate, I twist again and swing the wine bottle like a club, smashing it against the side of his head. The glass breaks; splinters fall down his face and over his shoulder. He groans and slips sideways, losing his grip on me. My feet touch the ground, and I stumble away from him, watching as he drops to his knees, blood running down his temple.

"Jenny!" Elise comes out of the trees. "I saw him follow you. I knew you would need me."

Still struggling for breath, I tighten my rope belt and pull my shirt down. "I hit him. I didn't know what else to do. We have to get out of here." I toss the broken wine bottle on the ground.

The man kneeling between us on the soft dirt groans. He holds one hand against his bleeding temple.

"You hurt him," Elise says in a low voice. "He will not go away and forget." She bends and picks up a jagged rock from the edge of the stream.

"What are you doing?"

"He must not follow us," Elise murmurs.

She steps closer, holding the rock over the man's head. Maybe he senses her near him, or her movement breaks through his pain because he suddenly opens his eyes and with his free hand grabs her ankle. She wobbles and tips over, but smashes the rock onto his face as she falls. When the rock hits him in the exact spot my wine bottle cut open his face, he groans and loses his grip on her ankle. His muscles relax; he shudders once and lies still. His face looks like bloody hamburger, his eye covered in blood.

"Did you kill him?"

"Yes," she murmurs.

My stomach churns. I swallow and try to fight it, but in another minute, I bend over a bush and throw up everything I ate an hour ago.

Elise ignores me. She kneels next to the man's body and begins searching his pockets as casually as if she kills people with rocks every day. "We must find what we can," she says to me while she carefully turns each pocket inside out, putting the items she finds in a pile on the grass.

"You can't steal from him."

"Yes, we can," she says.

I should leave her and run, but Elise is the only help I have. It's getting dark, and I don't know where to go, so I cross my arms over my chest and look away while she searches through his pockets.

She holds up some folded bills. "Look, money for us. We can buy food." She peels off several bills and hands them to me.

I hesitate, then take the money and shove it into my pocket. I'm committed. I'm robbing the dead.

From another pocket, she pulls out a folded knife. "Good," she says. The knife disappears into her canvas bag.

"Elise, we have to get out of here before someone comes for water."

She nods. "Yes. Help me turn him over."

"What?"

"We have to look in the back pockets. Hurry."

I take his feet so I don't have to look at his face. Elise grips his shoulders and looks straight into the bloody mess we've made of his features as she turns him—no hesitation on her part. Once his face is hidden against the grass, he looks asleep.

His back pockets hold a dirty handkerchief and some coins. Elise counts them and then hands them to me.

I add them to the bills in my pocket. "We have to go, Elise."

"Yes, yes," she agrees, but she keeps searching his pockets. "Look." She slides her finger under a long silver chain hooked to his belt and pulls out a round silver case.

"What is it?"

She flips open the lid. "Stones," she says, holding the case up to show me. Four deep red stones, different sizes and unevenly cut, but gleaming dark and fiery in the fading sunlight.

"Are those rubies?"

Elise shrugs, snaps the lid shut, and puts the silver case in her pocket. "I do not know, but the stones must have some worth because he tied them to his belt. We will take them."

I don't care if they're rubies. I don't care if they're worth a million dollars. I want to get away from the body on the ground, but when I turn back toward the meadow, Elise grabs my arm.

"No, we must go that way." She points across the stream to another field, lined with a row of hedges. "Hurry."

She splashes through the stream, never hesitating, every step landing firmly on rocks rising above the water. I follow as close as I can, but my feet slip off the rocks several times into the deeper water, and I'm wet up to my knees by the time we reach the other side.

"Run." Elise sets off across the field.

I stay close behind her, following her white shirt in the dim light as we run across the meadow. When we reach the other side, we find a dirt path leading to farm buildings, dark silhouettes against the sky.

"Where?" I gasp for breath, my heart pounding in my chest.

"There." Elise points, and we plunge through the door of a shed, shut it behind us, and collapse on bags filled with something grainy like sand.

"Sleep now," Elise says. "In the morning, we will find more food."

In a minute, she's sleeping as though we have nothing to worry about. Listening to her deep breathing, I stare into the darkness and think about everything I've done since I woke up in the cemetery. My legs start to shake and my teeth clench. I can't forget the man we left lying on the ground next to the stream—his hands pulling at me—his bloody face. I wrap my arms around my middle, curl into a ball, and close my eyes. I want to survive. I want to get home. Pieces of dreams—dark images of dead priests, burning houses, blood—keep me restless. I wake with a jerk, then fall back to sleep until Elise pokes me in the morning. I groan and roll away from Elise's fingers. Every joint aches.

"No one is on this farm," she says, "and no animals. The Germans took them." She pushes open the shed door. Sunlight floods in, blinding me for a minute.

I rub my eyes. "What should we do now?"

"We need food. I looked in the house, but there is nothing."

I lurch to my feet, a little unsteady, wishing desperately I had a bath, deodorant, a comb—anything that could make me feel like a reasonably civilized person instead of the grubby refugee I obviously am. "Is there water?"

Elise tugs at my arm, and I follow her into the deserted barnyard. Nothing moves; the silence in the bright morning is eerie.

"There," she points to a well halfway down a slope that leads to what looks like a tree-filled ravine with thick brush at the edge. "You get the water."

A cackle breaks the silence as a not-very-plump chicken waddles around the corner of the barn.

"A chicken!" Elise takes off after it, arms outstretched, zigzagging to follow it when the bird breaks into an awkward run, squawking with every step, staying just beyond her grip.

There's no chance I can catch a chicken on the run, so I head down the slope, aiming for the well, wondering if the bushes grow any berries I can identify and eat. Digging the priest's toothbrush out of my bag, I vow not to think about toothpaste.

I've just turned the well handle enough to bring the bucket to the top when voices cut through the quiet morning. They're coming from the ravine. My muscles tense. Am I crazy or are the voices speaking English? I have a brief debate with myself about safety or curiosity. After a minute, I'm sure the words are English, so I tiptoe away from the well, drop to my knees and crawl down the sloping ground until I reach the brush along the edge of the gully.

Two men are at the bottom. One, his left arm wrapped in a dirty bandage, is pinned under a thick tree limb at least six feet long. The other man is crouching over him, crawling back and forth, first trying to lift the tree limb and then trying to pull the other man out. But he can't lift and pull at the same time. They're soldiers in green khaki uniforms, but they aren't wearing helmets with those spiky things.

I push closer through the brush to see more, but it's muddy, and my hand slips to one side, sending broken twigs over the sloping edge of the ravine in a noisy rush to the bottom. The soldier struggling with the fallen tree limb stiffens, grabs his rifle, and swings it in one motion directly at me. I'm caught in the bushes. Is he going to shoot me? I'm sure I'm going to die here, right now. We stare at each other for the longest minute I'd ever lived through.

Dark brown eyes with amber glints, thick black hair. He lowers his rifle and reaches out to me. "Do you speak English? Help me," he says. "I need you."

A strange feeling sweeps over me—not panic exactly, but shock for sure. I recognize him instantly. He's my ghost.

7

Looking down at him, I'm dizzy for a minute, and the ground seems to roll under me. Lucky I'm on my knees because I'm sure I'd faint if I weren't, even though I've never fainted in my life. If this is a dream, it's definitely a long, complicated one, but the longer it goes on, the less it seems like a dream.

"My friend's caught, and I can't pull him out and lift the tree at the same time," he says. "I need you." He holds out his hand.

I wiggle out from the brush, collecting small scratches on the way, and slide into the ravine. He catches me as I come down. His forehead glistens with sweat, his hands grip my arms to keep me upright, and I feel the heat from his body as I press against him for an instant. He isn't ghostly now.

"Do you speak English?" he asks again.

He doesn't know me. My brain tries to sort out what's happening, but I can't. Focus, Jenny, focus. "Yes, I speak English. I'm an American."

Surprise and relief shows in his eyes. "Over there," he points. "I'll lift the tree, and you pull Pete when I tell you."

Pete clenches his teeth when I step behind his shoulders and get a good grip on his jacket under his arms. I dig my heels in the soft ground to get leverage. Now that I'm in the ravine, the tree looks bigger, a huge trunk with old rotted wood, and thick branches covering

Pete from his chest to his toes. One branch presses hard against his left leg, and blood has soaked through his pants where a pointed twig jabs him.

My ghost grunts and lifts the far end of the tree, getting a few inches of space between Pete and the branches. He signals to me, and I manage to pull Pete about a foot out of the tangle, but the overlapping branches keep him stuck.

"Wait." He gently lowers the tree trunk down, studies the branches, and walks slowly around the tree. Then he nods at me and takes the end again. This time, he lifts and pulls the tree to his right so the twig poking into Pete's leg pulls free.

I pull again, but, as Pete slides out toward me, I lose my footing and sprawl backward on the ground. Undignified. Worse, my sneakers, dirty but still very colorful, are in full view. I scramble up, twitching my pants down to cover most of the shoes.

Pete grunts and lets out a long sigh. "Much obliged, Miss."

We get Pete on his feet, but he's wobbly and holds his bandaged arm across his chest, so we stay in place on each side of him and exchange names as if we were having formal introductions under perfectly normal circumstances.

"Private Jackson Sommers, His Majesty's Army, 15th Brigade, 1st Cheshires. I'm very grateful for your help, Miss," my ghost says, looking at me over Pete's head.

Pete straightens awkwardly. "Private Peter Alphonse Cooper here, 15th Brigade likewise. That bloody tree just toppled right over on me from above when I fell in the gully here." He turns red. "I beg your pardon, Miss. Didn't mean to forget myself and my language."

I tell them a skimpy version of my story about visiting my aunt, and after we trade a couple more sentences, I realize they don't know any more about Belgium than I do. It's a relief and a disappointment at the same time. Before he kissed me, the ghost said he needed help. Did he mean help to move the tree? Or did he mean something more?

Pete swears his leg doesn't hurt, but I insist on unwinding a long cloth strip that holds his pants leg tight, so I can check the bloody spot on his leg. It's a jagged scratch but not deep. I start to rewind the cloth, but it gets tangled and I can't get it tight.

"What is this thing?"

Jack laughs. "It's a puttee, holds the pants tight for marching and keeping dirt out of our boots. We aren't marching now. Wrap it around the spot that's bleeding."

I wind the puttee around the bloody spot and tie it off, leaving the ends dangling down Pete's leg.

It's difficult to crawl out of the ravine because Pete can't put pressure on his wounded arm, so we struggle up the side, digging into the dirt with our hands and feet, while Pete hangs on to Jack with his one good arm and Jack drags him along. I put Pete's pack on my shoulder and carry his rifle in one hand.

When we reach the top and come out of the brush surrounding the ravine, Elise is walking across the grass toward the well, a dead chicken dangling in her hand. My stomach starts growling, and I'm suddenly so hungry I could eat the chicken raw. She sees the three of us and halts, the apprehension on her face so clear I can feel it transfer to me. I don't want Elise to abandon us. She's the only one who knows where we are and who can speak another language. And I want that chicken.

I wave my arms and run up the slope past Jack and Pete to get to her before she can bolt away. "Elise, I found these two British soldiers in the ravine. They'll protect us from the Germans."

She looks at me as if I've just been certified as a dangerous lunatic. "The Germans will shoot us if they find us with enemy soldiers."

"They have weapons."

"They will be our death." She backs away a step.

Jack and Pete stop at the well, and while Pete drinks from the ladle, Jack watches us, his rifle tilted in our direction. Would he shoot us?

"We can't leave them." I grip her arm. "One of them is hurt, and we don't know where we are or where we're going. Isn't four together better than two?" Without waiting for an answer, I point at the chicken. "Can we cook it?"

Her teeth gnaw at her lower lip as she looks from Jack and Pete to me and back again. Her silence makes me optimistic. "We don't have weapons, but they do. We're safer with them."

"Where are they going?"

"I don't know. We can ask—after we cook the chicken." My stomach is making embarrassing noises.

She hesitates—such a long minute. My breath stops. Finally, she nods and turns back up the slope, the chicken still dangling from her hand.

If the farmhouse ever had a stove, it doesn't now, and smoke coming out of the chimney would alert enemy soldiers in the area, so we can't use the fireplace to cook. Jack builds a little fire behind the barn where the smoke will drift out over the fields instead of down the lane leading up to the house. Elise strips the chicken feathers and cuts the body open with Jack's knife. She's as fast cooking the chicken as she was going through the pockets of the man we left on the bank of the stream. I don't want to think about the man. The smell from the chicken fat dripping into the fire sends my stomach into wild growling I can't control.

Jack grins and digs a tin from his pack. "Have a biscuit." He offers each of us a thin cookie. Elise takes a delicate bite from hers, but I can't wait. I cram the cookie in my mouth, chew it, and wash it down with a gulp of water. I've lost all my manners in this other time.

"Don't eat too fast when you're empty," Jack says. "Slow is best. Let your stomach get used to the food." He flips his tin upside down and hands the last cookie to me. "Take bites this time."

I know the others are as hungry as I am, but I stare at the cookie in my hand, wanting to pop it in my mouth and swallow it whole the way I did the first one. Instead, I carefully break it into four more or less even pieces and pass a piece to each of the others. I feel virtuous now, but there isn't enough left to take bites, so I swallow my piece in one gulp again. My growling stomach settles down, but the aroma from the cooking chicken reminds me I'm still hungry.

Elise slowly turns the chicken over the fire and studies Pete, especially his bandaged arm. "How did you come here?"

"Came from fighting at Mons in the south," Pete answers. "We got into it with German cavalry. Held them in the morning, but they got over the bridge and came up the road in the afternoon. We had to retreat—it was bloody tight, I can tell you." He coughs. "Sorry for my language, ladies."

Elise waves away his apology. Jack stamps out the fire while she carefully divides the meat with his knife. The hot juicy drumstick finally quiets my rumbling stomach, and there's enough of the chicken to make a second helping for each of us.

"Perfect, "Jack says to Elise when we've reduced the chicken to a pile of bones.

"If you retreated from Mons," Elise continues as if we hadn't paused to gobble food, "you should have gone south over the border to France. How do you come north?"

Jack stretches his legs and wipes his fingers on his puttees. "The weather was clear in the morning, but the fields got so thick with smoke by afternoon we couldn't see much. Gave them plenty of casualties though. Our Enfield rifles shoot fifteen rounds a minute, so the Germans probably thought we had machine guns, but after hours of fighting and moving around, we didn't know where we were."

"We bloody well held them at first," Pete says, "but there was always more coming. Right, Jack?"

"The French retreated, so we had to pull back, and our units scattered. Then Pete got hit."

"In me arm." Pete points to his dirty bandage. "Sun was getting low when we made it to a dressing station to get me bandaged. We had a wounded officer with us. Jack held him together to get to the station, but he died there. Felt close to Jack, he did, both being Canadians. Kept a hold on Jack's arm and didn't seem like he'd let go. By the time I was bandaged up, he was dead."

Jack nods. "Colonel Albert Warner—he was shot in the stomach. I knew he wouldn't survive, but he tried to hang on. He wasn't from our unit. He was an engineer with the command, but our officers were dead or as scattered as we were. We took the colonel as far as we could—got him to the surgeon before he died."

"So then you wandered north?" I ask. My fuzzy notion of where we are doesn't help me picture this fighting.

Pete grunts and pats his stomach. "Dodged through a village, slept in a barn, spent a day in a cornfield hiding from Fritz. Enemy was everywhere, poking swords into the corn trying to puncture us."

Images of soldiers and weapons and death keep us silent for a minute.

Jack looks at Elise. "Where are you from?"

She chews her lip before answering. "Charleroi," she answers.

"Heavy fighting there too," Jack says.

"The Germans pushed your army out and seized the town." She stands and kicks dirt on the trampled fire. "We cannot stay here."

"Where are you heading?" Jack stands and picks up his rifle.

"Brussels." She thinks for a minute. "If you get to Brussels and follow the canal to Antwerp, you can cross the border to Holland."

I help Pete to his feet. He isn't as wobbly as he was. "Can we follow the main road?" I ask.

Elise points at Pete. "Not in uniforms. The Germans will shoot if they see you. They will kill all of us. You must find other clothes."

I'm still wearing the priest's clothes, looking very strange myself. "Are there any work clothes in the house?"

"No," Elise shakes her head. "I looked, but the house is empty. The family took everything. There are no clothes, nothing."

"We won't put you in danger," Jack says. "We'll go on alone." He turns to me. "Thanks for helping us. And thank you for the chicken," he adds, tipping his head to Elise.

My hands curl into fists, and my muscles tighten across my shoulders as I try to think clearly. Jack's ghost must have had a stronger reason to find me a hundred years in the future than helping me out of a ravine, and if we separate now, I'll never know what I'm to do. I'm not going to leave him just because we don't have two shirts and two pairs of pants.

"We have to stick together. I'll find the clothes we need," I blurt out.

8

They look at me, expectation on their faces. I have no plan, and when I take a long shaky breath, they know I don't have one and disappointment shows.

"I mean, we'll find another house and we'll find clothes. The next farm or next village must have clothes left behind even if everybody's abandoned the place."

It's not much of a plan, but Pete nods as if I've said something very clever. "Jenny's got it right. We're bound to find some work clothes. People are running. They don't have time to pack up everything they own."

"We have to avoid the main roads even if we find new clothes," Jack says with a glance at me. "Elise is right. You'll be shot along with us if the Germans see us in uniform. They don't ask questions. I saw an officer try to surrender, and he was shot down where he stood." His deep brown eyes turn almost black. "I'll tell you the truth. You two might be safer traveling alone."

I send a significant look at Elise. "We can't protect ourselves from German soldiers with a wine bottle and a rock."

Jack looks confused, but Elise understands me, and she knows I'm right. Our fight with the man in the green scarf wasn't even close to what a fight with a German soldier would be. Still she hesitates, chews her lip, murmurs something to herself in French, and doesn't try to hide her obvious wish she could leave Jack and Pete behind.

"We can walk together—for now," she says at last. "It is best to cross fields and woods until you find new clothes."

Pete and Jack fill their water bottles at the well, and Elise fills a wineskin from the house with water for us. I sling the wineskin over my shoulder. The priest's big shirt covers me pretty well, but my face and hands feel fiery hot under the bright sun as we set out heading toward some woods. Before we walk more than a mile over the rutted ground under the sun, I'm so thirsty it's a struggle to swallow, and I can't work up enough spit to coat my throat.

I fall behind and take a long drink from the wineskin. The water is already warm and the taste is definitely unpleasant, but it's the only water we have. Before I can take another swallow, Elise snatches the wineskin away from me and slings it over her shoulder.

"Not too much," she says. "It has to last until we find a stream." She points toward the woods. "It will be cooler in there."

The crops have been harvested from the plowed fields, but Elise finds a few potatoes and onions and stuffs them into her sack. Two wooden plows lie smashed into pieces close to the edge of the field.

Without announcing he's in charge, Jack takes the lead and walks a step or two ahead of Elise, holding his rifle ready to shoot. I follow in Elise's footsteps and pray silently we don't meet any soldiers. They killed the priest in the village without hesitating—killing us wouldn't take any thought. When we reach the woods, the trees shield us from the sun and the air is cooler, so we stay under the trees the rest of the morning. My feet ache. I'm hungry again.

I halt and sniff the air. "Smoke," I hiss at the others.

Jack motions for silence, but it's not necessary because we all freeze in place while we stare at wisps of gray smoke curling around the tiny branches in the thick brush. Jack pushes through the bushes and follows the smoke. I stay close on his heels, with Pete and Elise behind me. After a minute we reach a row of hedges on the edge of what looks like a pasture, but there are no cows grazing and a low cloud of smoke floats over the grass.

On the far side of the pasture, a farm house has burned to the ground, and faint traces of smoke drift from smoldering piles in the rubble. I step forward, but Jack puts out his arm, stopping me.

"Soldiers might still be around," he whispers.

Pete swears under his breath, not bothering to apologize this time.

We circle the pasture, keeping the hedges between us and the open grass. The Germans must have taken the livestock because we don't see any animals. I cross my fingers, hoping I don't see any bodies. The farm buildings are charred, but some walls are still standing. Jack signals, and we sprint across the field to the well on the far side. We drink one after another. I linger until Pete finally takes the ladle away from me and mumbles something about too much water. Ducking my head in the bucket, I shake my wet hair and wipe my face on the priest's big shirt to clean off some of the grime stuck in my pores. I wonder if I'll ever have a shower again. Maybe the dirt will cake over me until I disappear.

The sun's directly overhead when we come through trees and reach another farm. This stone house isn't damaged. The heavy wooden front door is closed. Two lone cows munch grass in the pasture.

"The Germans might have missed this place," Jack whispers.

Pete grunts. "Might have, or the farmer's friendly with the invaders."

The house looks deserted, but we crouch behind the bushes in case someone comes back. A half hour passes with no sign of soldiers or farmers.

"I'll go in," I announce. "I'll snatch clothes and come back."

Jack shakes his head. "We can only see one side of the house. The family might be in the back fields. Soldiers could be inside."

"I don't look like an enemy," I point out. "I'm a lost refugee. If I see someone, I'll just say I'm lost."

Jack frowns. "You don't speak the language."

"I don't mind saying I've never seen a young lady dressed quite like you," Pete comments. "Could be the Germans wouldn't know what to do with you if they did catch you. How'd you get them clothes anyway?"

"I will go with Jenny," Elise nudges Jack. "You stay here in the trees."

Elise is a few steps behind me as we walk toward the house. My throat's dry again. I can't help expecting a round of bullets to come out of the building.

The rusty door latch creaks when I push it open. A double window in one wall provides the only light in the kitchen. A long rectangular wooden table sits in the center of the room with four mismatched chairs around it, and a tall, wide wardrobe, the door open, stands against the wall opposite one end of the table. The wardrobe is empty, and the upper shelves are missing. Dirty dishes and pans sit in the sink under the window. The priest's kitchen was more up to date. This sink has no faucet, just a hand pump. I hurry through the open door leading to a bedroom.

A trunk pushed against the foot of the bed looks promising. I raise the lid slowly in case there's some kind of trap inside. "Elise," I whisper, "there are clothes in here." Work clothes, neatly folded, stacked at the bottom of the trunk. Anyone could see the people who live here aren't rich, and I feel guilty about stealing, but I do it anyway because these clothes could save us. "Let's go," I hiss as soon as I've grabbed pants and shirts.

Elise ignores me. She picks through the clutter on top of a table tilted against the wall because of a broken leg. Pocketing a few coins, she inhales sharply and holds up a silver crucifix dangling from a long silver chain. "Look, real silver—worth much money," she says.

"Don't take that!" I clutch the clothes to my chest and edge toward the doorway. I can rationalize lying and stealing clothes that mean life or death for Jack and Pete, but stealing a crucifix isn't about saving people. "We don't need a crucifix."

She ignores me. She swings the crucifix back and forth in the light for a second and smiles as she tucks it in her pocket. "It is worth money," she repeats.

"Put it back," I hiss at her. "We can't take that."

Her expression turns dark. Her jaw sets in a tight line. "I am not stupid. We have to take what we can. Why should I leave it for the Germans to find?"

"Elise, leave it there. Maybe the farmer will come back. Maybe he isn't dead or gone. The crucifix is probably sacred to him. We need clothes not money."

She shrugs. Then she looks over my shoulder. Without a word, she turns, hooks one leg through the open window and slides out, disappearing over the window sill faster than I can ask her what's happening.

I spin around and stare in horror at a huge, muscular woman who's almost as wide as the doorway she's standing in. Her large, strong hands are on her hips, her feet spread. Her face is red. Her eyes glare at me.

9

We stare at each other. Her rolled-up sleeves show hard muscles bunched in her bare arms. Blocking the doorway, she says something in French, but she's pointing at the clothes in my arms, so it's not hard to figure out what she means. Her voice rises to a roar while she shakes her fist at me.

I'm pretty sure she could kill me with her bare hands, but I can't give up the clothes. No way to explain in French why I need them, and she might not be on my side even if I could explain. Her house wasn't burned, and two cows are grazing in the pasture, so for all I know she's friendly with the Germans. The only thought beating in my head is that Jack and Pete need me. I clutch the clothes tighter and murmur an apology, but she doesn't understand me or doesn't care about apologies because she yells and shakes her fist again.

I take a tentative step toward the doorway, but she moves inside the room, closer to me, blocking my exit. Her face gets redder, and without any warning, she hurls herself at me, reaching for the clothes or my throat—I'm not sure which.

I shriek and jump on the bed, still holding the pants and shirts. Her shouting gets louder, and she stumbles along the side of the bed, grabbing at me while I dodge and jump out of the way. The bed is like a soft trampoline, and she's strong, but not quick, so I stay out of her reach by jumping to a new spot while she's grabbing at the air where I was a second before.

With a couple of well placed bounces, I lure her to the head of the bed. Taking a flying leap, I reach the doorway before she can get around the bed. Inside the main room, I dash for the door, but my foot catches on the table leg, sending me to the floor, pants and shirts slipping out of my hands. In a minute, the woman is on top of me.

She punches me hard on the side of the head. Dizzy, I roll away from her fists and grab the edge of the table to pull myself up. She lunges at me, but I duck and hurl one of the chairs in front of her so she stumbles. I don't know how to fight. If she gets her hands on me, she'll crush me. We circle the table, weaving back and forth—she grasping, me avoiding. I hurl another chair at her, but she's ready this time and dodges it.

We're at a standstill. She's at the opposite end of the table, her back to the empty wardrobe. If I rush for the door, all she has to do is grab me with her huge hands as I go past her. I gesture at the pants and shirts scattered on the floor to show I've given them up. She doesn't even turn her head to look at the clothes. She's only interested in me now. We each grip an end of the table and watch for any move by the other one. I'm afraid of her strength, but her eyes terrify me more—she's full of rage.

I take a cautious step to one side, but she immediately steps in the same direction. I retreat, and she retreats, so our positions don't change—both stuck at opposite ends of the table. Desperate, I shove the table as hard as I can, ramming it into her so quickly and violently she reels backward. Knocked off her feet, looking dazed, she tumbles into the empty wardrobe, smacking her head against the back. I wedge the table hard against the wardrobe, trapping her. Once she gets her senses back, the table won't hold her for very long.

Snatching the pants and shirts, I race outside, running as fast as I can toward the trees at the far side of the pasture. I'm halfway across the pasture when Jack sprints across the short grass in full view of anyone close enough to spot him.

"You shouldn't be out here," I gasp as I reach him.

He puts his hand under my arm and half carries me at a run away from the house, past the cows, and through the brush into the woods. He drags me along until we are deep under the cover of the trees, surrounded by thick bushes that shield us from the view of anyone even a few feet away.

By the time we stop running, I'm shaking from tension and panting. Jack leans against a tree, and puts his arm tight around my shoulders. Without thinking, I collapse against him and rest my forehead on his chest, still clutching the clothes. For the first time since my strange trip out of Aunt Connie's garden, I feel safe—sort of.

"Why were you in the open like that?" I ask after I catch my breath. "You're in uniform—you have to stay hidden."

He looks surprised. "You were in trouble," he says. "You needed me."

I'm half irritated he took such a risk and half thrilled he didn't desert me. I take a deep breath and step back. "Did you see Elise?"

A dark expression crosses his face. "She said you'd been caught, and we should get out."

"If that woman had gotten her hands on me, she'd have broken my neck." I shiver at the memory of her huge hands. "I'm glad you didn't leave me behind."

He grins. "I'd never leave you behind, Jenny—you had the clothes."

We plunge through the woods, Jack in the lead, me stumbling behind, leaving a trail of broken twigs and trampled leaves, clutching the clothes against my chest, and praying the farm woman is still stuck in the wardrobe.

Elise gapes at us when we push through the trees and find her with Pete, sitting on the ground. I can't tell if her shock means she's happy or disappointed Jack found me.

There's no doubt how Pete feels because he leaps to his feet. "I knew you'd be back with Jenny!" He slaps Jack's back and turns to Elise. "Jack keeps his promises, he does."

"The woman was so big. . . ." Elise shrugs. "When you did not follow me out the window, I thought you were trapped," she says. "I went for help."

Jack's expression tells me he doesn't believe her, and I don't either. Pushing aside my memory of the woman's wild, hate-filled eyes as she grabbed for me, I act as if it was nothing to me. "She's probably on her feet by now. We need to get farther away."

We tramp through the woods in silence, putting distance between us and the farm, until Elise says, "I hear water that way."

I hear nothing, but by now I know Elise always hears water. She leads, and we fall into line behind her, pushing through bushes and trees. When we reach the stream, it's bigger than any we've passed so far, and it's rushing fast between the banks, so it's good to drink and it's deep enough to wash the grime off.

Pete sorts through the clothes and tosses a blue shirt to me. "This one looks small enough for you. You can throw away that black shirt."

I hold the shirt up to measure. It's smaller than the priest's shirt, and it's clean.

"Say, Jenny," Pete continues. "Jack and me can change here and wash up. You young ladies can go beyond the bend and take a dip yourselves if you want." He makes a little bow and laughs. "As gentlemen in His Majesty's army, we would never disturb you."

I'm lightheaded at the idea of having water all over me and washing my hair—or maybe it's hunger making me dizzy—but the notion of actually getting clean overrides my other needs for the time being.

Elise and I follow the bank until Pete and Jack are out of sight. Without hesitating a second, Elise strips off her blouse and skirt, a cotton slip, a camisole with pink trim lace around the neckline, and baggy panties—bloomers I guess—that reach her knees. In a second, she's stark naked and jumps into the water, squealing at the cold, but wading farther out until she's waist deep.

"Come!" She waves to me and splashes water over her shoulders.

I strip off the priest's shirt and hesitate because I'm not sure how she'll react when she sees my real clothes. I peel off my tee shirt, which I hope she thinks is a camisole. I don't have any idea when bras were invented, but she wasn't wearing one and she's staring at mine, so no matter what she says, I'm going to claim all Americans are wearing these odd pieces. I pull off my shorts followed by my pink bikini panties.

The water's too cold for me to jump in the stream the way Elise did, so I ease into it until I'm up to my waist. Elise laughs and splashes me with water until I stop shivering. The afternoon sun is hot enough to warm me once I'm used to the water temperature.

"I wish we had at least one cup of detergent," I remark while we beat our clothes on the rocks.

"A cup of what?"

"Um, soap, I wish we had soap."

The hot sun dries our underwear within minutes, but we soak in the water while we wait for the heavier fabrics to dry. When we crawl back on the bank, Elise is fascinated by my pink bra. She holds it up to study the straps and hooks.

"I like it." She glances at me over her shoulder. "Jenny, I was afraid when that woman found us in her house. I thought you would follow me out the window."

I don't know if she's telling the truth or just trying to smooth things over. She stole money and the crucifix from the farmhouse, a lot more than I stole, so staying around to help me when the woman came home probably seemed like a bad idea. She did help me fight off Green Scarf, as I call him to myself, so I'll give her the benefit of the doubt this time. She didn't want to travel with Jack and Pete, but she didn't desert us.

"I got away from her, didn't I?"

She looks relieved, and we pull our dry clothing off the rocks to dress without saying another word about the woman.

Pete calls from up stream. "Ladies! We're decent now, so you can find us when you want to."

I shake my head to get the water out of my hair and run my fingers through it to spread the curls. I'd like a blow dryer and deodorant but at least I'm clean again.

Jack and Pete are shirtless when Elise and I get back to them. They're crouched over a shallow pit, digging at the dirt with their bayonets, their uniforms in a pile on the ground.

"We have to bury our uniforms and rifles," Jack explains. "If the Germans find uniforms, they'll know we're here somewhere, and they won't let up until they find us."

"Keeping our pistols," Pete adds. "If we meet Fritz, we'll have to fight. I won't be a prisoner."

"The hole's deep enough." Jack drops his bayonet into the gap. Next, he tosses in their uniforms, the rifles, and Pete's bayonet before kicking the dirt back in the hole to cover everything.

I kneel next to him to help pat down the earth while Elise and Pete refill our wineskin and their canteens from the stream. When Jack bends and stretches his right arm to reach the loose dirt, I see the fiery red mark on the inside of his wrist. It looks like a dagger with the blade pointing toward his elbow.

I gasp and put my fingers lightly on the mark. He lifts his head and smiles. "It's a birthmark. Runs in my family."

I nod, but my mind churns with questions. Jack's birthmark is exactly like the one on Dan's wrist. When we were little and played in Aunt Connie's yard, Dan and I pretended his birthmark was a magical symbol giving him power to cast spells. It's not just a red mark; it's distinctive.

Once the sun sets, we roast the potatoes and onions over the smallest blaze Jack can make. Butter and salt would make the food perfect, but it tastes great as it is. We have to sleep outside, so I pick out an enormous tree near the stream and slump back against the trunk.

Jack settles next to me. "I've been wondering about you, Jenny. You don't look like any girl I've ever seen. Your hair is short as a boy's, and I've never seen shoes like those."

"American girls are different than Canadian girls."

"Not that different," he says. "Our farm was near the border across from Detroit. My father and I went there every month for supplies, and I didn't see any American girl on the streets dressed like you."

"You weren't paying close attention. I'm going to sleep now," I mumble as I close my eyes. The tenseness in my shoulders fades, and I let myself slip sideways until my head rests against Jack's shoulder. There's something so comfortable—so familiar—about leaning against him. At the last instant before I fade into sleep, Jack gently brushes his hand over the top of my head and ruffles my curls.

10

The next morning, we trudge across fields, wade across brooks, and push through straggly brush that scratches my hands and rips at my clothes. Jack walks ahead of me wearing the faded gray shirt I stole for him while questions flutter in my head. The birthmark on Dan's wrist matches the birthmark on Jack's wrist. Therefore, since I am in 1914, Jack must be Dan's—how many greats did Dan tell me were ahead of *grandfather*? I can't remember, but the bigger question is why Jack came to me as a ghost instead of to Dan's grandmother.

I wish I'd paid more attention to her story about the spirit she wanted to reach, but now the details are fuzzy except she said he wrote a war diary. Jack isn't keeping a diary now, so he must have written about his war experiences later. Aunt Connie's theory about living other lives and layers of time settles in my mind. Maybe I'm living another life. If we're all killed today, what would happen to Dan or his grandmother? What would happen to me? Would we all exist in the future time? Am I reliving what's already happened, or am I living it for the first time here? I groan out loud because the questions change every time I think them.

Jack looks over his shoulder.

I force a smile. "I'm all right, just a little tired."

Whatever the answer to this mystery is, I'm definitely not having a dream. The church cemetery was real. The woman punching me in the farmhouse was real. Jack touching my hair last night was real. The mud I'm stepping in is real.

We don't see a living soul all day. In late afternoon, Jack takes a chance and shoots a rabbit. Then we hide for an hour in the woods, waiting to see if any soldiers heard the shots. When the sun goes down, Elise skins the rabbit and roasts it over a low fire near another abandoned barn. I've never tasted rabbit, and no matter what Pete says, I don't think it tastes much like chicken. But I'm so hungry I'd probably eat skunk. I say that out loud, and Jack and Pete laugh.

No, you wouldn't, Luv," Pete says. "Not unless you was about to die of hunger. You might say skunk don't tempt the palate." The pants I stole are too long for him. He rolled them up but they unroll as he walks. "Got to fix these." Leaning back, he unties the puttee covering his leg gash, cuts the puttee in two with his knife and carefully ties each piece around one of his ankles, holding the pants legs in place. "Should do it." He winks at me.

I laugh. "Where are we?" I swallow the last bite of rabbit with a gulp so the taste doesn't linger.

Jack shakes his head. "I don't know. I lost my compass at Mons, but we're still heading north." He points to the sky, but every star looks the same to me.

"Elise, do you know where we are?" I ask.

"No," she shrugs. "We must find someone to ask."

In spite of their change of clothes, Jack and Pete don't look very much like local farmers, and Elise is the only one who speaks French. We know now she'd run if there's trouble, so we can't depend on her. I'm not too confident about getting help right now.

"We'll stay in the barn tonight," Jack says. "The roof has some holes in it, but it's going to rain, and some roof is better than no roof."

Before long, the rain starts. It's only a light spray, and we settle in the barn under the remaining part of the roof. The double doors hang half off their hinges, so we can't close them, but the fresh breeze is a relief because, although the animals are gone, their scent hangs in the air. Pete and Elise sit in the straw against one wall. Jack and I settle down opposite them on feed bags spread out on the rough floor. The mist sprays through the broken roof, making the dirt floor slick wherever the roof is open.

Pete whistles a tune I've never heard and leans back in the straw, his good arm behind his head. "I quite like the rain actually," he says. "Reminds me of home when I played with my chums in the mud."

I stretch out, thankful my sneakers are now covered with a thick layer of caked mud. "Where's home?"

"Sheffield." Pete sighs. "Miss it a bit, I do, even miss the noise from the steel mill. Me dad died in the mill, crushed by a slab. Brother George, older than me, works in the mill now, but mum didn't want me there, and I didn't want to be there, so I joined the army. Thought I'd see the world like Uncle Harry. He fought the Boers in South Africa—talked about it all the time." His grin fades. "I hope I live to talk about Belgium."

Jack punches a feed sack into shape so he can lean it against one of the posts holding up the roof. He keeps his pistol on his lap, aimed at the open door. "We'll get back to England, Pete. You'll have plenty to talk about."

Elise's gaze travels over me from my odd shoes to my short curly hair. "Jenny, where is your family?"

Keep it simple, I think. Don't get caught in an elaborate inconsistency. Make it nearly the truth—except for the hundred year gap of course.

"I'm... we live in Chicago near Lake Michigan. My father's a teacher, and I go to Washington Academy." I can remember *Washington* without much trouble, and if I said Kennedy High School, I'd have to explain who Kennedy was and how would I do that?

Elise stares, making me feel I'm pinned in place. "Do you have a sweetheart?"

What are the dating rules for 1914? "No, I don't." It's the safest thing to say. "My mother thinks I'm too young." I assume—hope—mothers in 1914 have a lot of control over what their daughters do.

Jack pays attention to our talk although he's seems to be concentrating on his pistol, making sure it's loaded, aiming at the open doorway as if soldiers are storming into the barn.

"What about you?" I turn attention on Elise. "Where's your family?"

She shrugs. "They are all dead."

"In Charleroi?"

"No, they all died long ago."

"In Charleroi?"

She looks irritated. "No, in Limburg. After my mother died, I worked for the English family in Charleroi."

I have no idea where Limburg is, so I stop tossing questions at her. I wonder what kind of family she had. Were they thieves like her? Maybe I'd be a thief if I had no family in the middle of a war.

"Do you have a sweetheart?"

She bites her lip. "No."

I wonder if she's lying about not having a sweetheart, but it hardly matters. I've probably lied more than she has. I can't resist another question. "Where will you go eventually?"

"Nowhere! You can go home to America, but I have no home now." She folds her arms across her chest and glares at me. That stops the conversation for a few minutes. Elise stamps on the straw to flatten it, sits, wiggles around trying to get comfortable, and turns her attention to Jack. "Where is your family?"

"Ontario, Canada," he replies. "We have a farm close to the Michigan border."

"Why are you in the British army?" I ask.

"I was visiting my mother's relatives in Salisbury, and my cousin decided to join the army, so I did too. I didn't think I'd be in a war so quick."

Pete chuckles. "Hasty decision for a Canadian fellow, Jack. Should have gone home after your visit, but instead you get shipped off to

Belgium, the Germans nearly kill you, and now you're sitting in a barn under a leaky roof."

"Can't see how you did much better." Jack grins. "You signed up to see the world—now you're sitting in this leaky barn with me."

Pete stretches out in the straw. "Right you are." He points to the doorway. "Are you taking first watch?"

"I'm not tired. I'll watch for a few hours."

The rain stops; the clouds break up; stars glimmer in the dark. Pete and Elise murmur to each other for a few minutes, but soon I hear deep, slow breathing coming from the other side of the barn. Jack puts another feed bag against the post, settles back and watches the open doors, his fingers resting on his pistol.

I wiggle closer, curiosity picking at me, and whisper. "What did your parents say when you joined the army?"

"I'm not sure they know. My mother's cousin might have written to her, but I haven't talked to my parents for over two years."

"Why not?"

"My father wanted me to be a farmer, to take over our farm eventually. We argued a lot, but he couldn't accept what I was saying, so when I turned seventeen and finished school, I took off. Got to England, visited my father's relatives, and when my cousin Charley joined the army, so did I."

"Where's Charley?"

"I don't know. He was at Mons, but in a different unit."

"Maybe your father isn't angry anymore."

"I have three sisters. I'm the only boy, and he always said it's my duty to take over the farm. He's not likely to change his mind about that."

"You have to do what you want."

"Get some sleep, Jenny."

We get to our feet, rearrange the feed bags, and punch them into a comfortable shape for us to lean against. When he shifts his body to gave me room, his loose shirt pulls open at the throat.

"What's this?" I whisper, running my finger over a flat, leather envelop hanging around his neck.

"It was Colonel Warner's—you remember—he was the officer who died after we got him to the dressing station. I promised him I'd bring it back to England."

"Very nice of you," I murmur. "You didn't know him."

He laughs deep in his throat. "It's only paper. I can carry it."

Reluctantly, I move my hand away, wishing I had an excuse to keep it on his chest because I like feeling Jack's heart beating under my palm. "Still, it's nice of you to carry a message to his family."

"Sleep!"

I curl up next to him. In a minute, he reaches across the rough cloth of the feed bag and takes my hand in his. I shift just enough to rest my head against his shoulder—I like it there. I don't know what he's thinking, but my mind shifts back and forth between the danger we might face tomorrow and how safe I feel when his fingers link through mine.

I'm tired, my legs ache, but I can't fall asleep immediately. What would Jack say if I told him I lived a hundred years in the future until he kissed me in a garden and brought me here? It's all a muddle. Finally, my eyes close, and I focus on the warmth from Jack's body before sleep blots out my confusion.

11

Soldiers shoot the priest in the street. I try to stop them, but then the soldiers turn and chase me. I run and run, the soldiers are behind me, getting closer. I wake up with a violent jerk, my legs kicking into the air.

The dent made by Jack's body is still on the feed bags next to me, but I'm alone in the barn. The floor is patchy with sunlight coming through the holes in the roof. Voices rise outside, and I let out a long breath, deliberately exhaling tension. I'm sure the only thing worse than existing in this place would be to exist in it alone.

Outside, Pete and Elise fill the canteens and wineskin at the well while Pete talks about what he'll do when he gets back to England. Elise rolls her eyes to the sky, but she nods and murmurs *ummm* whenever Pete stops for a breath. The bandage sticking out the sleeve of his shirt looks filthy. We should change it, but there's no drugstore with gauze, tape, and antiseptic cream nearby.

Jack dips his head in a low trough full of fresh rain water, then wipes his wet face on his shirt sleeve, and shakes his black hair like a shaggy dog.

"You shouldn't have let me sleep," I say.

He shakes his head again, spraying a few more drops in the air. "A few minutes doesn't matter. We'll leave as soon as we fill up with water."

I lower my voice and glance in Pete's direction. "Pete needs a new bandage. We can't hide in the woods forever."

"We might find a village doctor up ahead, but we have to be careful. If the Germans catch us out of uniform, we'll be shot as spies."

"You said you'd be shot if you were caught in uniform."

He runs his fingers over the butt of the pistol shoved into his belt. "That's right—we'll be shot in or out of uniform. The important thing is not to be caught."

In uniform—out of uniform. There are no rules to follow. I'm silent, wondering how I'm going to be any help for all of us.

"Jenny, if we get to a village," Jack avoids looking at me, "if we reach a friendly village, you and Elise should stay there. Pete and I—we can go on alone."

"It's safer if we travel together." I protest.

"It's not safe no matter how we travel," he mutters.

"We can help each other. You were stuck in that ravine when I found you. I helped you get Pete out and that proves we're safer together."

Of course, he doesn't realize he traveled across time to find me in Aunt Connie's garden, kiss me, and bring me here. To me, that proves we have to stay together, but if I say all that to him, he'll decide I'm crazy and find a reason to leave me behind.

He frowns again. "I don't think—"

A loud, long gurgle cuts him off. I flush and push my hand hard against my stomach, trying to stop the sound. Nothing stops it. The gurgle rumbles on and on until it fades away.

"That's what I mean," Jack says with a grin. "I'm grateful for everything you've done for me—and Pete. No denying you'd have more to eat if you weren't trudging around the countryside with us."

"My stomach doesn't know when it's hungry. It gurgles for no reason."

"Yeah, I'm never really hungry either, but we'd better find some food today. Go ahead and wash."

The rain water is cool and fairly clean, so I dunk my head in the trough the way Jack did, and wipe my face on my shirt. The coins Elise and I stole from Green Scarf jingle in my pocket, and a quick fantasy about buying toothpaste races through my mind. Instead, I rub the priest's stubby toothbrush across my teeth and dunk my head again in the trough.

We cut across the meadow behind the barn, tramp through woods on the other side, and reach a narrow dirt road along the edge of a cornfield where the stalks are as high as my shoulders. Elise snatches ripe cobs off the stalks and stuffs them in her bag. I feel stupid for not thinking of it myself, so I follow her, pull cobs off the stalks and shove them into my canvas sack.

In the distance, smoke from burning haystacks shoots up in black columns that separate into dark wispy curls against the clear blue sky. Tension tightens my shoulder muscles. The fields look empty, but the fires must have been started by soldiers, so they aren't far away.

Then we see them—six German soldiers riding horses along the dirt road. Elise hisses a warning, and we slip into the cornfield, hunching down between the stalks, trying not to knock over any that would mark a trail, staying close to the ground. The thump from the horses' hooves gets closer. I hold my breath, digging my fingers into the dirt. Through the corn stalks, I can see Jack's gray shirt. A splotch of blue farther away on the other side is Pete. My shirt is blue too. If they search at all, the Germans would have to be blind not to spot our colors in the corn. Elise is the only one wearing a light cotton blouse the same shade as the corn stalks.

The soldiers slow down and stop at the edge of the field, close to the rows where I crouch. The horses are nervous, snorting and stamping, so the soldiers have to shout to each other. The anger underneath the shouting is easy enough to understand. A soldier spurs his horse into the field between the rows where I'm hiding. It's too late for me to move back, so I flatten myself against the ground and hold my breath as he rides through the corn rows close to where I'm lying. Looking up, I see him clearly when he stops. He's young, like Pete and Jack. After a long, long minute, he turns the horse and rides out of the corn, shouting again to the others. I breathe just deeply enough to keep my lungs working while my heart pounds.

The horses paw the ground while the soldiers talk. Should I slither farther back into the rows? I discard that idea because any sounds or movement from the corn stalks will alert the Germans. A hiss and crackling—more shouts—then a flaming torch arches high into the air, over my head and lands in the middle of the cornfield.

Fire!

The corn stalks catch fire quickly, filling the air with sizzling, crackling sounds growing louder as the fire spreads. Smoke coils between the rows and between each stalk, cutting off clean air, and I press my face against my shoulder, trying not to inhale the smoke. The solders in the road have problems too because their horses are terrified of the flames—rearing and pawing the ground. The smoke is suffocating, and I struggle to keep a cough from exploding out of my stinging lungs. I have to get away. The fire makes enough crackling noise to cover whatever shuffling sounds I'd make if I move, and if I can't see the soldiers through the smoke, the soldiers probably can't see the field clearly. I slide sideways between the stalks, moving away from the thickest smoke, creeping across the ground. I have to leave my canvas bag behind. At a gap in the corn row, I see Jack.

Keep going, he mouths, pointing in the direction I've been moving.

A desperate need to cough rises in my throat, but I muffle the sound in my elbow while the heat builds around us. I can't see above my head—no way to tell if the soldiers have spotted us.

Jack reaches me, grips my arm and yanks me forward. "Pull your shirt over your nose," he hisses softly.

Keeping my head down and shirt pulled over my nose, I follow Jack, wiggling through the corn rows and over piles of broken stalks. The stiff leaves scrape my face and hands, so little trickles of blood mark my skin. My throat burns, and I press my shirt against my nose, trying not to cough, even though the cough is fighting to burst from my lungs. I slow down for a minute to catch my breath, but Jack tightens his hold on my arm and pulls me through an opening between two rows of corn stalks where we meet Pete inching slowly along the ground, leaning on his good arm and stifling choking sounds deep in his throat. Dirty tracks of tears from the smoke and heat streak his cheeks.

"Don't worry about me," Pete gasps. "I'll follow you."

I shake off Jack's hand and point to Pete. Jack hesitates and starts to reach for me again, but then he nods, grabs Pete's good arm, and pulls him along. Elise could be ahead of us, or behind us, or on fire.

"Where's Elise?" My throat is so dry I can barely get the words out.

"Don't know," Pete whispers.

As far as I can tell, we're crawling diagonally through the corn rows, heading in the opposite direction of the fire spreading toward the road where the Germans are waiting to flush out anyone foolish enough to try to hide from them. I can't hear much over the snapping sound of the corn stalks as flames race along the rows, and the stalks crumble into charred pieces. We crawl, twisting and turning through the rows of corn stalks. My face feels as if it's melting, the smoke stings my eyes, and I struggle to keep my shirt pulled over my nose while I creep along, following Pete's feet as Jack drags him ahead of me.

Jack must have a plan—I hope. If he doesn't, we'll be cinders before long. The fire could jump in any direction. My face is caked in dirt, and I can't get more than a puff of air into my lungs with every breath. Finally, we reach a opening in the rows of stalks.

Jack pulls his shirt down from his mouth and rises to his knees for a quick look ahead. "This is the end of the field," he whispers and points. "The woods are about a hundred yards that way. We'll have to run across the open ground." He drops flat on his stomach again. He tries to smile, but his jaw is rigid and his hands clench into fists for an instant.

I peer through the stalks at the clustered trees and the flat ground we have to cross to get there. Gray smoke from the fire hangs low across the grass, but the smoke isn't thick enough to hide us if we make a dash for the woods.

"Where are the soldiers?" My whisper is harsh croak.

"Don't know," Jack says. "I hope they're on the road where they were. Maybe they won't see us run for it. The woods look thick—hard to get through that brush on a horse. If we can get into the trees, we'll probably be all right."

Pete smothers a cough. "That's the rub, Jack. They'll catch us before we make the woods. There's no cover. Won't take a good horse but a second to cross that ground."

"It's Elise!" I half rise to watch her sprint out of the corn only a few rows from where we are and run in a zigzag pattern across the grass, heading for the woods.

Jack swears under his breath. "We have to go now!"

He pulls Pete to his feet, and we follow Elise across the open grass. Pete runs faster than I thought he could. I'm zigzagging, as I run, but it's not an evasion strategy. My sight blurs. My lungs are full of smoke, and I can't keep up with Jack. Tears from coughing and breathing in smoke run down my cheeks. I stumble over the uneven ground, but I can't resist looking over my shoulder.

The soldiers have spotted us.

Horses pound along the dirt road toward our end of the field. The woods look incredibly far away, but Elise reaches them first and disappears into the brush. A bullet hits the ground a few feet ahead of me.

"Keep running," Jack yells. "Don't look back."

Another bullet kicks up dirt on one side. Terror helps me run faster. The Germans aren't good shots or maybe their horses are too hard to control because of the fire. More bullets come close, but we dash into the woods before the horses can reach us.

The bushes are so dense there's no path for the horses. The soldiers shout, and one fires into the trees, but we stumble deeper into the woods. More shots. The soldiers turn their horses back to the road and trot in the opposite direction.

Nobody moves for a few minutes while we drink from the canteens, cough, and drag fresh air into our lungs. Elise lost the wineskin in the corn field, so all we have are the canteens. Pete takes long, shuddering breaths and holds his wounded arm tight across his chest. Jack leans against a tree, breathing slowly. We look terrible. Smoky, black streaks trail down our faces; our filthy clothes are torn. My arms and hands are bloody from the broken stalks that felt like knives on my skin. I'm desperate to wash off the blood and dirt, but I don't dare use drinking water for washing.

"We're alive," Jack says quietly. A brownish-red splotch of blood seeps through his shirt.

"You're hit." I crawl closer to him.

He grimaces. "It's not much. Bullet grazed me when we were running."

I pull his shirt up to look. The wound isn't deep, but it's a bloody streak about six inches along his side.

Jack winces. "It's not bad, Jenny. Don't worry about it. It won't bleed for long—it's almost stopped now." He pulls his shirt down and presses it against the wound.

Elise tries to talk, but nothing comes out of her mouth until she takes another long drink of water. "We are close to a village. I saw a sign when we walked on the road. Denappe." She makes a vague gesture.

"Do you know people there?" A coughing fit takes over and I collapse on the ground, struggling to breathe.

"No. If the Germans did not burn it, we might find food." Her voice is raspy with smoke.

"Where's the village?" Jack asks.

"On the other side of these woods," she says. "I saw the sign at the crossroads. See—this way."

She draws a little map in the damp dirt. I squint at the lines. If we walk straight through the woods, we should run into the village on the other side, but there's no way to know how big the woods are, and I'm not confident in her map.

Jack says what I'm thinking. "We need to find that village, but we can't take the road."

12

We trip over tangled roots, splash through puddles, and push past thick brush that rips at our skin and clothes. Pete and Jack check the sun to keep our direction. Elise, naturally, finds a stream, so we stop to drink. Our stomachs make gurgling sounds, but we lost the bags with corn in the fire.

"Where are we?" I ask, coming up for air after plunging my face in the stream.

Nobody answers. Pete flops on the ground, spread-eagled, his eyes closed. Jack puts his face in the water, gulps, and shakes his wet hair before he dips the canteens into the stream, refilling them and testing the caps for leaks.

Elise puts her head in her hands and groans. "The village is close." She points at the trees, which, to me, look the same as the trees we passed at least an hour ago.

I sit on the ground next to Pete while suspicions whirl in my mind. Are Jack and Pete pretending they can read the sun's position? Does Elise really know if there is a village nearby? We could be surrounded by hundreds of German soldiers right now. Maybe we'll wander in the woods until we're too tired, too dirty and too hungry to keep going.

Jack urges us back on our feet, and we push through more brush and more trees. The trees are farther apart than they were when we dashed into the woods, and at last we reach a clearing, find a road, and can see the housetops in a village ahead of us. There's no sign alongside the road, but Elise is sure this is the village listed on the sign at the crossroads.

It's quiet. No one's on the cobblestone street, no cars, no horses, no wagons. Two piles of charred wood and blackened stones seem to be what's left of two houses on the outskirts. Pale smoke rises out of a chimney on a small stone house with yellow trim around the windows. In the back yard, a little boy tosses a stick to a black dog while a woman pulls clothes off a line stretched between the house and a tree. When she sees us, she snatches the last shirt off the line and pulls the boy with her into the house. The dog barks and guards the back door, growling at us, a low rumble in his throat.

I move closer to Jack. He and Pete pull their pistols. My fingers curl into fists, my muscles tense.

At an intersection with another cobblestone street, a tiny church sits half burned, one side streaked black, windows broken, and faint traces of smoke hovering over the back of the church. As we stare at the damage, a priest walks out from behind the church, carrying a bucket, but halts when he sees us and slowly lowers the bucket to the ground.

I'm relieved to see the priest, but Jack and Pete keep their pistols steady as we walk toward him. When we're close, I notice the blistered burns on his cheek, bruises on his chin, and rips in his black robe.

Elise says something to him in French and points at Jack. She looks over her shoulder at me. "I told him we were refugees."

The priest carefully looks us over before he answers in English. "I am Father Delon. The Germans were here in the morning. They are gone now, but they will return because they want our village for. . . ," he hesitates, searching for a word, "a center for command."

"Father Delon, we need help. We're refugees from Liege, and we're walking to Brussels." I echo Elise's lie and point to Pete and Jack. "We need bandages and some food."

He shakes his head in a tired motion. "Not refugees," he says in a low voice. "Soldiers."

Elise sinks down on a low boulder at the edge of road and puts her head in her hands. I feel the same way. Everything in my body aches. I want to sleep for a month.

"We need help," I repeat in a low voice.

Rejection might as well be written in big letters on his forehead while he stares at the dried blood on Jack's shirt and Pete's dirty bandage. "French or British?" he asks after a long pause.

"British," Jack answers. He slides his pistol back under his belt. "We were at Mons, got separated from our unit."

"I'm an American," I mutter.

The priest points to the far end of the main road through the village. "I can help, but the Germans will return tonight. You cannot stay here. They will kill everyone if they find British soldiers with us." He motions to Pete. "Come with me. I will change your dressing and get food."

He leads us to the house where we saw the little boy and his dog. The priest knocks lightly. A woman opens the door an inch or two, peeks out, and begins to shut the door again. The priest murmurs a protest, puts his toe in the door opening and talks to her in French. He keeps talking until she nods, opens the door wider and lets us into the house.

"Her name is Corrine. Just one name is safer, so you will not know her," he explains as we step inside.

The house is cool. Dark blue curtains cover the windows. Corrine points to the sink, and we wash the blood and dirt off our hands. The boy sits in the corner petting his dog while Corrine puts heavy dark bread and hard yellow cheese on a platter in the middle of the wooden table.

Days of scrounging for food have destroyed all my manners. I grab a chunk of the bread and stuff it into my mouth. It's thick and chewy with some kind of seeds mixed in the dough. Delicious. After a few frenzied bites, I force myself to eat slowly so I can appreciate the sharp, tangy cheese and the grainy texture in the bread. I'm not sure what's more delicious—the cool water Corrine puts on the table or the food. It's been days—I've lost count—since I ate at a table.

Father Delon leaves and returns in a few minutes with fresh bandages. I nibble at the cheese while he changes Pete's dressing. At home, I'd never be able to eat across the table from Pete's raw, red wound, a bloody gash across his shoulder. Now the sight doesn't faze me. I help myself to another piece of cheese and slice of bread while Pete murmurs his thanks to Father Delon. Jack's wound is still seeping blood when he takes off his shirt. I watch the priest rinse the wound and cover it with a wide piece of cotton cloth wrapped around Jack's middle. I wish we had antiseptic. I wish we had a doctor.

I smile at Corrine and point to the cheese on my plate. "Wonderful. Thank you, thank you." A faint smile touches her mouth, and she murmurs to Elise.

"She says the Germans took the wine and the animals, so she has no meat for us," Elise translates.

Smiling, I help myself to another slice of bread from the platter. "So wonderful!"

"When did the Germans get here?" Jack asks the priest.

"Yesterday. Some stayed the night and took all our animals in the morning, but they told us a patrol will come back." Father Delon slides his fingertips lightly over the burns on his face. "They were brutal. Some men in the village. . . ." He stares at the ceiling for a moment. "We do not know where the men are now."

"Have you seen any other British soldiers?" Jack asks.

"Not British. A Frenchman came by a few days ago, and our own Belgian soldiers were here a week past. They left before the Germans reached us."

He speaks to Corrine. She shakes her head and tears shine in her eyes. "Corrine's husband was in the army at Liege, and she has heard nothing from him," Father Delon says. He walks to the window and moves the curtains an inch, so he can see the street. "We must not waste time. The Germans searched every house in the village and questioned all of us. They said they would pay a reward if we told them where British or French soldiers are hiding." His hand on the curtains trembles. "They will pay very well for information."

A cold shot of fear runs down my spine.

"It is a terrible time," Father Delon says, closing the curtain. "People will be desperate, and it will be dangerous to trust even neighbors we have known for years." He leans across the table toward me. "I will not reveal that you have been here. Corrine will not tell anyone."

"Someone else may have seen us," I mutter.

He makes a helpless gesture. "Perhaps."

"Thank you for your help." My thanks sound so weak. They're risking their lives just by giving us food and fresh bandages. One more bite of cheese and I push away from the table. "Jack, we should go."

"Not on the roads. The Germans control all the roads." Father Delon paces back and forth in the small room. "Brussels is taken. Antwerp—our army is fighting there, but the city will fall soon." He stops pacing. "I am sorry. We can do nothing more."

Jack adjusts his pistol in his belt and pulls his shirt over it. "Pete and I will go on alone. It's safer for you and Elise that way." He looks at the priest. "Can they stay here?"

Father Delon hesitates so long I think he's given us an answer without saying it. He murmurs to Corrine who turns to look at her son, sitting with his arm around the dog. Fear shows in her eyes, but she nods at Father Delon.

He touches her shoulder and smiles. "The young women can stay with Corrine. She will say you are cousins, but that one," he looks at me, "must not speak when the soldiers return. They might not believe you are American."

"I'm not staying here. Elise can stay if she wants, but I'm going with you two."

Jack frowns. "It's safer for you if you stay here. We don't know what we'll have to do to get out of Belgium. Pete and I should go alone." His voice is stern, but he smiles, and the fluttery sensation I always get when he does that takes over. Jack's ghost didn't come for me so I could abandon him while he was in danger.

"We met them by accident," Elise says. "You have no duty to go with them."

"We met each other by accident too, and I know I insisted we all stay together. Now you don't have to."

Elise taps her fingers on the table for a long minute, glances at the priest, and taps some more. "I will go," she says. "You need me to speak for you."

The priest exhales sharply, relief in his eyes. He opens the door to look outside. "No main roads," he says, turning to Jack. "In Brussels, perhaps someone can help you reach England."

Jack hesitates, his dark eyes on me. I stare back at him, and shake my head slightly, enough to tell him that I'm not going to stay with Corrine while he goes on. I'm coming with him. He nods and follows the priest. Elise thanks Corrine in French before we step outside and check the deserted street. If people are watching us from their windows, we can't tell.

"Which way?" Jack asks.

Father Delon flushes and rubs his forehead. "I am sorry I cannot help you," he mutters. "There is another way. Not the road. Go through the meadow," he points. "Find the countess—her estate is two kilometers west of the village. She has ways to help. God keep you."

We jog across the open meadow, and by the time we reach another cluster of pine trees, the sun is low in the west. Beyond the trees is another clearing, then more trees, then another clearing. This one has three concrete water troughs at least six feet long standing in open grass. The trampled grass around the troughs is dotted with mud puddles.

Jack signals a stop and looks around in the fading light. "We're on an estate," he says in a low voice. "Look at how clipped the grass is, and those hedges are trimmed."

"Can we drink the water in the trough?" I ask.

"No." Jack takes out his pistol as we walk closer. "The troughs are there to attract deer, maybe boars too. When the animals come for the water, hunters shoot them while they drink."

"Not overly sporting," Pete comments.

Jack motions us forward. We push through more bushes, stumbling in the growing darkness, and in the next clearing, we find a shed, nearly as large as Corrine's house. The single water trough nearby is full, a sign someone's tending it.

"Should we stop here?" Pete asks. He's holding his shoulder, his face pale. "I can keep on," he says when Jack doesn't answer.

Jack roams around the clearing for a minute before shoving his pistol in his belt. "We can sleep here tonight. No one's likely to find us in the dark."

The shed isn't locked. The cupboard holds a battered lantern and matches, and Pete gets a faint yellow light glowing for us. Heavy ropes and long poles lean against one wall. A search of another cupboard produces three cans of sardines and a big tin of crackers. Sardines don't appeal to me, but enjoying food isn't my standard any more. If we find food, we need to eat. Sitting on the bare plank floor, I chew and crunch through the little sardine bones, lick my fingers, and wipe the last traces of sardine juice on my long shirt. Will I ever be civilized again?

Pete leans against the shed wall, eyes closed. "Can't believe we're still on the run. We could use some help from those ghosts who gave us a hand at Mons."

"Ghosts?" My heartbeat spikes. Pete looks so pale, I scoot over and touch his forehead. It's cool. "What ghosts?"

A dreamy smile crosses his lips, and he pats my hand. "English bowmen—the old warriors from early times—they helped us when we had to retreat. I saw them in the clouds, shooting arrows into the German lines. You saw them, Jack, didn't you?"

"I don't know, Pete. The guns made so much smoke—the clouds—I don't know what I saw."

"What did the ghosts look like?" I ask Pete while I check his bandage. It's in place, no trace of blood.

"Centuries old they were," Pete says. He closes his eyes again. "They wore shiny helmets and carried longbows. Warrior angels to help us. You must have seen them, Jack—helping us get out alive."

"Maybe I did, Pete. We were desperate. The smoke and noise. Confusion. Could have been a miracle we didn't get captured."

Elise snorts. "Ghost warriors! How foolish!"

Pete's eyes snap open. "I saw them. They shot arrows into the German lines—supporting us. Things we don't understand can happen. Tell her, Jack."

"That's right," Jack says. "We can't understand everything. Get some sleep, Pete."

I insist on checking Jack's bandage and when he takes off his shirt, I find blood has seeped through—just a spot, but enough to show that we need more bandages.

"What is that?" Elise points to the leather envelope hanging around Jack's neck.

"It's a letter from a dead officer to his family," I snap at her, irritation obvious in my voice. "Jack's bringing it back to England."

"You carry it all this way for people you do not know." Elise makes a half-hearted attempt to cover her sneer as she curls into a ball on the wooden floor. "A waste of your time," she murmurs, closing her eyes.

Jack shrugs on his shirt and blows out the lantern. It's cold in the dark, and before long I'm shivering and hugging myself. Jack slides next to me and puts his arm around my shoulders. I lean into his warmth. My head settles on his shoulder and my eyes close.

13

The early morning mist rises nearly to my knees when I step out of the shed. I've lost track of time, but some of the leaves are turning yellow-orange so we must be in September by now.

In spite of the early daylight, the trees surrounding the clearing are so shadowy I can't see past them. The breeze swirls the gray-white mist into strange shapes and reminds me of ghosts and Pete's story about medieval English warriors in the clouds at Mons. After all the snickering I did when Aunt Connie talked about spirits moving back and forth through time, I'm perfectly willing to believe Pete saw what he said he did. Everything about ghosts and layers of time that shift over each other, letting us travel between them seems completely logical—Aunt Connie would be thrilled.

He hasn't made a sound, but I feel him standing behind me. My skin seems to have developed sensors to track his body heat, so I know when he's near without needing to look for him. I let the sensation spread over me, the warm rush across my skin, because he's close, and if I turn, he'll be there—the only pleasant sensation in the middle of the dangers around us.

When I do look back slowly, he's just a few feet away, smiling at me. Little spiky pieces of his dark hair stand up, messy from sleeping, and his chin has a layer of dark stubble. He'll have a beard if we're in the woods much longer. I smile, wishing I had a clean blouse instead of a dirty shirt and polished nails instead of broken ones, wishing I looked nicer for him.

"Did you sleep?" Jack asks.

"Pretty well. I'm sort of stiff." I rotate my shoulders and stretch.

He says something about the weather and finding the house on this estate. He points to the water trough. His voice is a soft murmur in my ears, but I'm not listening. I'm looking at his lips. When he kissed me in Aunt Connie's garden and started me on this weird journey, his lips felt cool and soft. Would they feel that way now? I imagine a different kiss—here—in his real world. In that kiss, his lips would be warm and press hard against mine. Do I imagine his kiss or do I remember it? I shake myself to get my head clear. This is no time to be thinking about kisses.

"Are you feeling all right?" He sounds worried and takes a step toward me.

"Sure. Just stiff."

I walk toward the water trough to put some distance between us, but something—a shiver in the bushes—catches my attention, and when I turn to stare into the shadows, my legs turn to stone, rooted to the ground.

It's enormous.

White splotches scattered over a huge black body—small wild eyes in its big head—looking straight at me. Gobs of spit drip from its jaws between two tusks sticking out of a long snout. I open my mouth to scream, but nothing comes out. My feet are locked in place. The monster snorts, raises its snout and squeals—a horrible piercing sound—while it shifts back and forth on stubby legs, hooves digging into the ground.

"Jenny, run!"

My legs unlock.

Another wild squeal. It charges me, and in a second I'm pinned on the ground. Drool spatters on my neck, hot, stinking breath fills my nose, and the snout pushes against my throat.

A shot. The monster crumples next to me—still alive—its head twisting, trying to reach me. Another shot. It sags, grunting, still twisting.

Jack grips my arms and pulls me across the grass. Then he steps over me and shoots the monster again in its ear. Another shot. Another. The monster shudders; his legs stop twitching.

I'm shaking so hard I can only manage to get to my knees. Jack lifts me to my feet and runs his fingers gently across my neck. "Did he bite you?" His fingers flatten against my shoulders, and he slides his arms around me, pulling me closer, as I sink against him.

"No, he didn't bite." My voice comes out in a squeaky whimper. I clutch his shirt, crumpling the cloth tight in my fist.

Pete stumbles out of the shed, his pistol in his good hand. "What happened?" He stares at the dead monster and gives a low whistle. "Look at it—a wild boar. Did it attack?"

"It charged Jenny."

My face is still buried in Jack's shirt while I take in a long, ragged breath. "Jack saved me," I manage to mutter as I lift my head.

Pete kneels on one knee next to the dead boar and runs his fingertip along a tusk. "It's bloody big and ugly enough. Looks like about four hundred, five hundred pounds."

"We should have kept a watch," Jack says. "That full water trough means the hunters are expecting game, and animals usually come in the morning. Jenny could have been killed." His arms tighten around me.

"Good shooting." Pete rises and circles the boar's body. "Not easy to get him in the shoulder."

"I was lucky."

Pete glances at me. "Could have been your end, Luv." His casual remark about my all-but-certain death under a wild boar releases whatever's holding me together, and my breathing becomes a string of ragged gasps.

Distress mixed with guilt crosses Pete's face. "Sorry, Luv, didn't mean to press the point." He awkwardly pats my back. "Lucky all around. Glory, I think this one's at least five feet long." He slides his pistol under his belt, walks along the boar's body, picks up the little tail, and stretches it out.

Another long shudder passes through me, but I straighten and loosen my grip on Jack's shirt. His arms slip away from me, and the morning chill spreads over me again. A puddle of blood has pooled under the boar's head, and his ugly pig eyes are open, staring at me.

"Good meat," Elise announces. "We can cook it over a fire."

"We can't butcher that thing," Jack says. "It's enormous, and we don't have the tools. We can't stay in one place long enough to do the job and cook it."

Elise looks disappointed—and irritated.

"Leave it here," I say. "Leave it here." I can't imagine eating anything connected to the boar. Those enormous jaws were only an inch away from my neck arteries when Jack got off his first shot.

"We should get out of here," Jack says. "The gunshots might—"

Loud crunching sounds from feet tramping through the brush. Voices. A shout. We're surrounded—guns aim at us.

A tall man with a clipped black beard shouts some kind of order. The other men say nothing but keep their guns pointed at us. Elise starts talking—a long stream of words matched with a lot of gestures.

I hate not knowing what she's saying, and I don't like the way she always points to Jack when she's talking. The tall man says something. She answers. He nods.

"He will take us to the countess," Elise says.

Will they help us or betray us? No way to know.

The leader keeps his rifle pointed at us while his men enter the shed and bring out the poles and ropes. Working fast, they tie the boar's legs to the poles and hoist it on their shoulders. Once they're finished, the leader motions, and we fall into place between the men carrying the boar and the leader, his rifle pointed at our backs.

A dirt path turns into a cobblestone walk leading through a garden to a house. It's a mansion, three stories, stone walls, balconies on the second and third floors, and gables—four of them. The double wooden doors at the entrance open, and a tall woman, about thirty, in a deep blue, taffeta dress with white lace trim at the neck, dark hair piled on top of her head, and long silver earrings dangling from her ears, gazes down on us from the top of the stone steps. She's holding a rifle pointed downward close to her long skirt. She's beautiful, but she also looks deadly. I sense she could flip up that gun in a second and shoot any one of us.

She walks down the steps and talks to the bearded man she calls Anton. He seems to give her a dramatic description of our capture, although I can't understand a word. She nods and spends a few minutes observing each of us, up and down, sideways, while we wait. To my shock, she suddenly speaks in English.

"No!" She shakes her head. "No, this will never do."

14

I'm in heaven.

I slowly slide down and sink up to my neck in warm soapy water. The claw foot bathtub is so big my feet don't even reach the other end. A yellow chunk of soap smelling like honeysuckle rests in a white porcelain dish hooked over the rim of the tub, and the bubbles I made with the soap float across the top of the water.

The countess's bathroom is the size of my bedroom at Aunt Connie's house. The bathtub sits under a wide window, so the sunlight shines in and down, creating rainbows in the soap bubbles. Along another wall two huge pedestal sinks stand side by side, and at the far end of the room is a very curious looking toilet in a separate narrow closet. The tank is a wooden box attached to the wall about six feet above the wooden seat. I flush by pulling on a handle at the end of a chain hanging down the side of the tank. After tramping through the woods for days and sleeping outside, I think the toilet is beautiful. Everything in this room from the white tile on the floor to the shiny brass faucet in the tub is beautiful.

Wiggling my toes to stir the bubbles, I wonder how long I can soak before someone comes in and makes me leave. I close my eyes, take a deep breath, and duck under the water. When I come back to the surface, I use the soap to wash my hair and plunge under the water again to rinse. In spite of my excitement about soap and a tub, the countess is on my mind. Can we trust her?

After asking our names, she sent Jack and Pete off with Anton, and Elise disappeared into the house with Katje the maid. Apparently, the countess's first concern was to get the four of us cleaned, and I got this glorious bathroom. My bra and panties are scrubbed and spread on the ledge under the window drying in the sun, but the priest's pants and the stolen shirt I've been wearing are in a dirty heap on the floor next to my sneakers. I don't think I can get the clothes clean, and the pants are useless, ripped in the knees and shredded around the bottom. It's also time to get rid of my shorts and tee shirt, so I've ripped those into shapeless pieces and buried them in the heap of dirty clothes. I shake my wet hair and step out of the tub, wrapping a big white towel around me.

A knock on the door. The countess calls, "Have you bathed, Jenny?" She opens the door a crack and peeps inside. In the bathroom light, she looks not younger but softer than she did when we met outside the house. For one thing, she's smiling at me, and for another thing, she's not carrying a rifle.

"Thank you so much for the bath. I was extremely dirty." I clutch the towel tight around me while water drips from my hair.

She closes the door behind her, walks into the room, and drops a bundle of clothes on a stool near the bathtub. My sneakers catch her attention, and she picks them up with that curious look everyone gets. The sneakers are in bad shape—the thick soles are splitting apart, and the leather is torn across the toes. Worse, the mud doesn't cover the colors entirely, so she can see the strange pattern.

"American style," I say quickly before she can question me.

She holds them up to the light, laughs, tucks the sneakers under her arm, and sweeps the pile of dirty clothes off the floor. A jingle from the pants over her arm catches her attention. It's the money Elise and I stole from Green Scarf. I'd forgotten about it. I should have given it to the priest and Corrine.

"You have money." She counts the coins and bills.

"We had no way to use it. We were hiding all the time from the Germans." Should I offer the money to her?

"Keep it," she says, putting the bills and coins on the edge of the stool. "It might buy bread and cheese when you need it. Money can often save you."

She rolls my sneakers in the dirty clothes concealing the colors. "You and Elise will dress as my maids while you are here. Your English soldiers must hide when German officers come to the house. They stop here every night—to eat. If they see two English men, they won't believe any story I can invent. The danger's always with us." Her voice is matter of fact, but her jaw clenches as she talks. She points to the fresh clothes and shoes. "Put those on when you're ready to come downstairs. Use the back stairway to the kitchen."

I want to ask her how she's going to help us reach Holland, but I'm nervous because she's entitled to ask me questions I probably can't or don't want to answer. She turns to leave but looks back from the doorway. "I'm sorry to be negligent. When we met, I forgot to introduce myself in a formal way. I am the Countess Fabienne de Carola."

"How do you do." I muster up my long-neglected manners. "Thank you for helping us, and please thank the count."

"The count, my husband, died more than a year ago."

"I'm so sorry," I murmur.

"He was ill with a weak heart for a long time. His death was sad because we miss him, but I'm glad he never saw his land taken by invaders." The coldness in her eyes startles me.

"I'm sorry," I say again. "You speak English very well."

A brief smile softens her face. "I had all my schooling in London. I met my husband there when he came to consult doctors about his daughter. We married quickly. I have a strong feeling—fondness—for the English."

"Is your husband's daughter here?"

"Yes. You'll meet her soon because I want you to be her companion while you're here. The servants are so busy, and Sylvie needs someone to be with her—a friend. The young woman who came with you can help Marta in the kitchen." She glances at my sneakers sticking out of the bundle in her arms, and runs her finger over the red leather on one toe. "Why are you traveling with two English soldiers? It's very dangerous."

I let the real answer run silently through my head—because Jack came to me as a ghost and kissed me. "We met by accident, and we've saved each other many times, so we're linked together."

She nods. "Linked. I understand how that happens. Now dress and come to the kitchen. The cook has hot food for you." The door closes softly behind her.

Food! Knowing hot food is waiting for me spurs me into a rush to dry myself and dress. The clothes the countess left are only a bit more fashionable than the priest's clothes. A gray long-sleeved blouse that buttons up to the neck. A dark blue cotton little-girl-style jumper reaching to my ankles. Brown high-top leather shoes with thick laces. Brown, knitted, knee-high socks. A soft cotton camisole with wide straps and a tiny pink ribbon woven through the cotton edge across the straight top. Shapeless white cotton pants. They tie at the waist, and the legs come down to my knees—panties in 1914? Hideous. I abandoned my shorts and tee shirt, but I'm not giving up my bra and panties, so they go under everything else.

I slip into all the layers and examine myself in the long mirror set in a wooden stand near the sinks. Do I look like a servant in World War I? My short curly hair isn't right. All the women I've seen in Belgium have long hair, but I have to be convincing if any German soldiers see me. The countess must know what she's doing.

Heavenly food aromas from the kitchen float up the stairway. My stomach rumbles, and I'm half running by the time I get to the kitchen door. Elise, dressed in a jumper like mine, is already at the table, dipping her spoon into a bowl of soup. A middle-aged woman with wiry gray hair in a tight bun smiles at me, one bottom tooth missing, pats herself and says, "Marta," before she ladles steaming soup into a bowl and puts it on the table in front of me.

I've never spent so much time thinking about food as I have these past days. Every move we've made was connected to finding food without getting shot. At home, I fed myself mostly with sandwiches or frozen pizza. Mom isn't much of a cook, and she's always on a diet. Dad eats at the university center most of the time.

The soup is delicious, big pieces of potatoes and carrots in thick broth with chunks of chicken. Dark brown bread flecked with caraway seeds sits on a platter. I tear off a hunk and dip it in the broth. Elise mops up the last of her soup by swirling her bread around the inside of her bowl. Marta sets heavy white mugs filled to the top with dark tea in front of us.

Elise takes a sip, blows on the tea to cool it, and watches me for a minute. "Be slow. If we eat too much or too fast, we will be ill," she says.

I put down my spoon and take a long breath. "Will the countess get us to Brussels?"

"She must know how to arrange it," Elise answers. She glances over her shoulder at Marta cutting sausages on a long table against the opposite wall. "The countess is very rich," she says in a low voice. "There are porcelain vases and clocks with gold trim. The inkwell on her desk is silver."

So Elise has managed to roam around the house. Instead of wondering whether we can trust the countess, I should have wondered if she could trust us.

Elise blows on her tea again. "She must have valuable jewelry."

Rubies from Green Scarf's pockets. The silver crucifix from the farmhouse. My muscles clench from nervous tension. "You have enough jewelry," I hiss at her. "We need the countess to help us. Don't think about her jewelry. That's not important."

Her gaze turns hostile. "You are an American. Maybe money is not important for Americans. For me, money is important. There is never too much money."

I glance at Marta, but she's still hunched over the table, chopping vegetables, and I'm pretty sure she doesn't speak English. I lean forward, whispering. "Elise, you have to forget about jewelry."

She shrugs and looks at the ceiling—her way of answering me and dismissing me at the same time.

"I mean it. We should concentrate on getting to Brussels and then to Holland."

"Why should I leave Belgium? Belgium is my country. You can go with Jack and Pete. I have no reason to go to England."

"I thought you'd want to leave—soldiers are everywhere—it's dangerous. Do you want to stay with the countess? She might keep you on here." I want her to say yes.

"Stay here? As a maid?" Elise drains her tea and lowers the mug to the table with a thump. "I was a maid in Charleroi. With money, I do not have to be a maid. With money, I can do what I want to do. In Brussels, a woman can live better than in the country. I am not a soldier. What does it matter to me if the Germans are on every street as long as I have money?" She pushes her chair back from the table and stomps out of the kitchen.

I follow her out the door leading to the back terrace convinced she's going to ruin whatever chance we have to reach safety. Jack and Pete, wearing fresh work clothes, stand at the bottom of the stairway leading down to the gardens. Jack looks up at me and smiles. My pulse speeds up as usual.

15

As I walk toward him, Jack bites his lip, but not fast enough to completely smother his laugh. "You look—very fetching." "It's clean." I hold out the sides of my ugly jumper in a mock curtsy so we both laugh.

He points to his black cotton shirt. "No blood stains." He's in fresh clothes from top to bottom, and he's shaved. His black hair, damp from washing and longer than when we met at the ravine, clings around his ears in half waves and droops over his forehead. I curl my fingers into fists, resisting the urge to push his hair off his forehead into a neat wave. I should say something significant about our circumstances, but instead I stare into his dark brown eyes and grin like an idiot because we've stayed together and we're safe for the moment.

The countess and Anton huddle near the stairs, heads so close together their foreheads almost touch. The countess murmurs softly, but Anton's voice rises to a shout. I ignore them.

Jack lightly touches the puffy sleeve of my blouse. "The first time I saw you," he says softly, "you looked like an angel coming to rescue Pete and me. You had a smudge on your nose and you had that ugly black shirt on, and I thought you were the prettiest girl I'd ever seen."

He catches my hand and traces a line in my palm, making me shivery and embarrassed at the same time. I love how he threads his fingers through mine, making sure we're really linked together. My mind gets hazy this close to him because I remember the way he kissed me in the garden when he was a ghost, and I wonder how he would kiss me here when he's alive.

He grins as if he knows what I'm thinking. "Anton got us fresh bandages. I'm nearly healed, and Pete's wound looks better now that it's not bleeding." He pulls me a few steps away from the others. "Anton told us to stay close to him, and we'll be picking apples in the orchards. If the Germans make an unexpected visit, they won't notice if there are extra men working."

"The countess told me I'm going to be a companion to her step-daughter, but I don't know anything about the girl. Elise is working in the kitchen. What happens to us next?"

"Anton said he and the countess have smuggled Belgian soldiers into Brussels in the past weeks even though the city is overrun with Germans. In Brussels, there are people who help allied soldiers get to Holland. The Germans haven't invaded Holland, and from there we can reach England."

"I thought Anton didn't speak English."

"I thought so too, but he does. Jenny, we have to trust them."

"We don't have much choice," I murmur. "Do you and Pete still have your pistols?"

"Yes. Anton told us to keep them hidden, but if we're cornered—" He stops. Images of guns and blood fill my mind until Jack bends closer to me. His breath ruffles the hair at my temple. "Pete and I— we're glad you came along with us. I'm not sure we'd have gotten this far without you. The first time I saw your face—"

A shout from Anton interrupts. "Good news!"

The countess puts her hand on Anton's arm and turns to us. "We've had word about a battle in France—near the Marne River. The Germans have retreated, and the French and British are hold-ing. As long as their lines hold, the German army can't reach Paris."

Pete whoops and slaps Jack on the back. "There you go! Our boys will take care of them now that we've got our bearings. We're taking charge now. Fritz won't break through this time, and we'll have him running back to Berlin before he knows what happened."

The countess doesn't look as excited as Pete does. She shakes her head slightly. "The news is good for France, but our Belgian army is surrounded at Antwerp, and the German army controls nearly all of Belgium." Anger sizzles in her voice. "The success in France makes me hopeful, but fighting can last a long time."

I try to look surprised and excited with the others. I don't remember exactly how long the war lasted, but I know it wasn't finished in a few weeks. The armies settled into trenches and attacked each other over and over without much success until the United States joined in. The fighting isn't going to end soon.

"Should we go south, Jack?" Pete shifts back and forth on his feet, as if he's already marching. "Get to France and join up with one of our units? Don't want our boys to think we're a couple of deserters, do we?"

"No!" I can't stop myself. "That's crazy. Soldiers are patrolling every road in the country. It's miles to France—wherever the Marne is. You'd never get there, and how would you find a British unit? Besides, you're both wounded."

Pete pats his bandage. "Wound isn't so much. I'm not a bloody invalid, and Jack's hardly scratched." He frowns at me, but I don't care because Jack's face shows he's taking Pete's idea seriously.

"Jack." I squeeze his hand. "You won't be any good to your army if you're dead." I hate saying the words because a picture of Jack lying bloody in a deserted field immediately flashes in my head. "You should go to England."

Jack slowly pulls his hand out of mine and thinks for a long moment while he absently slides his fingers over the front of his shirt, tracing the outline of the leather envelope that holds the officer's letter. "We aren't deserters, Pete. We've been trying to get to England and our army."

"Maybe going to France is the right thing?" Pete looks uncertain now.

The countess shakes her head. "Jenny is right," she says in a tone that sounds like a command. "You can't go south. You'll be caught and shot on sight long before you get to France. It's a true miracle you've gotten this far without being caught. In England, your generals will send you where they need you. You will be fighting—wherever you go." She crosses her arms and stares into the distance for a moment. "Naturally, you must do your duty as you see it," she adds, sending a chill through me.

Pete shuffles his feet, disappointment on his face. "What do you say, Jack?"

Jack shoves his hands in his pockets and stares at the ground. "It's a hard thing to decide," he says, looking at the countess. Heading south could be the right thing to do . . . but the countess makes a reasonable point. We won't be much good to the army if we're lying dead on a dirt road, or if we can't find our units. In England, the army can decide where to send us."

A long quiet whoosh of relief escapes me.

"A good decision," the countess says. "Now, there's work. Jenny, come with me. You must meet Sylvie. She's been left alone far too long." She spins on her heels and walks toward the house. Half way up the stairs leading to the back entrance of the chateau, she halts, turns, and makes it obvious she's waiting for me.

I squeeze Jack's hand and run to catch up with the countess.

16

Following her up the dark curving stairway to the second floor, I stumble in the dim light, but when we reach the top, enough sunlight shines through the long, narrow windows to light the hall and glint off the polished wooden floor. Slowing my steps, I stare at the opposite wall covered with portraits of men wearing white wigs and women holding large colorful fans spread out against their elaborate gowns. They must be ancestors of the late count. Would they approve of the countess and her secret plans to outwit the invading army and rescue lost soldiers?

We turn off the main hallway and stop at the end of a short passage where the countess takes a long key out of her pocket, slides it into the door's heavy metal lock, and leans forward to add pressure as she turns the key. It takes a second or two before the lock turns with a rusty, crunching groan. Before pushing the door open, she turns to me and smiles. "Sylvie has always been special. She sees worlds the rest of us do not, and I will be easier in my mind if she has a companion. Her governess fled back to England when the Germans invaded." She leans on the door and pushes it open.

The room is a child's fairy kingdom. The bedroom walls are covered in murals of gardens, lilies floating on a pond, tall green trees, pink and yellow flowers, squirrels, rabbits, chipmunks, and little girls with fairy wings spinning on their toes among the animals. Long gauzy, white curtains move slightly with the breeze at the open balcony doors. The same gauzy material decorated with embroidered yellow tulips and purple violets loops around the four posts of the canopy bed.

"Sylvie? Where are you? I want you to meet someone." The countess glances around the room, a frown cutting between her eyebrows. "Perhaps on the balcony," she murmurs. At the open doors, she gasps. "Sylvie! You are too high. You must get down at once."

A girl balances on the wide stone railing enclosing the balcony, her arms outstretched, her feet in pink ballerina slippers, toes hooked over the edge of the railing. She smiles at the countess and waves.

The countess puts out her hand to hold me in place. "Jump down now, Sylvie." The girl giggles, and the countess smiles. "Our new friend Jenny is here to play with you."

Sylvie fixes her gaze on me, then jumps onto the balcony landing on her pointed toes. Her laugh is the closest sound to a bell I can imagine. When she speaks to the countess in French, the countess nods and gestures toward me.

"English, Sylvie. Jenny speaks only English." She glances at me. "Sylvie is skilled at languages—she speaks six."

"Wow."

Wispy is the only word that fits her. We look each other over, tentative smiles on our faces. Sylvie's straight, blonde hair swirls around her shoulders like feathers in a breeze. She's so thin, her pale pink dress seems to be draped around a shadow.

I hope my expression is friendly. "I'm very pleased to meet you, Sylvie. My name is Jenny."

Her light blue eyes fix on me intently. "I'm twelve, how old are you?" She doesn't look twelve. There's no shape to her.

"I'm sixteen."

She claps her hands and twirls once on her toes. "All my friends are so old. You will be my youngest friend."

The countess laughs. She explains where we can walk in the garden, shows me where Sylvie's paints and easel are stored, gives me instructions about when to eat and what to ask for in the kitchen. I try to file it all in my head, but there are so many details, I give up trying to remember all of it and just keep nodding.

"You'll sleep here." The countess points to a narrow bed and little dresser fitted into an alcove off one corner of the room.

"Here?"

"Yes, Sylvie needs to have someone with her as much as possible." She strokes Sylvie's long hair, running her fingers through the light strands. "It was luck you found us because Marta was trying to keep watch, but Sylvie gets tired of the kitchen."

"I like to be in the garden." Sylvie twirls again, her arms above her head. "Do you like flowers?" Her gaze becomes intense while she waits for my answer.

"I do like flowers, and I'd love to see your garden."

She claps her hands again. "I'll show you—we'll look at all the flowers."

I remember what the countess said about getting medical treatment in London. "Is there medicine to give?" Please, no shots.

"There's no medicine." The countess slips her arm around Sylvie's shoulders and drops a kiss on her head, while Sylvie's eyes stay fixed on me. "I'll leave you now," the countess says.

She's nearly at the door, when Sylvie stops her. "I saw Papa this morning. He told me he would be home soon."

Silence hangs over us for an instant. I don't know what expression I have on my face, but the countess's gaze flicks briefly in my direction before she turns back to her stepdaughter. "Did you see him today? I'm glad to know he'll be home soon. Have fun with Jenny."

Sylvie has dozens of dolls, and she introduces me to each one. She shows me her paints and how she mixes colors. For lunch, we eat tomatoes and cheese in the kitchen where Marta chatters in French. Sylvie answers her in French and giggles. She's happy with everything Marta says, and I'm glad to have an excuse to keep silent. Their voices are a soft babble in the background while my mind is on Jack and how we'll get to Holland. Elise is nowhere in sight. When I ask about her,

Sylvie translates Marta's explanation—Elise is peeling potatoes in the vegetable storehouse. I smother a giggle. Elise must hate that chore.

After eating, we walk in the gardens behind the house. It's early September so there aren't many flowers left, but Sylvie shows me where the flowers would be growing if it were June and she names every shrub and tree while she skips along the tops of the marble benches that line the stone paths through the gardens. She seems to float in the air when she twirls on her toes. Fortunately, she doesn't ask me any questions about where I came from or what I'm doing. I'd like to avoid the combination of lies I've had to repeat over and over since I woke up in a Belgian cemetery. It's hot in the afternoon, so we sit on the balcony while I watch Sylvie paint with her watercolors.

"Why do you paint fairies?"

Sylvie points into the distance where trees cluster at the edge of the gardens. "I paint what I see there."

"Do you see fairies in the trees?"

"In the trees and in the garden too—near the pond." She carefully places her paint brush on its stand, sits back in her chair, and turns to me.

My breath stops. My chest tightens. She's looking intently at me, and her light blue eyes have turned so dark they look almost black. I wonder if she's dangerous—if she has fits—if I need to call someone.

"You're not really here, are you?" Sylvie whispers.

"Of course, I'm here."

"No, I can see through you, so I know you're not truly with me." She rubs her forehead. "You're somewhere else, somewhere very far away."

If only she could explain how I got from Aunt Connie's garden to 1914 Belgium. Probably no one believes anything she says, but I don't dare tell her how Jack kissed me and brought me through time—it's too risky.

I put on a broad smile as if we're joking. "So tell me where I am."

She studies me, her eyebrows knit in a straight line. Finally, she shakes her head so hard her blonde hair sprays out in a fan. "You're between places, between times. I wish you could stay with me, but you have to go soon."

"You're right. My friends and I must leave here before long."

"I'll miss you. I'll be sad."

Maybe I should take a chance and ask her. "Do you know how I—"

The bell for the evening meal echoes through the hallway. Sylvie giggles and claps her hands. "I hope we have custard tonight!" She spins on her toes to the door, leaving me to trail after her,

We eat alone in the kitchen again. The workers must eat somewhere else, and there's been no sign of the countess. Marta pours tea and puts crusty chicken pie in front of us. The flaky crust melts in my mouth, and the chicken breaks apart when I put my fork into it. I never liked Brussels sprouts at home, but they're actually delicious with carrots and potatoes mixed in the thick gravy. Marta does have custard for us—creamy vanilla with raisins and nuts. Sylvie squeals, claps her hands, and demands two helpings. She's scraping the last raisin from her bowl when engines roar up the driveway.

Marta turns pale, clutches her chest, and motions us toward the back stairs away from the main hallway.

Sylvie skips up the stairs two at a time. "The German officers eat here every night," she explains. "Marta makes me hide in my room when they come. The officers like Marta's cooking, but they are very rude." She waits for me to unlock the door. "They took Papa's automobile and won't give it back. Marta says they drink our best wine and never say thank you."

"That is very rude," I agree, closing the door and sliding the bolt in place, My adrenaline spikes. Where are Jack and Pete?

"Do the officers search the house every night?" My throat is dry and tight.

"Oh no." Sylvie spins on her toes for a minute, lifting her arms in a ballerina pose. "They eat and make noise. The countess has to eat with them. She has to taste the food and drink the wine before they do. After she doesn't die, they eat and drink everything on the table. I'm glad I had two bowls of custard." She laughs and spins a few more times. "We should sit on the balcony. I'll draw the pictures in the clouds."

On the balcony, Sylvie concentrates on her pencil drawings, while I sit next to her listening for every sound, wondering if I'll hear boots in the hall, wondering what I'll do if a German soldier asks me something and I can't answer.

A laugh floats up from the back terrace. I slide off the chair and crawl to the railing, keeping my head down. Ignoring me, Sylvie draws the cloud shapes and hums to herself. Low voices speak German and then laugh. Kneeling, I peek through the railing posts to the terrace directly below us.

Two soldiers sit at a small table, and Elise is serving them chicken pies, bread, and tea. The soldiers are young, like Jack and Pete, and they're relaxed, collars open and caps tossed on the table next to their plates. One of them grabs Elise's hand as she puts a cup in front of him and says something to her. Elise laughs and pulls away. She answers him in German, and he laughs too. When she comes back to the table with the teapot, she lets him take her hand and doesn't pull away for a long time.

"The drivers eat on the terrace, and the officers eat in the dining hall," Sylvie says very quietly as though having soldiers in her house was entirely normal. Maybe for Sylvie everything was normal—fairies, soldiers, and me traveling through time.

I hold my finger over my lips to make sure she whispers. She puts her pencil next to her drawing, crawls across the balcony, and kneels next to me. "That one," she points at the blond soldier who's flirting with Elise, "makes jokes and laughs when he eats here, but he's afraid when he drives the officers." She points to the other soldier. "He's afraid all the time. He worries about home."

I stare into her eyes, a clear light blue again. "How do you know these things? Have you talked to them?"

She shakes her head. "I'm not allowed to talk to them. I know what they hold in their heads."

We sit on the balcony until the light fades and the officers' cars roar down the long drive to the road. Sylvie shows me her pencil drawings of the clouds in shapes I've never seen. The stars are out when the countess knocks on the door. She places a white, cotton nightgown on my bed.

"Did the officers question you about escaping soldiers?"

"When they are here, they eat and brag about their army." The countess sighs and shrugs. "They searched the house the first time, but they haven't done it again. One never knows of course. They are. . .unpredictable."

"So they might search again sometime."

"Perhaps."

The countess admires Sylvie's drawings and kisses her good night while she tucks her in bed under the quilt. She manages to giggle with Sylvie as if there's no danger outside the chateau, as if the officers who enjoy her wine and food every night wouldn't shoot her if they discovered us.

I flip through the illustrated pages of Sylvie's picture books before putting on the white nightgown and getting into bed in the alcove. Lying there, I stare at the ceiling, listen to Sylvie's deep, steady breathing, and wonder what will happen to us. Sylvie's description of me caught between places and times seems close to the truth although I can't understand how or why it happened. Aunt Connie would love to hear about Sylvie's explanation for my adventure, and she's the only one I could safely tell. I miss Jack. After so many nights of sleeping side by side, I feel strange to be alone at night. Holding his hand helped me forget the dangers for a little while because he was with me.

17

"When we send the next shipment of apples to Brussels, Anton will take you to our contact in the city. That person will get you to the border so you can cross into Holland."

The countess's voice is soft and perfectly calm as she explains her plans to the four of us.

We're in the library. Jack was alone, paging through a poetry book, when I got there, but the others followed me in so quickly I didn't have time to talk to him. The room is elegant, decorated the way I always thought a library in a mansion would be. The early morning sun shining through the leaded glass windows throws a mix of shadows and bright light on the gold and green carpet that covers most of the polished wood floor. Hundreds of books bound in tan and maroon leather fill the shelves behind glass doors in the bookcases.

Jack sits next to me on a love seat upholstered in green and gold to match the chairs. Pete slumps in a chair near the fireplace, holding his arm in a way that tells me his wound is hurting. Elise pushes her stool into a corner so far away from the rest of us the countess has to move her head back and forth when she talks as if she were at a tennis match.

She sounds confident, but after a minute, I realize she's not actually promising that we'll escape—she's only promising she'll get us to the next person who will help us. Jack slides his hand across my arm in a reassuring gesture. He smells like soap, and his black hair is damp from washing. I wish I could lean against him while he puts his arm around me, but I'm supposed to be listening intently to the countess's plans, and my guess is PDA is really frowned on in 1914. So I smile but hold myself stiff and upright.

"Anton will drive our biggest wagon late in the afternoon, so you'll reach the rendezvous in Brussels when the streets are dark," the countess explains. "The wagon has a false bottom—a place for you to hide."

Pete sucks in his breath, grimaces, and shifts his arm uncomfortably across his chest. "Don't mind hiding in a wagon. I've done worse since we've been on the run."

"We should go as soon as possible," Jack says. "You're taking a very great risk for us."

"Right," Pete agrees. "No point in dallying around, as me mum always says."

Elise fidgets on her stool, rubbing the toe of her shoe over a green leaf in the carpet pattern. "Where is the rendezvous?" It's not a friendly question.

The countess pinches the bridge of her nose and sighs before she answers. "It's best you don't know the place. We must protect those who are helping soldiers reach the border, so we tell nothing ahead of time. If information were to reach the German command, people will be arrested, shot, and probably tortured for information."

"We don't want to put anyone in danger," Jack says quickly. "We just want to get on with it."

"We should know where we are going and who is there," Elise grumbles.

The countess stiffens. "I must decide such things."

The atmosphere in the library turns suddenly hostile, distrusting, and a long tense silence settles over us while we avoid looking at each other. I push back my uneasiness and put on a false cheerful smile.

"The countess knows what's best, Elise. She has experience helping refugees and lost soldiers."

Elise glowers at me. "Maybe you want to get into an apple wagon without knowing where you are going, but there is danger everywhere, and I want to know what I will face. Where are we going and who is in Brussels helping people get to Holland?"

It takes some effort to remind myself Elise picked me up on the road when I was alone and saved me from Green Scarf. In spite of her complaints about traveling with British soldiers, she's helped us. Our early friendship has disappeared, and it's probably my fault because all my attention turned to Jack when I found him.

The room is quiet with tension. "Do you want to go to Brussels with us?" I ask.

She pouts. "I want to know who to trust."

The countess's gaze is cold, but her voice is smooth as cream. "These are dangerous times—the enemy is patrolling every road, every village. We must take precautions, but we must trust each other also. In a day or two, we will take you to Brussels." She hesitates for a long moment. "You may stay here if you wish, Elise. The Germans won't question how many kitchen maids I have."

We wait, silent, while Elise digs her toe into the carpet. "I will go to Brussels," she mumbles.

"Good," the countess says. Her shoulders relax. "Go back to your chores now. The Germans could decide to search the house at any time—we can't rely on their coming only to eat our food and drink our wine."

"Thank you, Countess," I say quickly.

Jack and Pete each thank the countess several times, shake her hand, and praise the way she's hidden us so far. Elise mumbles an awkward thank you and leaves the room. Pete follows her down the main stairway, but Jack pulls my hand and steers me to a paneled wooden door at the end of the hallway. It opens into the back stairway that leads two flights down to the kitchen. Marta's laugh comes faintly up the stairway. Spicy smells from her stew drift upward.

Jack stands close to me on the shadowy landing. "I looked for you last night," he says in a low voice. "I wandered around the garden and then I sat in the library and read for a bit, hoping you would turn up."

"I was with Sylvie, the countess's stepdaughter. I have to sleep in her room so she isn't alone."

"Too bad." He grins and takes my hand. "That apple wagon will be a tight fit, but as long as you're next to me, I'm going to like it."

Heat crawls up my neck, spreading across my cheeks. I'm blushing. Maybe he won't see it in the shadows. When he slides his rough fingertips across the back of my hand, I'm jittery and relaxed at the same time. I turn my hand so we can link fingers. "It's dangerous for you to roam around the house or the gardens. What if the Germans come unexpectedly?"

"It was dark. I was careful. Anton warned us yesterday when he saw them turn into the road leading up to the house, and we hid in the carriage house. They stayed a long time. The countess shouldn't feed them so well."

"They make her taste the food and wine first, so obviously, they don't trust her. She laughs at their jokes and pretends she's happy to feed them and talk with them every night, but I have to keep Sylvie upstairs with the door locked until they leave."

"She knows the danger—they could arrest her whenever they feel like it. She's risking a lot by helping us."

"Elise flirted with the soldiers—the drivers—when she served their food."

"Did she?" Jack moves so close to me I have to tilt my head to look at him. My pulse starts racing. It pounds so loudly in my head I'm sure he can hear it.

"Yes, she did," I whisper. "She was laughing and flirting with the soldiers on the terrace, and she speaks German. I couldn't understand what they said to each other." Jack slides his free hand around my waist, sending my heartbeat into an uneven flutter. I should step away but I don't want to. "Are you listening to me?"

"I'm listening," he says with a soft laugh that sends my pulse into a thumping rhythm.

His breath stirs my hair. Anticipation blots out every worry about Elise, about danger, about escape. Jack's finally going to kiss me. He bends his head, his eyes on my mouth only inches away. The only thought drumming in my head now is how warm Jack's lips will be when we kiss. His breath touches my lips. My hand tightens on his shirt sleeve. Fear catches me. If he kisses me now, will he send me back to Aunt Connie's garden? Is that the way this time travel thing works?

"No!" I jerk away, pulling my hand out of his.

His expression goes from surprise, to confusion, to embarrassment. "I'm sorry. I didn't intend to be forward." He steps back and runs his hand through his dark hair. "I guess I did intend it, but I thought. . . you. . . wanted—it seemed—"

He stops talking, his face red, and we stand awkwardly apart in the dim light in the stairway. I want to explain, but of course that's impossible. I want to kiss him, but I don't dare.

"It's all right," I mumble. "I just can't."

"I'm sorry, Jenny."

Another embarrassed silence takes over. We stand close but not touching. Neither of us knows what to say or do. In the kitchen below us, pots clang. Marta shouts something. The noise releases us.

"I need to find Sylvie." Turning away, I flee down the stairs toward the kitchen.

18

Marta's stew fills the kitchen with a strong, spicy aroma, but for the first time since I woke up in that cemetery, I'm not tempted by food. Jack looked so confused and hurt when I pulled away from him. I want to run up the back stairs and tell him I didn't mean to push him away. What good would that do? Maybe I've ruined everything.

Sylvie, her long blonde hair pinned on the top of her head and a ruffled apron tied around her neck, stirs chocolate in a small pot. "I'm making chocolate custard!" she announces when I look over her shoulder. "Marta said I could have custard if I helped make it."

"That's wonderful." I don't put enough enthusiasm in my voice because Sylvie stops stirring and looks at me.

"You're not happy," she says. It's not a question.

"I think I'm tired."

She shakes her head and goes back to stirring the chocolate custard. "No, you're sad about something."

I don't have to create a new lie for her because Elise enters the kitchen through the outside door, and Marta immediately says something in French pointing to a tub of potatoes. Elise wrinkles her nose, but she picks up the tub and turns to leave, making a point of ignoring me.

"Elise, wait a minute." I stop her at the door. "Please don't worry because the countess won't tell us the details of her plan. It's not that she doesn't trust us."

That's probably another lie. The Germans are searching the villages and countryside for British soldiers and others trying to get to Holland. One mistake could get us all shot. So I do suspect the countess doesn't trust any of us completely.

Elise looks down at the tub of potatoes in her arms and then up at me. "You," she says with a hiss, "are upstairs in a beautiful room, and I am downstairs peeling potatoes."

"It's only for a few days until we can get into town. I'd help you, but I have to stay with Sylvie."

"I am not a maid," she spits out the word as if it was a curse.

"You said you were a maid in Charleroi," I remind her.

"I am not in Charleroi now, and I will never be a maid again."

She looks so fierce, I change the subject. "I saw you with the soldiers last night. You were speaking German. Did they tell you anything that will help us escape?"

"You saw me?"

"Sylvie's balcony is over the terrace. I heard voices, so I looked over the railing. The soldiers didn't see me—you had their complete attention—and you were all laughing. Did they tell you what's happening in Brussels?"

Elise's angry expression fades into a blank stare. "Why would they tell me anything? They were hungry." She hesitates. "You saw them. They made jokes with me."

"You were laughing with them, so I thought—"

"No," she cuts me off. "They said nothing important." She balances the tub of potatoes on one hip and slips out the door.

Sylvie stirs her custard and chatters about the fairies in the garden she saw this morning while my thoughts flutter between how I'm feeling about Jack and why I don't dare kiss him, and German soldiers who are far too close to us. Jack takes precedence. He was a ghost in Aunt

Connie's garden but when he kissed me, I ended up here where he's real. Therefore, his kiss must be the key to sending me back and forth across time. I didn't walk through any secret doors or pass through a mirror. My purpose must be to help him escape, and instead of thinking about what his kiss would feel like when he's flesh and blood, I should concentrate on getting safely to Holland. It's ridiculous for me to feel romantic about someone living in 1914. That thought doesn't last longer than a second. I'm in 1914 too, and he's not a ghost now.

Squeezing my eyes shut doesn't help to block Jack out of my mind. Guilt seeps through me. I rub my temples, wondering why I don't have a migraine from trying to sort out what's possible and what's not. In fact, I haven't had a headache since I woke up in the cemetery with bullets crashing around me. My concussion must have stayed behind in my other life.

Sylvie finishes stirring her custard, pours the smooth chocolate into white cups, and sets them on a marble-topped table against the wall to cool. "Let's walk to the river," she says with a serious tone. "You won't be sad in the sunshine." She unties the apron, lets down her hair, and takes my hand.

"I'm not sad," I lie again.

She takes my hand and pulls me out the door, across the back terrace, and along a path between rows of shrubs. "When I was little, Papa took me for rides in our big carriage—it had red velvet seats and bells on the back that made a pretty sound when we drove. It's gone now. The sleigh is gone too. Everything. I'll show you the carriage house before we visit the ducks."

"Ducks!" I fake enthusiasm. "Can we feed them?"

She holds up a sack. "Marta gave me stale bread."

Sylvie pulls me between hedges as high as my shoulders. Enjoy the day, I think to myself. Pretend it's Jack's hand holding mine instead of Sylvie's. We make another turn, and the carriage house shows through the trees ahead of us. I expected a garage, but the carriage house looks like a smaller version of the mansion—turrets, a porch on the second floor. Under the porch two huge double doors are big enough for vehicles to enter. We walk closer, but Sylvie stops the same moment I do.

The countess and Anton stand under a tree on one side of the carriage house. Her arms are around his neck, her head resting on his shoulder. His arms are tight around her waist, and his lips press against her temple where her hair sweeps back in a twisted coil at the back of her head. They look like a scene in a romantic movie, and a picture of Jack's arms wrapped around me the way Anton holds the countess immediately grips my imagination.

"Come this way," Sylvie whispers, tugging at my arm. When we get a few yards away, she says, "Anton loves her very much."

"Do you know everything about everyone?"

She giggles. "Mostly I do."

"Does the countess love Anton?"

Sylvie sighs. "It's so romantic. They think no one knows, but everyone does."

"Did your papa like Anton?"

"Anton came to our house after Papa went away," Sylvie says, "but Papa likes him now. He tells me so."

"That's nice." Knowing the countess was faithful to the count gives me more confidence we can rely on her.

"Loving is difficult." Sylvie's eyes flash dark blue again as she looks at me out of the corner of her eye. "You know about loving." She skips ahead of me. "Look, there's the river."

What Sylvie calls a river is a stream about the size of the one Elise and I waded across when we left Green Scarf behind, but it's big enough for ducks—mother ducks followed by six or seven baby ducks swimming in triangle formation behind her. Sylvie kneels at the edge of the stream, tearing the bread into small pieces. Big brown ducks waddle up on the bank and snatch the bits from her hand. The mothers and babies stay in the water, but they dip and bob for the bread bits when Sylvie tosses them close to the edge of the stream.

The ducks keep Sylvie entranced for a few minutes while my mind loops between uncertainties. Will Jack forgive me? What is

Elise saying to the German soldiers every night? What will happen when—if—we get to Brussels?

The evening routine is the same as yesterday. We eat Marta's thick stew, and I give my dish of chocolate custard to Sylvie, which makes her very happy. The German officers arrive before we've finished eating. Marta hurries us upstairs before the officers climb out of their cars.

Tonight, I have no qualms about spying on Elise from Sylvie's balcony. The soldiers speak in German, and Elise laughs with them. She stands very close to the blond soldier when she puts his plate on the table—definitely flirting. She's taken apart the braids she usually wears and tied her long hair back with a blue ribbon so her hair hangs in ripples to her waist. She smiles at both soldiers, but her attention is especially on the blond, and finally she calls him Carl and calls the other soldier Hans, so I know their names but nothing else.

When she pours their tea, Carl slides his arm around her. She giggles and lets him pull her on his lap. She stays there, one foot swinging, and smoothes his thick blond hair while he drinks his tea. When an officer calls to them from the house, Hans and Carl jump to their feet and salute as he crosses the terrace, heading for the cars. Carl grabs his cap, buttons his collar, and snatches a quick kiss from Elise before he follows Hans down the terrace steps to the driveway.

"She likes the soldiers," Sylvie says, watching me drop into a chair.

"Why does she like them?" My knees are numb from kneeling on the stone balcony floor.

"They tell her she's pretty. That makes her happy."

"What else do they tell her?"

"They talk about home and food." Sylvie holds up her drawing so I can admire it. "Hans has three brothers in the army, and Carl has two little sisters, and they hope they can go home very soon."

"Is that all?"

"Carl's grandfather makes good sausage."

Home, sisters, and sausage—not exactly top secret information. I hold Sylvie's drawing up to the light—a castle nestled on a cloud and a fairy hovering over it. "Do you see fairies in the clouds?"

"Sometimes, but they like dancing with the flowers and birds in the garden more than flying in the clouds." She yawns.

When the countess opens the bedroom door much later, I put my finger against my lips. "She's asleep."

She straightens the edges of Sylvie's pink cotton blanket. "Are you tired also?"

"Not much." Proper young women probably don't ask about the sleeping arrangements of young men in 1914, but I can't resist. "Where are my friends Jack and Pete sleeping?"

"In the carriage house at night—it's far from the main house and if the Germans want to inspect it, your friends will have time to run to the orchards and then, if needed, they can run to the woods." She lingers at the door. "Your friend Elise sleeps in the room next to the kitchen. The Germans won't be concerned with house maids." She closes her eyes for a second. "They found a French cavalry officer hiding in a farmhouse yesterday. They shot him and the family who was hiding him."

"I know it's dangerous for you."

She manages a slight smile. "Anton and I will get you to Brussels. Anton has done this before; he knows the way. You've been strong— and very lucky—to get this far."

After she leaves, I lie on the bed, still dressed, and drop into a restless sleep, dreaming about fairies and soldiers until chimes from the ballerina clock wake me. The ballerina spins around her tiny platform twelve times. Midnight. A faint thud sounds in the hallway.

I turn the heavy door knob slowly, praying the door won't squeak. Tiptoeing down the short hallway, I turn into the main corridor where moonlight streaming through the tall windows lights the hall in a silvery glow. A figure walks toward the stairway, stops, half turns, the light shining on her face.

"Elise! What are you doing here?" My voice carries through the corridor in spite of my whisper. Something in her hand glints in the moonlight before she closes her fist and shoves it into her pocket.

"Go back to bed," she hisses back at me. "This is not your business."

"What do you have?" I reach her before she starts down the stairs. "Where have you been? Are you stealing from the countess?"

Elise narrows her eyes and retreats a step. "It is not your business what I do. You can bow to her if you want to, but I will not. She has everything—more than she needs."

"She's helping us! You should be grateful." I step closer. "What did you put in your pocket?"

She tries to shove past me and take the stairs, but I grab her arms and hold her back. I'm taller, so I can outreach her, but she squirms and maneuvers making it difficult to keep my grip on her. We twist and pull at each other while I struggle to search her pocket. She spins, jerking backward to protect whatever she's holding, but with a desperate pull on her arm, I yank her hand out of her pocket. A gold chain wrapped around her fingers glitters in the faint light.

"Does that belong to the countess?" I grip her wrist with as much pressure as I can until her fingers open, and I snatch the chain holding a pendant—a pear-shaped pearl. Under the dim light, it looks bluish-gray—and valuable. "Is this real?"

Glaring at me, she rubs her wrist. "Yes, it is real. The countess is rich—she does not have artificial jewels."

"You already have the rubies you took from Green Scarf. You don't need any more. Are you crazy to take a chance like this?"

"Money is protection. There is never enough protection."

Hostility flickers in her gaze as we stare at each other. We aren't friends anymore if we ever were—too much divides us.

"What will you tell the countess?" she asks. "Will you abandon me?"

19

We lock eyes in the half light while I waver, suddenly undecided. Her constant thieving puts us in danger, but I owe her some loyalty. I glance up and down the hallway. We're still alone. "No, I won't abandon you."

A slow smile. "We can share it," she says. "In Brussels, we will find someone to buy the pearl and share the money."

The chain is antique gold links and the pearl is set in spirals of gold—it must be a family heirloom. Maybe the count gave it to the countess on their wedding day. "No, we're not going to sell it and share anything. You're going to put it back where you found it."

Her smile fades—her gaze turns hostile. "You are a fool, Jenny. You think you are going back to America, but maybe the countess has no good plan. Maybe Jack and Pete will be killed. Maybe you cannot leave Belgium. How will you live? Jewels like this can keep us rich enough to survive."

She's listed my deepest fears because I have no idea how this race to the border turns out. If I'm killed here, how will I get back to my present? I push back a flash of terror and manage to shake my head. "I don't need to be rich. Jack and Pete don't need to be rich. They need to get out of Belgium and back to England. The countess says she has a plan, and I believe her. Stealing jewelry is not the way to show gratitude." I'd like to shake Elise into some common sense, but we've already made enough noise in the hallway to attract an army.

"I do not need to go away. I need money to survive in Belgium. The war could be long."

She might have stolen other things from the countess already, but she wouldn't confess if she had, so there's no point in asking. "You have to put this necklace back where you found it, and I'm going to watch you do it." I check both directions in the hallway, hoping no one's heard us yet. "Which room?"

She sets her jaw, obviously angry, but she points to the double doors at the other end of the hall. "That one."

"That's the countess's bedroom."

"She is not in it." Elise smirks. "Your saintly countess must have a lover to be gone from her room all night."

I don't know if the romance between Anton and the countess holds any danger for them, but I don't trust Elise enough to tell her anything. "She's a widow. She can do what she wants. We have to put this necklace back before someone comes."

The bedroom drapes are closed, so the only light comes from the moonlight slipping through the narrow opening where the drapes separate. I squint, trying to adjust to the dark, but Elise moves without a stumble across the room straight to a dark wooden chest of drawers near the bed. When she switches on the brass lamp on the chest, the tinted glass globe sends a rosy light into the room.

Silently easing open the top drawer in the chest, she removes a black lacquered jewelry case. The cover is decorated with bright green leaves surrounding a gold initial F in the center. The case fastens with a solid-looking double hinge, but Elise flicks it open easily. When she lifts the cover and swings the velvet-lined compartments apart. I suck in my breath. Bracelets, earrings, hair clips and rings, gleam in the soft light.

"Beautiful!"

Elise smiles. She looks at me over her shoulder and puts her fingertip on a silver butterfly pin. "We can take this small brooch—to buy food in Brussels."

"No, we can't."

"This ring?" She slides a gold ring set with two emeralds on her finger and holds out her hand to watch the light glint on the stones.

"No."

Elise frowns but slips the ring off. When she takes the necklace from me, she carefully positions the pearl so it touches another gold chain. Then she adjusts the tiny barrel clasp at a slight angle. "It belongs just so." Before she closes the compartment, she strokes a gold bracelet. Lowering the lid of the case, she reattaches the double hinge and puts the case back in the drawer.

I wonder again what else she's stolen from the countess.

"Let's go," I whisper.

"I did what you wanted," Elise says when we reach the top of the stairs. "Now, I must go to my small room next to the kitchen." Venom rings in every word. "You go to your soft bed with beautiful quilts." She tiptoes down the stairs without waiting for an answer and disappears into the darkness at the bottom.

The rest of the night, I twist in my bed, shifting restlessly under the light quilt. By the time daylight streaks across the floor, I know I have to talk to Jack about Elise. I can't keep this secret to myself.

After breakfast, it's not hard to convince Sylvie to help Marta make biscuits in the kitchen. Once her hands are deep in flour and she and Marta are giggling, I slip out and retrace the path Sylvie took me along to reach the carriage house. Jack is behind the building chopping wood into fireplace size pieces, while Pete, using his one good arm, carries each piece to a woodpile. It's hot, and their shirts, soaked with sweat, cling to their chests and arms, but they're laughing at something—as relaxed as I've seen them since we met in the ravine.

Pete waves at me. "Jenny! Come to chop wood with us?" Laughing, he points to another ax propped against a rusty carriage wheel leaning against the building.

Jack's hello is polite as if we barely know each other. I feel the chill, but at least he doesn't look angry.

Pete makes a joke about learning a new trade as a wood cutter. Jack and I stand stiff, awkward, embarrassed, glancing at each other, then looking away, not paying much attention to Pete. Prickles of tension travel through my shoulders to my neck muscles. After a minute, Pete gives up his attempts to joke. "I might rest the arm a bit. Mum always told me to leave when I wasn't needed."

I feel guilty for ignoring him. "How's your arm today, Pete?"

"I expect to be tiptop before long." He sends me a little salute and disappears into the carriage house through the back door, leaving me alone with Jack.

Jack sweeps his wet hair back from his forehead and clears his throat. "I'm. . . I want to apologize." A red flush crawls up his throat. "I shouldn't have tried to kiss you, and I'm sorry I upset you." He props the ax against the wood pile and wipes his hands on his pants.

"No, it's my fault." My voice comes out in a nervous squeak. If only I could be smooth with guys like some of my friends are. I have no instincts for saying the right thing to make the awkwardness go away.

Jack rubs the back of his neck and stares at the line of trees in the distance. "A gentleman doesn't take advantage of a lady." When he turns back to me, his dark eyes are full of regret.

A lady. A gentleman. A warm, melting sensation runs through me, and my urge to explain why I can't kiss him almost takes control of me. But I stifle it in time because I don't want to disappear and lose him.

"I didn't want to push you away." I slide my hand into his, and he closes his fingers over mine. "I wish I could explain, but it's too complicated."

"You don't have to explain anything."

We stand silent, close together, a perfect time for a kiss—if we could. I imagine his lips would be tender and exciting, and his arms would be tight around me. Maybe he's imagining too because he exhales and steps back, letting our fingers slip apart.

"Anton told me we'll leave soon if nothing interferes."

"I hope we go soon." I hesitate, then blurt out my story. "I caught Elise stealing jewelry last night." The more details I add about my midnight confrontation with Elise, the more uneasy Jack's expression becomes. When I add a description of how Elise flirts with the German soldiers every evening, his mouth tightens.

"I told Elise I wouldn't tell the countess I caught her stealing, but I don't know if I should keep the secret."

"Whatever Elise does makes sense for her," he says after a long pause. "She's a Belgian. She needs to live through the fighting until the Germans are defeated or until they win. Being friendly with the soldiers—she could be making sure she can survive no matter how the war turns out."

He's thinking rationally, but I'm not in the mood to excuse Elise. "That's no reason to steal from the countess after she's taken us in. I'm afraid if I tell the countess, she might drop the escape plan and throw us out."

"The countess seems to know what she's doing and who to trust. Look how she handles the German officers every night. She hasn't made any mistakes yet."

"Elise won't tell me if she's stolen other things, but I can search her room. If I find anything, we can decide what to do next."

"That's too dangerous. What will you say if you're caught?"

"I won't get caught, and no one else can do a search. You and Pete have to stay out of sight. I'm in the big house day and night. I can look through her room while she's working. Marta keeps her busy peeling potatoes and scrubbing pots."

"Peeling potatoes?" A faint smile crosses his lips.

"She hates it." We grin at each other for a minute.

"It's too risky. She might go to her room for any reason during the day."

"I can search while she's serving the drivers their food on the terrace. She stays with them every second until they leave."

"That's risky too." Jack grimaces. "The officers are inside the house, and they might see you. To be honest, I'm more worried about them than whether Elise has stolen jewelry. Don't forget there's a bounty on enemy soldiers—and people who help them. We can't put the countess in more danger than she is already." He thinks for a moment. "I wish we knew exactly what Elise talks about with the two drivers. Maybe it's nothing but flirting."

"Sylvie says the soldiers talk about their families." I grind my shoe into the dirt, unable to shake my sense of impending doom. "Elise's room is next to the kitchen, and I can use the back stairs. The officers in the dining room won't see me. They're too far away, and the drivers can't see from the terrace. It's the best time to search her room."

"All right. Be careful. Don't take a risk. Swear to me if there's any chance the Germans will see you, you won't try to search her room."

Knowing he's afraid for me is extremely satisfying. I can't help moving closer. "I swear. If there's any change in the routine or where they eat, I won't go downstairs at all."

His puts his hands on my shoulders. "We can't create an uproar over stolen jewelry when the countess is arranging our connection in Brussels. If you find any jewels in Elise's room, put them where the countess will find them later, after we've gone."

"Yes, that's best—if I find anything."

We stare at each other. His eyes focus on my mouth, and his expression tells me he wants what I do. For a moment, we both seem to stop breathing. Slowly, he takes his hands off my shoulders and shoves them in his pockets. "Good luck."

Waiting for evening, I plot what I have to do in Elise's room. Sylvie notices I don't eat much, and I make up a story about an upset stomach. The German officers arrive for their evening meal earlier than usual, sending Marta into a nervous fit as she shoves pots from one burner to another in her effort to speed up the cabbage and sausages. She hurries us out of the kitchen while Sylvie grumbles about missing the apple cobbler. Upstairs, I watch from the balcony, and as soon as Elise is serving—and flirting—with Hans and Carl, I tell Sylvie I've forgotten something downstairs.

Creeping down the servants' stairway, pressing close to the wall where the steps are less likely to squeak, I listen for the voices from the dining hall. Fortunately, Marta is making so much noise in the kitchen, a squeak or two from me on the stairs would never reach the officers.

Elise's room looks the way she described it—plain and little furniture. A bed with a brown coverlet, a four-drawer dresser, a wash basin and pitcher, several wall hooks for clothes. The only pretty object in the room is hanging on a wall—one of Sylvie's water colors of the garden with flowers and birds in an antique gilt frame. The room is neat and clean, and the scent of strong soap lingers in the air.

I've seen enough movies to know I have to search systematically, so I start with the dresser, although that's so obvious I don't expect to find anything. Elise was extremely careful when she touched the jewelry in the countess's case, so I assume she'll notice if anything in the drawers is even slightly out of place. I run my hands over the clothes as lightly as I can and then check the bottom and back of the dresser.

Nothing.

The wash basin sits on a small table. Stooping, I check the underside of the table and run my hands along the square legs and edges. The only drawer in the table is empty, and there's no sign of a false bottom or back. Then I check the wash basin and pitcher. Nothing underneath.

There's no closet, so the only thing left is the bed. Through the thin door I can hear Marta still muttering as she slams another pot on the stove. I don't dare mess the bedding. Elise would notice the minute she flung back the coverlet.

I run my fingers under the pillow, inside the pillow cover, along the edge of the mattress, and under the mattress as far as I can reach along both sides. After patting the sheets to check for suspicious lumps, I drop to the floor and peek under the bed. The springs are clean--nothing stuck to the mattress and nothing on the floor under the bed—not even a dust bunny. The only window in the room is square and low. I check the sill and feel under the ledge and along the grooves where the window slides up and down.

Nothing.

I've searched everything. Relief followed by a twinge of guilt take hold. Jack was right—Elise is just trying to survive. Last night could have been her first attempt to steal from the countess, and I stopped her. She was angry, but she's probably over it by now. Flirting with the soldiers—especially the blond one—will cheer her up. If—when—we reach Brussels, Elise will probably stay there. Maybe she'll find a job. Maybe the war will end quickly.

At the door when I turn for a final look, my eye catches Sylvie's painting again. Running my fingers along the bottom of the frame and along the sides, I feel a cloth-covered lump glued to the back about two inches from the edge. It pops off easily when I pry at it. The torn piece of white linen shows part of an embroidered initial like the embroidery on the countess's napkins. Unfolding the cloth, I'm not surprised to see a gold ring—the same one Elise tried on last night, a wide band set with emeralds. She must have gone back to the jewel case.

My doubts about her were right on track. I slip the ring into my pocket, so I can hide it somewhere to be found later. Elise will discover it's gone when we get ready to leave, but she won't be able to admit what she's looking for.

Turning to leave, I reverse myself. Don't overlook anything. The picture frame is heavy, but it's easy to slip off the hook in the wall. When I see folded papers stuck in the edge of the frame at the top, a chill runs along my spine. My fingers tremble so much, I have trouble gripping the papers strongly enough to yank them off the back of the painting.

One sheet looks like a letter, but it's in German and I can't read it. The other sheet is a map. It's a map of the house and the gardens, including the path to the carriage house.

20

The meaning of the map slowly sinks in.

Horrible images flash through my mind—Jack and Pete lying dead along with the countess and Anton. Sylvie and Marta might be shot too if Elise delivers this map and letter to the officers. I could be shot. Maybe she planned to give them these pages tonight, but the officers came early, and she wasn't ready. More likely, she knows I'm watching her from the balcony, so she's waiting for a better moment. Soon she'll think of another way to tell the Germans we're here, and she'll be ready when they come again.

Boots clatter overhead, shouts for the drivers echo through the house. The officers are in a hurry tonight, not lingering over the countess's wine the way they usually do. Stuffing the papers in my pocket, I hoist the picture frame up to the wall hook. The wire stretched across the back settles on the hook, but the frame slants, showing the marks on the wall where it usually rests. Matching the frame to the marks means shifting the picture back and forth along the hook to get it perfectly in place while the house echoes with shouts. Finally, the frame settles into place.

When I step into the hallway, I come face to face with Carl and Marta in the kitchen doorway. He's holding a plate piled high with sausages. Marta gasps when she sees me, then presses her lips together.

Carl glances at her, a puzzled frown on his forehead before he turns and sees me. "*Fraulein?*" He smiles, friendly.

I dip into an awkward curtsy and sprint for the stairs. By the time I unlock Sylvie's door and race to the balcony, the officers are climbing into their cars. They speed down the front drive and disappear between the hedges where the drive meets the main road.

Sylvie looks up from her painting. "Did you find what you were looking for?"

"Yes"

"But you didn't like it," Sylvie murmurs.

"No, I didn't." I drop onto the chair near her, my heart still thumping. "What did Elise and the soldiers talk about tonight?"

She swirls her brush in a paint pot and lightly dabbles pale green on the paper—leaves in a brown tree. "Beer and picnics—and hunting."

"What kind of hunting?"

A shrug. "I don't remember. Papa came and talked to me."

I draw a deep breath and close my eyes for a minute. "That's nice."

Sylvie carefully tightens the covers on her paint pots, washes her paint brush in a small dish of water, and sets the brush on a little grooved stand to dry. "Elise did something bad in Charleroi."

"What did she do?"

"Papa told me all about it. When the Germans came, she told them the English family hid French soldiers. The Germans were very angry."

"I'm sure they were." Dread seeps through me.

Sylvie giggles and begin to practice her ballet positions. While she spins on her toes, I dig through memories of what Elise told me about herself when we met. She worked for an English family in Charleroi, and when the Germans took over the city, the family died. There's a bitter taste in my mouth. Am I going to rely on the report of Sylvie's dead papa? I smother a groan. No point in showing Jack the papers I found; he can't read German. There's only one person I need to tell—and the faster I do it, the better. Tension makes my head spin.

I waver between blaming myself for convincing Elise to travel with Jack and Pete in the first place and wondering if all of us are doomed because of my mistake.

When the countess comes to say goodnight, Sylvie spreads her watercolors on the bed so we can admire them. The countess sits on the bed while she studies each watercolor and points out some object or color or brush stroke that's exceptionally clever. "Your paintings are beautiful, Sylvie. I like this tree and the ducks in the pond."

I sit on the bed with them, smiling cheerfully and echoing the countess's praise. The last painting Sylvie shows us is a watercolor of the German officers and their cars. One officer stands next to the car in his black boots. Sylvie's painted him in brown and black colors making him look like an ominous spirit growing out of the pink and yellow garden flowers behind him in the watercolor.

"This painting is very fine," the countess murmurs. "The officer looks like Colonel Schroeder who comes to eat every night."

"Are you afraid when they come to our house?" Sylvie leans against the countess, curling into her arms.

The countess looks over Sylvie's head into my eyes. Her lips move silently, *"Always."* Then she laughs and smoothes Sylvie's hair, "The colonel appreciates Marta's good food—he enjoys eating here."

"Does he like us?"

"Yes, he does, and he especially likes Marta's delicious roast pork and the wine in our cellar. Colonel Schroeder is very important, so we must do whatever we can to keep him pleased when he visits. You and I and Anton and Marta—we'll stay together and be happy and safe."

That overly-pleasant explanation sends Sylvie to sleep under her pink quilt, but when countess rises to leave, I follow her. "I need to tell you something. Can we go to your room?"

Inside her room, I blurt out my suspicions about Elise—the way she flirts with the soldiers every night—her complaints about money—my search through her room. I return the ring to her. Finally, I thrust the papers into her hands. "I don't know what the letter says, but the second sheet is a map of the house and gardens. I decided you needed to know."

She glances at the map and reads the letter, her expression calm and unworried as always. "It says nothing important," she answers at last. "You have no reason to worry, I do thank you for showing me the papers and for finding my ring. One must be extremely alert every day."

My shoulders relax. "I was afraid—"

She puts her arm around me. "I understand. Everyone is afraid in these times. But we must concentrate on our schemes to protect ourselves and our friends. Anton and I have your escape to Brussels carefully planned. We've taken other soldiers—Belgians and British—to Brussels." She thinks for a minute. "Early tomorrow, before the workers come to pick apples, we'll meet at the carriage house. I want you to examine the wagon Anton has rebuilt especially for hiding. You can try it for size—all of you fitting together. In the afternoon, Anton will take past the German patrols and into the city."

"Tomorrow?"

"Yes, Anton tells me it is the best time." She sighs. "Sylvie will miss you so much."

"I'll miss her too." It's the truth. She fascinates me with her odd bits of information, and she's become like a little sister. Everyone assumes Sylvie is a bit crazy because she talks about fairies and her dead papa, but I think she can sense things most people can't—I have no idea how she does it. I kissed a ghost, so I'm not going to dismiss everything Sylvie claims she's heard from her dead papa. She knows what no one else does—I'm not really here.

"You could stay with us if you want," the countess says. "The Germans don't care about my servants. Sylvie would be so happy to have you stay."

For one second, I'm surprised how tempting her offer is. In spite of the Germans coming every night for food, the estate is like a sheltered oasis in the middle of a war, but the comfort the countess offers me isn't strong enough to make me leave Jack. I don't think I'm finished with what I'm destined to do. He says I've already saved him, but I wonder—I think—there must be more for me to do. "Thank you, but I can't stay. I have to go to Brussels with Jack."

"Your face when you look at Jack—I understand you must go on with him—and with Pete of course." She smiles at my blush. "Sylvie says your face is easy to read because you think with your heart. It's a fine quality." She slips the ring on her finger and gazes at it. "This ring was my husband's last gift to me. I want to give it to Sylvie one day. Don't worry. Everything will be as it should be."

When I tiptoe back into the bedroom, Sylvie rubs her eyes and sits up in bed. "Are you leaving?"

I climb on the bed and take her hand. "Tomorrow."

She hugs me and puts her head on my shoulder. "I'll miss you," she says with a sigh.

I tighten my arms around her. "I'll miss you too. Promise me you'll take good care of the countess and help her when she needs it."

"I promise."

We both cross our hearts and swear we'll be good and careful. After we hug again, Sylvie slides under the quilt and falls asleep almost immediately. I stretch out on top of the quilt, her hand in mine, while I stare at the ceiling, wondering what will happen in Brussels and wishing Jack was holding my hand.

When the countess taps on the door in the early morning, I follow her quietly down the stairs to the kitchen where Elise waits for us. Her face is blank—no nerves. She must not have discovered the ring and papers are gone.

The countess isn't wearing her usual lacy blouse and long dark skirt. She's in work clothes, a plain blue shirt, boots, men's pants, and a big heavy cotton jacket with pockets the size of dinner plates. Elise and I trail behind her through the garden to the carriage house. Anton stands with Jack and Pete next to a wagon roughly ten feet long and five feet wide. Behind the driver's seat, a small open area is piled with loose apples, but most of the wagon bed is covered by a wooden platform loaded with bushels of applies, packed close together.

The countess plunges her hands in her pockets. The rising sun streaks through the surrounding trees and dapples the ground with light and dark patches. "You four should examine this wagon so you understand how you'll travel," she says. "There's enough space, but you'll be tightly pressed together."

Anton runs his fingers along a seam between wooden boards, and a panel opens under the raised platform revealing a low space padded with old quilts. There's no room to sit—we'll have to lie flat during the trip. We take turns peering into the opening.

Elise is the last one to check the space, and after a long look, she snorts and shakes her head. "It is too small. How can we stay so close without moving for so long?" She stamps away from the wagon and folds her arms over her chest. "This is a stupid plan. The wagon is not big enough for four people."

"It's big enough for three," the countess answers in a soft voice.

She pulls her hand out of her pocket, points a heavy black pistol at Elise, and shoots her square in the chest.

21

Someone screams. Jack steps behind me, wraps his arms around my waist, and pulls me tight against him. I'm the one who screamed. Elise doesn't move. A red stain on her blouse spreads over her chest, blood dribbles out the corner of her mouth. Her open eyes stare at the sky, a startled expression on her face. She's dead.

I'm shaking, and if Jack didn't have his arms around me, I'd sink to the ground because my legs are like wet string. "I—I didn't—I didn't—" My throat closes, my mind won't form a clear sentence. I clamp my hands around Jack's wrists, so he won't let me go, so I can stay upright. How many times have I seen dead bodies in the past weeks? Too many, but I didn't know them. Elise, bloody on the dirt in front of me, is a new kind of horror. It's my fault she's dead.

Pete swears under his breath and shuffles his feet. "Bloody surprise that," he mutters softly.

The countess casually slides her pistol back into her pocket, no trembling, no guilt or regret on her face. She glances at Anton, who does not seem at all surprised to have a dead body lying at his feet. "It was necessary," she says quietly, her gaze holding mine. "Elise would betray us—if not here, then in Brussels."

"The letter?" My voice cracks.

She gestures in the direction of Elise's body. "Yes, her letter to the Germans was a betrayal. She would have had all of us killed and gotten a reward." The countess's expression is serene as if she hadn't just shot someone in front of us. "We'd have had no warning. You stopped her when you found that letter."

I don't want her praise for stopping Elise's treachery. Guilt runs through me, and if Jack weren't holding me up, I'd collapse. When do people like the countess feel guilty? "It's my fault," I murmur.

Jack puts his head close to mine and whispers in my ear. "Jenny, you did the right thing. If Elise was going to betray us, it's best this way. It would have been worse if we'd had to kill her."

My mind goes blank for an instant. I've lied and stolen to keep us safe, but I could never kill anyone. That idea fades pretty quickly. Maybe I'm lying to myself because I didn't hesitate to give the papers I found in Elise's room to the countess. The letter was a mystery, but I knew the map was dangerous. Worse—I didn't care what might happen to Elise as long as Jack and I were safe together.

Jack arms stay tight around me. I focus on the trees in the distance and avoid looking at Elise lying bloody on the ground no more than two feet from me. Finally, I turn to the countess. "We should bury her." My voice sounds like the countess's voice now—calm and steady.

The countess and Anton exchange glances, sharing some kind of intuitive communication without speaking. Anton stoops and lifts Elise's body. "One of you," he says, "come with me."

Pete glances at my tight hold on Jack. "Right then, I'll come," he says. He and Anton disappear into the woods behind the carriage house.

"Anton knows what to do," the countess says in a low voice. "The Germans cannot find anything suspicious if they search the estate."

"Will they bury her in the woods?" My fingers unlock, releasing Jack.

"There's an old well in a clearing. It's deep, and no one uses it now. Anton will put rocks on top of her, so she will have a burial of a kind. No one will find her, and the well is too deep for animals to bother her."

The bottom of a well. Elise was a planner. She must have worked out what she wanted to do when she got the money for betraying us. She never said if she had a sweetheart. If she planned to meet someone, he will never know what happened only that she didn't show up as promised. "How do we know the letter I found was her only message to the Germans?"

"We don't." For the first time, a hint of fear shows in the countess's eyes. "I couldn't be sure it was her first letter. She might have said something to the drivers about you or about our plans. If Colonel Schroeder behaves strangely when he arrives tonight, I'll know. That's why you three must leave today with Anton."

In the afternoon, a light drizzle begins as we crawl into the wagon, wiggling in side by side, touching shoulders, hands, hips, and trying not to breathe too deeply. Anton tucks my skirts around my legs. "Rain is good," he says. "German soldiers do not search every wagon on the road when there is rain."

He closes the cover over us and rearranges the bushels of apples across the top. The wooden platform covering our hiding place creaks from the weight of the bushels, but the bushels conceal most of the platform except for the cracks letting in air, so we can breathe. I wanted to say goodbye to Sylvie again, but the countess ordered me to stay out of sight with Jack and Pete at the carriage house until it was time to leave.

Pete awkwardly shifts his bad arm, bumping my shoulder. "Sorry, Luv, it's a bit tight."

"Don't worry about it, Pete," I whisper.

When my hand touches Jack's, he threads his fingers through mine in the comforting way he has, and my pulse slows down to a steady rhythm. It's seems safer to be on the move than relying on the countess to keep the German officers from searching the estate.

I move my head so it rests against his shoulder, and he squeezes my hand.

Rain sprinkles through the cracks in the wood, making us damp but also giving us some moisture to lick off our lips. Pete goes to sleep while the wagon lurches down country roads, starting and stopping. Anton is right about the rain. German patrols stop us several times, but they never do more than look at the apples piled in the front of the wagon and tap a few bushels on the back while we hold our breaths. Anton gives away apples and jokes with them.

It's black as the darkest night inside the wagon, but the darkness makes every sound sharper—birds chirp in the trees on the side of the road, rain drops ping on the apples, horses clomp on the roads, Anton whistles under his breath, and small animals scratch in the dirt on the side of the road. Gradually, the sounds outside the wagon change to rumbling automobile motors, shouts, arguing voices, clattering wagon wheels, and—most alarming—marching, heavy boots.

Jack whispers against my ear, "We must be in the city."

The wagon rumbles on, turning corners, until the rain gets heavier and muffles the street sounds into one wet, splashing noise. "Quiet," Anton hisses when the wagon comes to a stop. We wait in the dark, hearing nothing outside. Anton finally begins to move the bushels of apples. He flips up the cover over our hiding place and peers in. "The sky is dark," he whispers. "No one is out."

Pete groans and stretches while Jack helps me out of the wagon. Our legs are stiff from the hours in the cramped space. The wagon is parked in a narrow alley running along the side of a building. The drenching rain makes it nearly as dark outside as it was inside the wagon.

"Quick." Anton leads us around the corner to four attached row houses. Shutters cover the windows, and when I glance across the street, I know why. A huge German flag—horizontal black, red, and white stripes—hangs outside a large square building. The streets are empty—no soldiers in sight.

Anton pushes us ahead of him. "Keep heads down," he says. "Quick."

On our side of the street, the door marked 149 opens, and a thin woman beckons us inside. Her brown hair, streaked with gray, is swept up and knotted under a starched white cap. The long sleeves on her blue dress end in stiff white cuffs, and her white apron has a bib reaching nearly to her starched white collar.

Anton bends close to her ear and mumbles a few muffled sentences. The nurse listens and nods while she looks us over. We shake off the rain drops and wipe our faces on our sleeves. The nurse murmurs something to Anton, and he slaps Jack on the back. "Much luck," he says, pulling his hat down and slipping out the door.

The nurse quickly shuts the door behind him. "Welcome to our clinic," she says softly in an English accent. "I'm the director. My name is Edith Cavell, and you may call me Matron. Anton told me your first names, and I will use them. You'll stay in the clinic for a few days while I find a guide to take you north to Holland."

"There's a German garrison across the street," Jack says.

A calm nod. "This is a Red Cross clinic, but we have only wounded German soldiers here at the moment. When the Germans took Brussels, they also took over our clinic. They inspect often but not well, and they've never discovered any Allied soldiers I've hidden here. At the moment, a Belgian soldier is staying in the cellar. Eventually, a guide will take you to the border with Holland." She folds her hands as if she's going to pray. "Wartime is difficult, but one does one's duty the best one can." She looks pointedly at my short hair. "Do you intend to go with the two young men to the border?"

"Yes."

A slight frown. "You can't stay with the men in the cellar. It isn't proper. There's a room on the top floor near the back stairs, and I'll give you a uniform so you can work in the clinic." The frown disappears, and she smiles.

I can't argue with her—what would I say? *Don't worry about being proper. I can't kiss Jack because if I do, I'll whirl through a mysterious time transfer and vanish.* She leads us down a hallway and out the back door to a cellar entrance. A soldier, who looks younger than

Jack, stands up when we enter the low room, and we exchange first names.

"Louis's been alone for a few days, but now he'll have companions." Miss Cavell tone is pleasant but formal, as if we've all gathered in the clinic for some old-fashioned social event.

She leaves us alone, and in a few minutes another nurse arrives with a tray of food. She introduces herself as Millicent but tells us to call her Sister. We sit at a rickety table eating as though we've been starving for days instead of a few hours—carrots, slices of beef, thick bread. Millicent leaves and comes back with three mugs of beer for the men—she gives me a cup of tea. Louis is a Belgian soldier who was in one of the forts at Liege and in very broken English tells us how the Germans overran them in only a few days. Jack and Pete tell him about fighting at Mons in the south, and the three mutter about ammunition and maneuvers.

I don't want to leave them, but I have no choice when Miss Cavell in a firm voice tells me it's time to go upstairs. The room on the third floor is small with a plain bed and dresser, and a half-curtain on the bottom of the square window facing the street below. A folded, heavy cotton nightgown with long sleeves and a ruffled collar at the neckline lies on the bed. Hooks on one wall hold a clean white apron and a blue dress.

"I don't know anything about nursing," I say, looking at the uniform.

"You won't have difficult tasks. You'll work as an aide to the nurses. When the Germans inspect the clinic, they'll pay no attention to you."

"Do they inspect often?"

"Every day." Nothing in her clear gray eyes indicates that she's worried about the horrible danger she'd face if one day the Germans decide to check the cellars.

"Do the other nurses know you're hiding soldiers from the Germans?"

"One or two—those I trust implicitly. You must keep silent about what you know and say very little to the staff. Say nothing at all to the Germans even if they speak in English. Tomorrow, I'll introduce you to the nurses as a refugee I've taken in and put to work. We're short-handed now. Most of my English nurses went back to England, and we get more wounded in every day, so everyone will be happy to have help in the clinic."

She explains how to find the kitchen and says Millicent will give me instructions in the morning. After she leaves, I shrug off my clothes, put on the nightgown, and lie on the plain blue coverlet, staring out the open window at the stars. No noise comes from the garrison across the street, but through the rain I can see into a third-floor window and watch uniformed figures moving around in a lighted room. The street is silent and dark—no cars, no rattling wagons, no voices.

A faint knock on the door sends me to my feet, heart pounding in my chest. Rushing barefoot across the floor, I open the door a crack. Jack stands in the shadowy hallway, a half grin on his lips. "Let me in," he whispers.

I pull him inside and close the door as silently as I can, my breath catching in my throat. I'm insanely glad to see him, and I stifle a giggle. In spite of Miss Cavell banishing me to the third floor to protect me, I'm alone with Jack in the dark with only the moonlight coming through the window, and I'm in a nightgown—a very heavy, ugly nightgown—but still a nightgown.

"How did you find my room?"

"I found my way from Mons to Brussels—finding your room wasn't that hard. Miss Cavell said it was at the top next to the back stairs, and I followed my instincts—which are very good where you're concerned."

Thank goodness it's dark because I can feel the blush shooting up my throat to my cheeks. "There's another door on this floor, across the hall."

He laughs low in his throat. "I tried that one first. It's a storeroom, full of bandages and bedpans and bottles."

"So maybe your instincts about me aren't exactly on target."

"My instincts about you are on target all right," he says. He takes a half step closer. "Jenny, we have to talk about something."

"What is it?" A familiar chill jolts through me.

There isn't any chair in the room, so we sit on the bed. The faint light coming from the window across the street gives my white nightgown a ghostly look. Jack takes my hand and runs his thumb across the pulse in my wrist, a gesture that always makes me quiver to my toes.

"We have to be realistic. We're in Brussels surrounded by the enemy. If Pete and I get caught—it's even more likely here than in the country. I guess I don't have to explain what would happen. If we're caught, you need to take care of something for me."

"The Germans won't find you. Don't say that."

Jack glances out the window. His hand tightens on mine. "That garrison is filled with soldiers, and they inspect the clinic every day. Miss Cavell says she's gotten British soldiers to Holland safely, but we're not there yet, and anything could go wrong. You have to promise to do something for me if I can't get across the border with you."

22

"What is it?"

He presses my hand against his chest, so I touch the outline of the leather envelope under his shirt. The heat from his skin radiates through the cloth, and my fingers automatically spread out, feeling his heart beat rapidly under my hand. I hope it's beating so fast at least partly because we're sitting so close, and it's so dark. That's definitely why my heart is thumping in my chest.

"If I'm caught," he whispers, "you have to get this envelope to England—to an army office."

"The dead officer's letter to his family?" I trace the edges of the envelope with my fingers. We're only feet away from dozens of German soldiers, and Jack's worrying about delivering a letter to a family he doesn't know. "Nothing's going to happen to you or Pete. We've gotten this far, and we'll get the rest of the way."

"It's nice to think that."

"Sorry." My attempt at optimism doesn't fool either of us. "I promise. If anything stops you from getting to England, I'll find a way to get the officer's letter to the army no matter what."

"It's not a letter, Jenny."

"You said it was. You said when the officer was dying, he gave you a letter for his family."

"You said that, and I let you and Pete think it was a letter."

"If it's not a letter, what is it?"

"I'm not sure." Jack unbuttons his shirt, pulls out the envelope, and jerks the cord over his head.

When he spreads three sheets of paper on the bed, we stare at a jumble of figures and formulas that don't look like anything I remember from algebra or geometry. One sheet is covered in squiggly drawings—squares and loops and rectangles.

"What did the officer say these papers were?"

"He didn't say. Dragging him to the dressing station took all my energy, and he was too wounded to talk and walk at the same time." Jack arranges the sheets in a neat row. "The station was in turmoil. The Germans were advancing on it, our men were shot to pieces, doctors were shouting orders, and Pete was hurt. I knew the colonel wasn't going to make it. He was shot in his stomach, losing a lot of blood. A surgeon tried to stop the bleeding but couldn't help, so he left us alone. With the noise and gunfire, it was hard to hear, and the colonel was gasping for breath, but he managed to say the papers had to get to England because they were vital to the army."

I point to one of the squiggly drawings. "This looks like a tank."

"Tank?"

When did armies start using tanks? Think fast. I trace the outline of the drawing. "It looks bulky, like it's loaded with something."

Jack studies the drawing and shrugs. "I can't make sense of it. The colonel was an engineer. When the Germans broke through our lines, units got mixed together. Men ran in every direction. He got separated from his unit—we did too."

We stare at the papers in silence until I give up. "The colonel's dead—he can't explain these formulas—how can these papers be any help to the army?"

"I don't know, but the last thing he said to me was that papers had to get to England."

"What about Pete. Should you tell him?"

"If I'm caught, Pete likely will be too," Jack says. "If the worst happens, you'll be the one who can get to England. America isn't in the war. If we're discovered, the Germans would send you home—they don't want Americans mixed up in this war."

"I promise," I whisper. "I promise I'll get the papers to the British army if it's up to me to do it."

We gaze at each other for a long time without speaking until Jack wraps his arm around my waist and pulls me close enough to put my head on his shoulder. I close my eyes and slip my hand inside his open shirt collar, so I can feel his heart beating. His breath stirs my hair, while he gently runs his fingers through the stray curls at my temple.

We lean against each other, listening to our breathing, feeling the warmth from each other, and just for this minute, I can pretend we're the only people who matter, nothing exists outside this room, and we have all the time in the world to be together.

The lights in the upper garrison windows go out. "I'd better go back to the cellar." Jack folds the papers, puts them back in the envelope, squeezes my hand, and leaves me sitting in the room alone.

It's hard to sleep. I thrash around the bed, under the coverlet, over the coverlet, wiggling uncomfortably on the stiff mattress, rearranging the flat pillow, wondering about the future and secret papers. When I finally fall asleep, my dreams is full of British soldiers running from bullets spraying around them thick as rain drops, and Jack is in the crowd, blood running down his face. I wake up violently, breathing hard, kicking my legs in the air, and sweat covering my forehead and arms.

Millicent comes to my room before any light shows in the dark sky and directs me to the bathroom on the second floor. I've been spoiled by the chateau's luxurious bathroom. This one is clean but tiny and plain and shows the wear of many people using it—small cracked sink—missing pieces in the tile floor under the clawfoot tub. The tub isn't as large as the one at the chateau, but it's big enough for soaking, and I sink into the warm water up to my neck. In spite of the warmth, chills take over when I can't stop myself from remembering how close Elise came to betraying us and the horrible moment when she died. Every time I tell myself we're nearly out of danger, we have a new hazard to face. Now it's Jack's papers we have to worry about. Pushing them out of my mind, I concentrate on rubbing the bar of soap into my wet hair.

Drying vigorously with the stiff, rough towel brings the blood to my skin, and my optimism manages to rise again. Brushing my hair and squeezing the curls into shape, I glance in the half mirror over the sink at my naked body, and my breath stops. A warm breeze floats through the half open window, but I've turned cold and shivery.

Slowly, carefully, I run my fingers through my hair, stretching out the curls to their full length. Next, I raise my arms above my head and stare at my reflection. Bending, I run my hands along my legs. I'm not sure how much time has elapsed, but I deliberately focus on events and count the days and weeks to estimate how long it's been since I woke up in the church cemetery. A little over four weeks.

Sylvie's voice echoes in my head. *You aren't really here.*

Nothing on my body has changed. I haven't used a razor for a month, and my skin is as smooth as if I'd just come out of Aunt Connie's bathroom. My hair hasn't grown. I haven't had to search for a tampon. Running—hiding—stealing—lying. Each day was too frenzied for me to notice that nothing about my body changed. Jack and Pete had stubbly beards and longer hair by the time we reached the countess. Except for being dirty and tired when we got there, I was in the same condition as when I dashed into the garden to meet my ghost. Not needing to shave my legs should be a good thing, but it's like discovering I haven't been eating or breathing.

In spite of the shock, an eerie calm settles over me while I put on my uniform and go down the stairs to the clinic's main floor. Miss Cavell gives me instructions for handling the cart I'm to push along the rows of beds filled with wounded German soldiers.

"You look very efficient," Miss Cavell says while she adjusts the collar on my blue cotton dress and smoothes the tie on my white apron. "I'm glad it fits you well enough. The officers aren't likely to notice anything unusual about you when they inspect the clinic today. They probably won't notice you at all if you stay far away from them." When I don't answer, she tilts my head up to look in my eyes. "Are you all right, my dear? You seem distracted."

Her soft voice has a motherly tone, the kind that makes me want to put my arms around her. She's managing an entire hospital in the middle of a war and smuggling soldiers to safety, but she looks as unruffled as if she had all the time in the world to listen to my problems.

I attempt a smile. "I'm sorry, Matron. It's so much to remember."

She puts her arms around me, and I sink against her, grateful. A lavender scent from the handkerchief tucked in her pocket is unexpectedly soothing. It reminds me of Aunt Connie.

"It's frightening to be in a war, I know," she says. "You've been strong to come this far. Why are you traveling with the English soldiers? You're an American. I could tell the German commandant about you and he can arrange—"

"I can't leave Jack!" A blush crawls up my neck. She doesn't have to be a genius to figure out my feelings about Jack.

"I see," she says quietly with a smile. "Then we must be sure you both stay together all the way to the border."

My first task in the clinic is pushing the cart loaded with bandages and medicines behind Millicent as she goes from soldier to soldier in one of the two long wards lined with beds on both sides. Millicent has flaming red hair piled so high her nurse's cap perched on top looks as if it's about to fly off her head. She's gorgeous. The soldiers—the patients—brighten, sit up if they can, and smile when she walks down the aisle.

At first, I try to hold my breath because of the strong smell of alcohol, blood, and body odor although the patients look clean. They wear flannel nightshirts, and most have thick white bandages somewhere on their bodies—chests, arms, legs, heads and ankles. Out of uniform, they look young and helpless, and they mutter *Danke!* while Millicent changes their bandages and swabs their wounds with hydrogen peroxide from one of the bottles on my cart. We don't speak in front of the soldiers. She points to what she wants, and I hand it to her. After stopping at a few beds, I anticipate fairly well what she's going to need after she unwraps the wound—*Peroxyde d'hydrogène* and then the clean bandage.

The patients with small bandages covering wounds on their arms or feet sit upright in their beds. When we reach a soldier lying still, his eyes closed, his leg bandaged from ankle to knee, my stomach starts to churn from the sickening smell rising from his wound. The odor is overwhelming. Millicent strips away the gauze layer by layer. The last layers are soaked with pus. I bite my lips hard to keep from vomiting and fix my eyes on a point in the ceiling far down the room when she pulls the last strip of gauze off the patient's leg. Millicent is efficient and completely unaffected by the horrible smell and ugly, pus-filled wound. For this soldier, she wants the bottle marked *Solution saline stérile*, then the hydrogen peroxide. The soldier grimaces while she washes out the wound, but he stays silent, bearing the pain better than I would have.

At noon I push the food cart along the rows of beds. Every patient gets the same meal—a slice of dark bread, a bowl of thick potato soup, two slices of veal, and a cup of tea. One patient with a chest wound is too weak to feed himself, so I have to sit next to the bed and feed him by spooning up the soup and cutting the meat into small bits.

The soldier swallows the last piece of meat and sinks back on his pillow as Millicent rushes to the bed and pulls me into the aisle. "The Germans are here for the inspection," she whispers.

Heavy boots thump on the wooden floor.

23

"**M**ind your cart, stay away from them, and don't catch their gaze," Millicent adds in another whisper as she runs to join Miss Cavell meeting the German officers at the entrance to the main ward.

I push my medicine cart to the back wall, and slowly, as if there's some purpose to it, I rearrange the bottles on the upper shelf, moving them from row to row while all my senses track the two officers as they walk down the center aisle between the rows of beds. The faintest sounds reach me although my heart pounds in my ears. A silent prayer the grim-looking officers won't decide to check the cellar repeats over and over in my head. After moving the bottles back and forth on the cart three times, I fiddle with the stacks of gauze bandages, cutting them like cards, shuffling them into new piles, cutting and shuffling them again, fumbling the piles, so I have to collect the pieces before I can restack them. My body is half-turned away from the officers, but I'm intensely aware of where they are and what they're doing.

Miss Cavell walks next to the officer with a short gray beard and a monocle in one eye. She speaks to him in French, pointing to some of the soldiers, apparently giving progress reports about their injuries. When they pause at the bed of a young soldier with a wounded arm, the officer speaks to him in German. The soldier answers and salutes awkwardly. The younger officer trails behind, looking bored, until he notices me and slows his step.

I shuffle more gauze squares and rearrange more bottles, keeping my head down, but I can't ignore him because he strolls over to my cart and speaks to me in German. Trying my best to fix a wide-eyed innocent look on my face, I smile and shake my head slightly, so I'm friendly but can't communicate. I wait, wide-eyed, smiling, my pulse jumping. Do I look innocent or guilty?

Miss Cavell saves me—hurrying toward us and speaking to him in French with an urgent tone. He nods, answers, looks me over again, and hesitates, but she manages to steer him back to the older officer who's at the door, arms folded, tapping his boot on the floor. The two give Miss Cavell a polite salute and leave.

"What did you say to him?" My fingers are still trembling when she reaches me.

She glances at my cart and sorts the bottles back to their original order. "I said you were an Irish maid working for me in the clinic. Fortunately, neither of those officers speaks English." Her attempt at a smile doesn't fool me. Her hands are shaking too.

I rub my damp palms over my skirt. "If they discover what you're doing here—I don't know what—"

"Yes, yes" she interrupts, "of course, it's dangerous. We must be on our guard every minute. The German army controls everything in Brussels, and they can search the clinic whenever they want to. It's our duty to stay composed and focus on our mission." Her usually calm voice quivers just enough to reveal her nerves.

"When I was in the kitchen this morning, I saw—I think the cook is—is she a German? Can we trust her?"

"Hilda? Hilda's been with me for years. I don't know all her loyalties, but I can't send her back to Germany because her husband is Belgian and works in the city. She wouldn't leave him." She takes a long breath, calmer now.

"Does she know?"

"I'm not sure what she understands. None of the soldiers who passed through the clinic were in uniform, and she never talks to them or has any contact with them. I've told everyone the men who come and go are refugees and need food for a few days. No one's questioned that story, and I can only hope Hilda believes me."

Safety depends on so many small bits fitting together, like a giant jigsaw puzzle. We have to hope Hilda isn't very observant, the Germans won't search the cellars, no one will question the refugee story, and someone will be able to guide us to the border. "Why didn't you go back to England when the Germans invaded? You might have reached home before Brussels was taken."

"I wasn't here when the invasion began. I was visiting my mother in Norwich when the war broke out, and I came back to Brussels at once." She folds her hands together. "My duty is completely clear to me—my place is in the clinic and while I'm here I must save as many of our soldiers as I can."

"Jack has to get to England," I say in a low voice.

"How long have you been with him?"

"I found him in a ravine, helped him pull Pete out, and we stayed together. They have to escape."

She touches my hand for an instant. "Jack is lucky you found him. Have faith. He'll get back to England, and you'll go home to America. We must pray for success in these matters, but now, we'll concentrate on our patients. I know you'll be strong no matter what happens." She smoothes her hair and walks quickly away without waiting for my whispered promise. The noise from her tapping heels fades down the hallway.

After two more days in the clinic, I'm used to the daily inspections by the German officers every afternoon—the leather boots thumping into the ward, the questioning glances. The visits don't last long, mostly because Miss Cavell walks with them, shows them new patients, and manages to bore them with details about hospital supplies. The tedious information concerning gauze, saline solutions, medicines, and battered flesh sends the officers out of the clinic as quickly as they can manage, and they never investigate the kitchen, the cellars or the storage shed in the tree-shaded yard behind the clinic.

The German soldiers don't look especially fierce or frightening lying wounded in their beds although in uniforms and with their weapons they must have been as terrifying as those we saw while we tramped along the roads. In their hospital shirts, they look like boys who should be in school not lying in a hospital wrapped in heavy bandages. When I push the cart behind Millicent as she makes her rounds, they grin and talk to me in German and don't seem disappointed by my failure to answer them as long as I smile and laugh a little.

Some soldiers are silent. They stare at the ceiling, ignoring us, but jumping nervously if I push the cart too close to the bed or when Millicent puts her fingers lightly on their foreheads to check for fever. They don't have wounds; they don't eat much; they lie still with eyes open but vacant. Some are dizzy if they try to stand. Some don't know their names. Some shiver and shake for hours.

"They suffer from neurasthenia," Millicent tells me.

"Is that like post traumatic stress?"

She looks blank. "What?"

Another mistake. I stumble over an explanation. "I mean, these patients aren't wounded. They seem to be stunned—maybe by the guns or the battles—and now they can't speak clearly or concentrate. It could be because of the horror they've seen."

She gazes at one of the soldiers. "You might be right about the reason they can't communicate," she says. "The fear and the terrible guns have shaken them into silence. The patient in the small room at the end of the hall is only sixteen. He arrived one day shivering and gasping, but he's never spoken." She smiles. "*Traumatic stress*—an interesting way to put it. Very clever."

The boy with the chest wound died after the evening meal. As usual, I sat next to the bed and fed the beef soup to him, but he sipped only a spoonful or two before he dropped his head back on the pillow. He was feverish—his blond hair matted wet on his forehead, and his breathing turned into long raspy gasps. I patted his forehead dry, but the cold sweat beaded again immediately. Millicent wasn't in the ward. Sister Gregson was behind a curtain tending to another wounded man. The German boy and I were alone with each other, but we had no words we could share. He turned his head on the pillow to look into my eyes, and for a moment, we gazed at each other. I smiled at him. Then his hand trembled on the bed, and I reached for it. Although his breathing grew shorter and harsher, his grip was strong and tight, crushing my fingers. *"Danke"* The soft whisper came on his last breath.

24

Jack climbs the stairs to my room late every night. When I hear his step, I rush to open the door so he doesn't have to knock. We whisper in the dark and spread the sheets of paper from the leather envelope on the bed, trying to understand them. But the pages show a meaningless jumble of lines, circles, and numbers with a few words we can't interpret jotted in the margins.

After we give up trying to decipher the formulas, Jack slides his arm around my waist and rests his cheek lightly on the top of my head, while we look out the window at the moon or at the building opposite the clinic where we can see German soldiers, drinking and playing cards. Holding Jack's hand and feeling his warm breath rustling my hair proves there's nothing ghostly in this room. Just for now at least we're safe and together. We've been at the clinic five days. Miss Cavell tells us she's arranging for fake identification papers we'll need if a patrol stops us in the street.

"Louis left for the border just before I came up here," Jack whispers tonight.

My dreamy mood abruptly ends. "How did he leave?"

"A man—looked like a fisherman—big boots—came to the back of the clinic behind the storage shed. Miss Cavell gave Louis his papers, a passport, and some money and said the man would take him to the border—or close to it."

"Who was the man?"

"No names. If Louis gets caught, he won't know the name of the man who guided him."

"How long does it take to get to the border?"

"I don't know. Probably depends on the route, how many stops, and if the Germans get suspicious."

Suspicious—horrible word. "She told me most soldiers reach the border without being stopped."

"Sure, but each escape is different. She's going to take our pictures for the passports."

"How long does it take to get passports?"

"A couple of days I guess. She'll tell us when she's ready." He shifts closer to me, takes my hand, and strokes his thumb over my wrist in his special way, so a warm flush runs up my arm. "Jenny, when we get to England, will your parents insist you sail for America on the first available boat?"

It's tempting to blurt out the truth and confess I don't know what happens to me in this life or how long I'll be here. It's tempting, but if I explain all that, he might stop holding my hand, and this delicious closeness will end. More likely, if I tell the truth, he'll think I've lost my mind.

"I'm not sure. I haven't thought about it." Another lie, but I've told so many lies after all, what's one more?

"I guess you miss your family." He turns my hand over and traces my life line in my palm.

I search my memory for lies I've told about my family. "Of course, I miss my parents." A lie. "I'm sure they're worried about me." Another lie, but Aunt Connie might be worried. "I have no way to contact them." That's certainly the absolute truth.

"Your pulse jumps when I touch you here. Do I make you nervous?"

"Not at all." Another lie. My voice wavers because his fingers stroking my palm and wrist increase that warm sensation into a burn that spreads along every nerve ending. Definitely hot enough to make me melt.

"I think you might be wrong." He grins and presses his thumb over my wrist again. "Your pulse seems to miss beats when I touch you here."

I snatch my hand away.

He leans so close to me his breath stirs the curls at my temple, and if I turn my head the smallest fraction, our lips will be so close, I won't be able to resist tilting my head just enough to reach his mouth. "Don't go home to America when we get to England," he murmurs against my cheek. "Stay with me as long as you can."

"Will you have to go back to your army unit?"

"Yes, but maybe we'd have a few days together. We could—" He hesitates, grins, and starts over. "London is full of famous places," he says, in a tourist-guide tone. "There's Westminster Abbey and London Tower. We could take a boat to Greenwich. Maybe the war won't last very long. Maybe we'll be lucky." While I chew my lip and search for an answer that sounds rational, Jack plays with my hair, winding the curls around his fingers. "Don't go back to America right away," he whispers. "Stay with me in England."

When Jack's this close to me, I get a little lightheaded, but it's too soon for me to disappear. He isn't safe yet. According to his diary, Jack reaches Holland before I disappear. Or do I die in Holland?

While I'm searching for a reasonable answer, he runs his finger along my jaw, dips his head, and kisses my cheek. My heart flutters. For a second, I turn toward him—but I catch myself, curl my hands into fists so I don't touch him, and get to my feet. Fear surges through me now. He kissed my cheek—is that strong enough to send me back to my other life? Waiting for the whirling darkness to capture me, I hold my breath until I have to gasp for air. Nothing happens. My legs feel wobbly, but relief slowly puts me back together. A kiss on my cheek isn't going to send me back to Aunt Connie's garden. The kiss for that transfer has to be like Jack's kiss when he brought me here— his lips firm against mine, blotting out every thought until my head spins, and I lose my balance.

"Sorry," he says, getting to his feet. "Didn't mean to upset you. I thought after all the time we've been together, we could. . .I was wrong."

"You didn't upset me. I just can't. . . ." Embarrassed—I hurt him again—conjuring up an adequate lie to explain my strange behavior is impossible.

He gazes at me, waiting for a better answer I suppose. An awkward silence descends. Finally, he straightens his shoulders. "Probably time for me to go downstairs."

At the door, I put my hand on his arm to hold him back. "I promise I'll stay with you as long as I can."

It takes me hours to fall asleep, twisting on the bed, wishing my promise meant what Jack thinks it does.

25

"Louis was captured last night."

Jack props the mattress he's carrying against the hallway wall and runs his hands through his thick black hair in a gesture I recognize by now. He's worried. We're alone in the hallway outside two small rooms at the back of the main ward. The daily inspection is over, so Millicent has Jack dragging beds and mattresses from the cellar storerooms to the clinic's main floor. More patients are on the way. My cart is piled with sheets, blankets, and pillows to make up the beds.

A familiar rush of apprehension shoots through me. "How do you know Louis was caught?" If Louis can be caught so quickly, then our escape is no sure thing either. Miss Cavell's confidence about her network of people getting us to the Holland might be extremely misplaced.

"A messenger came to the back gate. Miss Cavell is in the yard with him now."

"Where was he captured?"

Jack's mouth tightens. "Don't know," he whispers. "Not far—the edge of town. They stopped for food, and the place was full of German soldiers. Louis looked suspicious to them—who knows why? Louis is Belgian. He should have blended in the crowd without any trouble. The guide got out of the cafe while Louis was being arrested and came straight here."

If we were alone, Jack could put his arms around me, but we're only a few feet from the open ward full of nurses and patients. Instead of hanging onto him, I clutch the handle of my cart until my knuckles turn white. "Will Louis tell the Germans about us, about the clinic?"

"He's a soldier. He knows what to do."

"Will they shoot him?"

Louis is only seventeen. With his curly brown hair drooping over his ears, and his shy smile, he looks even younger. Why would anyone shoot him? But I remember the priest in the village lying in the street, his blood oozing out into the dirt. Anyone can be hurt in a war.

We stare at each other over the pillows on my cart.

"They won't shoot him," Jack says softly.

He's saying it to calm me, but he sounds so certain, my dread eases enough so I can think clearly. "Will Louis getting caught stop us from escaping?"

"We'll have to wait and see what Miss Cavell says. She'll know when the time is right for us to go north."

He hoists the mattress on his shoulder, and I follow him into the small one-bed room. He drops the mattress on the bed frame, straightens it, and pauses for a moment before turning back to me, his smile fixed in place. "We'll get out of Belgium. We won't be caught."

I nod. "I know." We need hope and confidence, so we lie to each other.

The only light in the room shines through one small, high window. The diamond-shaped glass panes create a criss-cross pattern of bars on the wall as if we were trapped behind them. Jack reaches for my hand.

"Inspection! Inspection!"

The warning winds like a snake through the wards, passing in a hiss from nurse to nurse. A surprise inspection. I run into the hallway to look. The officers aren't alone as they usually are. They have soldiers with them—all stand grim and forbidding at the entrance to the ward. Even the patients look alarmed and hastily shove card games out of sight, straighten sheets, lean back on their pillows, and fold their arms across their chests to look as much like helpless invalids as they can. Feet thump across the floor, voices rumble, and Millicent rushes to the doors to greet the officers in a burst of French and many gestures.

Jack is trapped. He can't reach the stairs to the cellars without passing through the middle of the ward, and the Germans are already inside. At the other end of the ward, Millicent is putting on a show of welcoming the same two officers who inspected the clinic only an hour ago. Five soldiers in their spiked helmets, weapons resting in the crooks of their arms, begin walking along the rows of beds.

Frantic, I rush back to the room to search for a hiding place. Jack points to the bed, grabs a sheet from the cart, flips it into the air, and drops it over the mattress. I roll the cart into the room and block the doorway with it, tossing a pillow to Jack. In a second, he's in the bed, lying flat, arms at his side, while I spread another sheet over him up and tuck it around his body up to his neck.

In the ward, there's a rush of activity. Miss Cavell comes into the clinic's main floor, her voice rising over the competing sounds of soldiers and patients. She dashes to greet the officers and repeats the enthusiastic welcome Millicent offered, sounding as if she's thrilled by a second visit in one day. Her fluttery comments and nervous laughter manage to keep the officers from getting more than a few feet into the room.

Jack's boots rising underneath the sheet are too high to be bare feet in the flat slippers the patients wear. I snatch a blanket from the lower shelf of the cart and spread it over the bed where his feet make a tent of the sheet. The blanket doesn't entirely conceal the mound his feet create, so I grab another blanket, shake it out, and toss it in an untidy mess on the bed, rumpling it into bunches of fabric over Jack's boots.

Better.

There's no time to do more. The soldiers tramp between the aisles, elbowing the nurses aside, and rummaging through the trays, side tables, and carts. The German officers with Miss Cavell chattering alongside walk between the rows of beds and pause next to random patients. They aren't making conversation with the men—they're asking questions in harsh demanding tones. The patients shake their heads and say *"Nein,"* frequently. Adrenaline surges through me. When I peek into the ward again, the soldiers are getting closer, looking in doorways and stepping in and out of the smaller rooms that hold one or two patients. Miss Cavell and Millicent keep a stream of conversation going as they follow the two officers, but this visit isn't like the others. The officers don't seem bored this time. Frowns crease their foreheads. There's no smiling, no courtesy, no flirting with the younger nurses.

I hurl a third blanket over Jack, managing to conceal the outline of his body in the bed. He fixes his eyes on me. I point to the ceiling and wave my hand over my face, to indicate a blank expression. He shifts his gaze to a crack in the plaster in one corner and focuses on it.

A German soldier in the doorway kicks my cart and hurls rough demands at me, gesturing with his rifle. I nod as if I'm trying to hurry while I make an clumsy attempt to move the cart out of his way. I bungle the move so the wheels lock, keeping the cart blocking the door. Another push or two, and the wheels lock a second time. The soldier growls impatiently, shifting his rifle to a more threatening angle. My skin is like ice, but I force a smile and gesture an apology for being so awkward. After another improvised struggle with the cart, I wheel it aside, so he can enter the room. Jack lies motionless on the bed, staring blankly at the ceiling.

Looking around the nearly bare room, the soldier snaps something in German. I spread my hands, making a helpless motion of not understanding but keeping a smile painted on my lips. When the soldier steps closer to the bed, I remember one of the French words I've learned in the clinic.

"*Pou,*" I say, pointing to Jack. Lice.

The soldier steps back and for the first time I look directly in his face. It's Carl, the driver Elise flirted with at the chateau. My palms are damp. Will he remember me? We only saw each other for an instant. Carl stays a good distance from the bed but hurls what sounds like a question at Jack. Jack never takes his eyes off the cracked plaster in the corner of the ceiling, perfectly copying the expression of the patients who can't talk. Carl repeats the question, shifting his rifle again in the direction of the bed. At the chateau, he was relaxed, laughing and making jokes with Elise, but now his expression is grim and unforgiving.

"*Fievre.*" I make an elaborate gesture of wiping my forehead.

Carl hesitates and stares at me. The barest flicker of recognition shows before his expression changes to bewilderment. "*Fraulein?*"

"*Achtung!*"

The young officer who inspected my cart during my first day in the clinic appears in the doorway. Carl stiffens and salutes while the officer takes a quick look around the room not showing much interest. For weeks, he's seen clinic patients who don't move or talk.

"*Fievre,*" I repeat, pointing at Jack.

He nods and barks an order at Carl. I hold my breath. Carl hesitates, looking at Jack and then me again. He opens his mouth but closes it. His face becomes an expressionless mask, and he walks out of the room without another glance at the bed. Lingering, the officer pokes at the sheets and blankets on my cart before turning his attention to me. His gaze moves slowly over me traveling from my toes to my hair. My shapeless cotton uniform doesn't give him much to look at. He mutters under his breath and strides out of the room.

The noises of the inspection swirl around us. Cabinets open and close. Doors open and slam shut. Miss Cavell keeps up a nervous babble in French, but she gets no responses from the officers. When they speak, they talk to each other in German. Long minutes drag by. I'm afraid to look at Jack, afraid we'll reveal ourselves at the very moment another soldier decides to check the room. When the harsh voices and banging drawers finally stop and the doors to the clinic slam shut behind the Germans, I lean against the door jamb, breathing hard, shoulders stiff, knees weak. Every muscle in my body is stiff with tension. We escaped this time, but the Germans can inspect the clinic as often as they want to.

"You managed very well." Miss Cavell pauses in the doorway and looks at Jack still wrapped head to toe in the blankets. "It was clever to pose as a patient." She puts her arms around me for an instant in the comforting, motherly way she has. "They found nothing and they're satisfied—for the time being at least. We must count our blessings."

"What happened to Louis?"

"He's taken prisoner, I'm afraid. Everyone is suspect now. We need to be cautious. The Germans must not discover even a hint about what we do here. Fortunately, they have never thought to inspect the cellar." She straightens her uniform. "I have duties to manage." As she walks away, she calls for Millicent.

Jack kicks off the blankets and gets to his feet, his face pale. Relief because we've escaped capture one more time swamps me.

"You were so clever. He didn't suspect anything." Jack's voice is hoarse.

I stagger blindly toward him, tears forming in my eyes, nervous tremors beginning. Pulling him close to me, I slide my arms around his neck. His arms tighten around me, and we hold each other without speaking. I don't ever want to let go. His body trembles, or maybe the shivers I'm feeling are mine.

Lifting my head, I look into his dark eyes. His face is only a breath away. His head lowers, and our lips brush. For a minute, I'm awkward and breathless, and then a little dizzy, but Jack pulls me closer, and the kiss I've been imagining so long happens. I thread my fingers through his silky hair while the room spins around me. He's alive, and his lips are warm and tender and exciting all at once, and we're together.

My mind suddenly clears. "No!"

Horrified, I push him away. He blinks, confused again, and his arms drop to his sides. I squeeze my eyes shut and wait for the spinning darkness to take me into a black pool. How could I have forgotten even for a second? Tense, afraid, hands curled into fists, I wait. But I feel nothing, and when I open my eyes, Jack is still in front of me, a confused look on his face as he stares at me.

"Nothing is happening," I whisper.

He whistles softly. "Not true. Plenty's happening—although I wasn't sure it ever would."

If kissing Jack didn't send me back to Aunt Connie and my life there, what will? Moving closer, Jack puts his arms around me again, kisses my forehead and drops soft, little kisses across my cheek and along my jaw. "Don't be afraid," he whispers. "We're lucky together."

His breath stirs my hair. I rise on my toes and tighten my arms around his neck, reaching for another kiss.

26

I'm deliriously happy.

I shouldn't be. The German officers have changed their routines—they send soldiers to inspect the clinic at unpredictable hours, so Jack and Pete have to stay hidden most of the time. Brussels is clogged with soldiers patrolling the streets, setting up checkpoints, demanding identification papers from Belgians, searching every cart and basket. Shops shut down early. People stay off the streets after dusk. The streetcars run at odd times. Because Louis was captured so quickly, Miss Cavell hasn't found a guide to take us to the border. The men who were willing to guide soldiers to the border a week ago are afraid now of being caught and sent to a prison camp—or worse.

While I push my medicine cart up and down the rows of patients, I wonder about my other life. Kissing Jack wasn't the trigger to send me home as I expected, so I have no idea how or if I'll return to Aunt Connie. Even more confusing, I'm beginning to sense I've been in the clinic before. It's nothing I can put my finger on exactly, but I'm almost sure I've seen the bandages and bottles stacked on my cart and inhaled the antiseptic smells in some other place or time. Aunt Connie's theory that we've all lived other lives keeps running through my mind. If she's right and I'm in a previous life, how does it end? Am I reliving what's most important in that life or what happens just before I die? Do I have a choice to stay in this life or go back to the one

I was living in the future? Trying to analyze this situation should give me a headache, but it doesn't. I haven't had a headache since Jack brought me to my other life, as Aunt Connie would call it.

Confusion doesn't cut into my happiness. Now that I know Jack's kisses aren't going to send me into a black darkness, we kiss as often as we want to. Quick kisses in the cellar where Pete teases us and calls us "lovebirds." Laughing kisses when we pass in the hallways whenever Jack does chores for Miss Cavell. Long, slow kisses on the bench in the garden after dark, until both of us are breathless and not thinking at all about German soldiers or crossing borders. I know this incredible mood has to end, but now I exist in a kind of joyful space suspended between dangers.

Now there's only Jack.

Miss Cavell says we have to be patient because she needs to arrange false papers for us and find someone trustworthy who's willing to risk taking us to the border. When she photographs us for our passports, I can't help smiling, and she tells me to put on a serious face, so the picture will be appropriate for a passport. Apparently, people don't smile for photos in 1914.

Pete has grown a mustache. "Makes me look a bit more sophisticated, it does. I'm betting the female population will like it when I get back to England." He smoothes his finger over the wiry brown hairs above his lip like a villain in a silent movie. "Probably I'll have several young ladies seeking my attention."

Jack laughs. "They'll have to seek your attention quickly because the war office will have us back in our unit the minute we show our faces in London."

I don't laugh. Any reminder that we're putting all our energies into escaping from Belgium, so the army can send Jack and Pete into new dangers puts a shade over me. Jack sees my frown and reaches for my hand. I lock my fingers around his while Pete speculates about where the army will send them and wonders if most of the war will be over before they get back to it. Jack rubs his thumb across my wrist.

Usually, this gesture makes my nerve endings tingly, but my mind is locked on future dangers, and I barely feel anything.

Nights in Brussels are very dark because most street lights don't work. When the sun goes down, the only light on the street comes from lamps shining through open windows. After the evening meal, I collect the trays, smile at the patients, and refill the water pitchers. Outside, shadows spread across the streets. When I finish my work, Miss Cavell calls me into her office.

She's neat and organized in the clinic, but in her office, clutter takes over. Overlapping piles of papers and folders cover the top of her desk and more folders balance hap hazardously on chairs. Boxes filled with papers line the floor along the walls.

"Can I do something for you?" I point to the desk. "Shall I help you organize your files?"

"No, I rather hate this mess, but it's best to keep the office this way in case the officers decide to examine the clinic records. I know where specific records are, but it would take an outsider a long time to find whatever he might be searching for." She smiles, but tired lines show around her eyes and mouth.

Shuffling through the messy piles on her desk, she pulls out some thin blue sheets. "Please take these to the kitchen for Hilda. They're grocery lists." She puts both hands to her head and massages her temples. "Food is becoming more difficult to get, especially butter and eggs—and meat. The pork was very bad this week."

Guilt stirs. I've been so happy with Jack, I've forgotten what other people are worrying about. We've been here nearly two weeks. Two Belgian soldiers came last night looking for a place to hide. Running the clinic and smuggling soldiers to Holland under the eyes of the Germans—no wonder she has dark circles under her eyes.

"I'm sorry it's so difficult. Maybe we'll be able to leave soon, and you won't have so many burdens."

Her clear gray eyes center on mine. "I don't mind the burden. Saving the men is what matters. I'll be sorry to lose you, Jenny, but the passports should be ready in a day or two. I think I've found a guide for you. I'll know tomorrow." She hesitates, sighing. "I want to talk to you about something else. You know, I hope, I'm very fond of you, and I wonder—the garden bench. Of course, it's quiet there for you and Jack to talk."

Heat crawls up my throat—my cheeks start to burn. "It's still warm in the evening," I say weakly. "We like to be outside after being inside all day."

"Yes." She taps her fingers on the desk, keeping her eyes on the glass paperweight resting in a lopsided slant on a stack of papers. "The garden is certainly a better place to talk than in your room. A young lady must always be careful."

I want to dissolve on the spot. She knows Jack came to my room the first few days we were here, and she knows we kiss in the garden. My behavior must be shockingly unsuitable for 1914, and I've disappointed her. "We didn't. . . uh. . . we never. . . nothing. . . ."

She starts to smile but bites her lip instead. "I'm glad to hear that. These are terrible times. Battles—horrible injuries—death—uncertainty. Young people sometimes make bad decisions when emotions are high." She rubs her temples again. "Ask Hilda if she needs anything before I buy supplies at the end of the week."

The kitchen is at the back of the clinic with a door that leads directly to the garden. Jack and I use the main door off the hallway to reach the garden, but the kitchen door is useful because Hilda takes the garbage along the side path stretching behind the shed and leading to the trash bin at the edge of the alley. I miss the warm, spicy aromas that lingered in the kitchen at the chateau. In the clinic, after the last meal of the day, Hilda's kitchen has a heavy soap and ammonia odor, overwhelming any scents left from the cooking.

Hilda's English is a little choppy, but we communicate well enough. I hand the sheets to her and ask about supplies.

"Beer," she answers. "More beer. Wait, I look pantry."

While she disappears into the large storage room, I gaze aimlessly around the kitchen. It's spotless but stark, not like the cheery atmosphere in Marta's kitchen. Then my breath stops, and a slow paralyzing fear spreads through me like flood waters seeping under closed doors.

A row of pegs for coats lines the wall next to the back door. The early October weather is still warm, so there aren't any coats hanging there, but looped around one wooden peg is a long silk scarf—green with gold fringe and tiny gold tassels on the ends.

I'd recognize it anywhere.

I close my eyes to blot out the sight, but I can't blot out the sickening memories. Struggling. Hands fumbling over my clothes, under my shirt. Stale breath against my face. The wine bottle. Blood splattered on my hand. Elise and the rock.

We left him dead—I thought. Elise went through his pockets, but I can't remember if either of us checked for a pulse. Much as I hate it, I force myself to piece together the memories in order. I didn't check his pulse, and Elise didn't check it either. When she finished emptying his pockets, we waded across the stream and ran to the deserted farm on the other side. The last time I saw that green scarf, it was around the neck of a dead man.

Hilda steps out of the pantry. "More flour," she says. "Tell her more flour."

"That green scarf," I lick my lips, forcing myself to sound indifferent, "it's very unusual."

She glances at it. "*Ja*, my husband. He forgets it yesterday."

Yesterday. He's been in the clinic. He could walk through the door at any second.

"Does your husband work at the clinic?"

"*Nein*." She gives me a peculiar look. "Metal—he sells."

I'm afraid to ask more questions because her expression is turning suspicious. I thank her and walk slowly back to the clinic office, insides churning, mind buzzing.

Miss Cavell makes a note about beer and flour on a slip of paper after I repeat Hilda's requests. "Thank you, Jenny." When I don't leave, she looks up. "Was there something else?"

My mouth is dry. I lick my lips and try to smile. "Hilda and I were chatting about her husband." A lie, but that's nothing new for me. "She said he comes to the kitchen to see her."

"Yes, Maurice often stops in later in the evening, and she gives him the same meal we serve patients." She runs her finger over the edges of the glass paperweight. "I don't object although if the food shortages get worse, I may have to. When she can feed her husband easily, Hilda's happy, and I need her in the kitchen."

"What kind of man is he? She said he sells metal."

"He collects metal trash and sells it. I've long suspected that Maurice collects other things as well, perhaps not entirely honestly, but he does nothing odd in the clinic. That's all I can worry about."

"So he works in the city," I murmur.

"Yes." She leans back in her chair and thinks for a minute. "He's often gone for long periods doing some other kind of business. I don't know exactly what. He got caught in the first wave of the German invasion and had a terrible accident on the road back to Brussels. I never got all the details. I doubt Hilda got all the details. His eye was badly damaged. He can't see much out of it and has to wear a patch. Very unfortunate injury, but these things happen in war time. Everyone suffers in some way."

A terrible accident. My last vague hope Hilda's husband was not the man who attacked me fades. I picture Elise smashing the rock into Green Scarf's face, leaving him bloody next to the stream. His eye destroyed. What would he do if he found me here? I can't control a shudder.

Miss Cavell notices. "Is something upsetting you? Something about Hilda's husband?"

I raise my shoulders in an elaborate shrug to indicate I don't have any serious interest. "I saw his beautiful scarf in the kitchen. The green one. It caught my attention."

"Ah, the scarf. It's one of a kind. Hilda made it for him."

I shiver again.

When I meet Jack in the garden later, my thoughts are as black as the night sky. The moon is covered in clouds, and the light is so dim I find Jack more by instinct than by sight. He holds out his arms. I walk into them, wrap my arms tight around his neck, and bury my face in his shoulder.

"What's wrong?"

"Nothing." I mumble into his shirt.

I briefly consider spilling out the story of Green Scarf, but I don't. Jack doesn't need more things to worry about. Maybe, with luck, I'll never see Green Scarf. We might be gone before he shows up in Hilda's kitchen again. Miss Cavell said his visits aren't regular. Maybe he'll go to another town for whatever business he conducts when he's not selling metal.

"Don't say *nothing* to me." Jack drops a kiss on the top of my head. "We've been together too long for me to swallow that. I know when you're worried or scared. You can tell me anything."

I keep my face buried in his shirt and my arms tight around him, so he can't pull away. Discovering Green Scarf is alive and not far away has exploded the fantasy I invented after our first kiss—Jack and I have all the time in the world. I'm a fool. We have almost no time.

He ruffles my hair, and I blink back tears, determined not to cry, determined not to think about the time when he won't be close enough to touch my hair or kiss my cheek, when I won't feel his warmth, or hear his heart beat.

"Sit down." He pulls me down on the bench and puts his arm around my shoulders. "Now tell me." The tightness in my neck slowly eases as I nestle against him.

"Miss Cavell says we'll be leaving soon, and I'm wondering what will happen next."

"I've been wondering too. Staying or going—it's all a risk. Louis got caught in the first couple of hours." He kisses my temple. "Do you want to stay here? I'm sure Miss Cavell would keep you. As a matter of fact, she could get you to an American embassy. You'd be safe and could go home."

"I don't want to leave you!"

I sit up and twist sideways, so I can kiss the edge of his jaw and smooth the wave across his forehead. He trimmed his hair at the chateau, but it's getting longer again, drooping around his ears, curling around the back of his neck. Does he ever wonder why my hair stays the same length?

"I shouldn't have made you promise to stay with me. It wasn't right."

"I wanted to promise." My voice rises in the quiet dark. I change to a whisper. "I won't leave you until I have to."

He puts his hands on either side of my face, staring into my eyes. "I want you to be safe. Nothing can happen to you. You're precious to me."

Precious. The word flows around me like an embrace, the way his ghostly presence did when I first felt him in Aunt Connie's garden. I put my hands over his, holding them in place. "Listen to me. I'm not going anywhere before we've crossed that border. I'm definitely not letting you go alone after all we've been through together."

"That's what I mean," he says, pulling his hands away. "You've already been in too much danger. You're an American girl who happened to be in Belgium at the wrong time, and somehow you got mixed up in my problems, and you've been caught in rough patches ever since we met."

"I was in danger before we met," I remind him. "You kept me safe." I lean close and brush his lips so lightly I can barely feel his breath against my mouth. "We were meant to be," I say softly.

"Do you believe in fate?" He smiles.

Do I ever! I also believe in Aunt Connie's explanation of mixed-up time, all the minutes swirling together, in and out, putting people in any time they're destined for—any time they have a purpose. I can barely see his smile in the darkness.

"I believe in our fate—being together," I whisper.

He pulls me close again, burying his face in my hair. We wrap our arms around each other, and I listen to his steady heartbeat, realizing the sensation spreading through every corpuscle of my body is love. Total, complete, and enduring love. In the middle of a war, in the wrong place, with no possibility of a future involving *forever*, I'm in love. I want to tell him.

But he says it first, lips against my temple. "You know I love you, don't you?"

27

"You three will leave tomorrow," Miss Cavell murmurs, her voice so low I can barely hear her. She pretends to straighten the bottles on my cart and leans closer to me. "At midday."

"Are you coming with us?"

"I'll take you to the first rendezvous. I don't want a stranger coming here—there are too many inspections at present."

Our third surprise inspection of the day has just ended. Nerves are starting to shred under the tension of never knowing when the Germans will come through the door. Millicent, usually as serene as Miss Cavell, has a sharp edge in her voice when she gives me instructions. Some of the nurses snap at each other. In the kitchen, Hilda is cranky. Even our patients, all of them German soldiers, are jittery. One tells me in broken English he's afraid they'll send him back to fighting before his wounds are healed. I tell him the fighting will be over soon. It's what they all want to hear.

"Should we leave in the daylight? Isn't it safer at night?"

"Daylight is safer. We probably won't be stopped, but if we were on the streets at night, we'd be questioned immediately."

This news should make me happy. Getting to the border and out of Belgium has been our only goal, but, in spite of the daily inspections, I've felt the safest in the clinic with Miss Cavell watching over us.

"I'll tell Jack and Pete." I try to sound eager, but I can't call up any emotions except vague fear and loss.

"I've already told them about the plans." She looks closely at me. My face must show my reluctance. "Do you want to stay with me? I could get you to an American embassy, and I'm sure you'll be sent home."

"No, thank you, Matron." I'm firm on this answer no matter what else I'm worried about. "I'm going with Jack and Pete."

"I knew you'd say that." Understanding glints in her eyes. "I'll put new clothes for you in your room tonight. You shouldn't wear anything that looks like a uniform. It could attract attention. Jack and Pete will dress like ordinary workers, so there won't be anything distinctive about any of you."

"I still have the clothes I wore here."

"Those clothes won't do. What the countess gave you is too fashionable. You need to dress like a girl from a farm to match Jack and Pete."

A plain brown cotton skirt reaching to my toes and a plain white shirt buttoned up to my neck are too fashionable? After weeks of dodging soldiers and hiding, the only style I have left exists in my pink bra and panties, which I wash out every night, praying the elastic will last forever. There's no point in discussing fashion with Miss Cavell because her uniform always looks as if it's been dipped in starch—never wrinkled, never dirty. The first time Jack saw me I was wearing the priest's clothes. Then I wore the shapeless jumper and the plain travel clothes the countess gave me. Then the hideous nightgown the first night here, followed by this aide uniform, which is slightly too big for me. Just once I'd like to look pretty for him, but it's not going to happen.

I glance at the patients—no one is listening to us. "I understand. Thank you for the clothes. I really am grateful for everything you've done for us."

Miss Cavell is like Aunt Connie, but in an entirely opposite way. Aunt Connie is flamboyant and wildly emotional, hugging me a dozen times a day, spreading love around her. This English nurse is quiet and controlled, but she's as warm and giving as Aunt Connie in the way she cares for people. I'd like to hug her, but she's so proper I don't have the courage.

Her eyes show her worry, but she smiles. "These are difficult times, but helping you has been a pleasure." A soft sigh. "You three are cooperative and careful, not like some others. It's dangerous for all of us when some ignore the realities of our circumstances."

She's more on edge these days because the Germans have increased their surveillance on everything and everyone in the city. Random inspections take place in every hospital and business. Another worry for her is the two Belgian soldiers who arrived at the clinic a few days ago and insist on drinking every night at a tavern in spite of the risks. The Belgians come and go through the gate leading to the alley behind the clinic. If a German patrol came along at the exact time the two are leaving or returning, we'd all be exposed.

"Where will we go tomorrow?" I deliberately put some enthusiasm in my voice.

"We'll meet your guide at a café I know. I'll explain more when we get there. It's best not to know too much beforehand." She pats my shoulder. "I'm confident you'll reach Holland, Jenny. Be strong."

I spend the rest of the morning pushing my cart through the ward, forcing myself to look cheery and relaxed, but my nerves are jumping again, and my imagination creates a long list of possible dangers between here and the Dutch border. Maybe we'll be captured as fast as Louis was. Tension makes me grip the handles on the cart so hard my fingers turn numb, and I have to stop pushing to shake out my hands until the feeling returns.

My head is full of Jack, danger, and the unknown route to the border, and I forget to keep track of the bandages and alcohol bottles on my cart. Millicent heaves a sigh and orders me to the supply room in the back hallway near the kitchen. I wheel the cart inside the supply room, and an arm slides around my waist, startling me into a squeaky gasp.

"Thinking about me?" Jack's whisper in my ear sends goose bumps over my skin.

"Yes, no, yes. You shouldn't be on this floor. The Germans—"

"They inspected fifteen minutes ago. They won't be back for at least an hour. Do you know the news? We're leaving tomorrow."

"Miss Cavell told me." I lean against him, feeling the steady rise and fall of his chest under his thick cotton shirt.

"Don't worry. We'll be lucky. We'll have tea and biscuits in London before you know it." His arm tightens around me.

"I love you." We both murmur the words at exactly the same time. He chuckles deep in his throat while I muffle my laugh against his shoulder. His lips brush across mine so lightly I feel the warmth but no pressure.

The rest of the day I think about tonight—our last time in the garden, probably the last time Jack and I will be alone to whisper about love. The other worry running through my mind is the question of how I'm going to leave him when the time comes. We've kissed enough in the last few days to send hundreds of spirits back and forth across Aunt Connie's shifting layers of past, present, and future. In spite of toe-curling kisses, breathless kisses, no swirling darkness has rushed me back to Aunt Connie's garden.

After a light rain late in the afternoon, the clouds separate and the moon shines as bright as a street light. While the patients quiet down for the night, Jack hauls boxes to the store rooms for Miss Cavell, so I wait outside for him and wander along the small empty flower bed and the bushes near the back fence. Lights flicker off in the wards. Hilda's kitchen is dark already. No sign she's expecting her husband tonight, and tomorrow we'll be gone.

I settle on our bench and smooth my skirt around my legs. My feet in ugly brown shoes stick out below the hem. Jack probably doesn't think my clothes are particularly awful since most of the women on the street are wearing the same drab, dark, heavy cloth. What would he say if he ever saw me in shorts and a tee shirt?

At the back of the garden, the hinges on the gate next to the trash pit squeal. Footsteps tramp behind the shed along the path next to the fence. One of the Belgians must be returning from the tavern. The footsteps stumble a bit—he's probably drunk. A bulky, muscular figure steps around the corner of the shed and starts across the grass, heading for the back door of the clinic. The moonlight catches his face—the black patch over one eye has a glossy sheen in the moonlight.

Green Scarf.

I rise from the bench at the moment he sees me. My feet won't move. I'm nailed to the ground, staring at him while he stares back at me. Does he know me? A growl comes out of his throat. I turn to run, but he's faster. Two long steps and his beefy hand clamps over my upper arm, wrenching me backwards closer to him.

"You!" he grunts in rough English.

I swing violently away, twisting to get out of his grasp, but his fingers clamp around my arm, and he easily dodges my attempt to hit him with my free hand. Desperate, I stamp my foot backwards, but he's in heavy boots, and I can't feel his feet through the thick leather no matter how hard I stamp. My skirt tangles around my legs, making me immobile, unable to kick.

When he attacked me at the stream, he pulled me close, and I found a way to hit him with the wine bottle, but this time he holds me in a grip I can't break, and just far enough from his body, so I can't do any damage. I don't have a weapon anyway. I don't dare scream for help. Shouts would bring the soldiers from the barracks across the street.

"You," he growls again. "My stones."

I'd love to give the rubies back to him. Elise sewed them into the hem of her skirt when we were at the chateau. They're at the bottom of the well with her body.

"I don't have them! They're gone!"

He jerks me closer, twisting my arm behind me so I'm facing away from him. Pain shoots from my wrist through my shoulder into my neck. "Stones!"

"Lost—they're lost." I shake my head, trying to convince him I'm telling the truth.

His grip shoots knife-like pain up my arm. I'm dizzy with it. The harder I struggle, the harder he twists my arm. He's going to break it for sure. A violent shake snaps my head, and for a second, I see a cloud of white sparks in the night sky. His other hand closes over my free wrist, stopping any possibility I can hit him. Another brutal shake.

"Stones?"

"Gone, all gone. The rubies are lost!" Gasping, I try to turn my head toward him, but I can't move. "The patients!"

He halts, holding me in place, and stares at the dark windows in the clinic. There's no sign we've been heard. Then he releases one arm and slaps me hard, spinning my head to the side. I taste blood at the corner of my mouth as he shakes me again.

A sudden jerk. He's wrenched backward and loses his grip on me. Fresh jolts of pain shoot up my arm from the sudden release—I stagger and fall to one knee.

Jack wrestles Green Scarf to the ground where they roll silently, heaving at each other, punching when they can. Struggling to my feet, I look around desperate for a weapon, but only grass, bushes, and a bench too heavy for me to move are available.

Jack is taller, but Green Scarf is heavier. As they turn one way and then another, Green Scarf's fist slams into Jack's stomach and then into his face. Curling his body to one side, Jack raises both feet, kicks them hard into the Green Scarf's stomach, and rolls away putting space between them. On his feet, blood dripping down the side of his face, Jack lands a punch that sends Green Scarf lurching backward and crashing into a bush near the bench, but when Green Scarf gets to his feet again, the moonlight catches a silvery glint in his hand.

A knife.

Breathing hard, Jack backs away while Green Scarf presses closer, making little circles in the air with the knife. The grass is still slick from the rain, and their feet slide when they jump sideways or back, each one trying to get an advantage. With a deep grunt, Green Scarf closes the gap in a single leap and swipes his knife across Jack's chest, slitting open his shirt, leaving a long, thin bloody streak on his skin, spreading into the cut edges of his shirt. Jack backs away.

Frantic, I run across the garden to a huge flower pot, empty at the end of summer, but still half full of dirt. It's nearly three feet tall and heavy. Struggling with the pot, I finally pull it over on its side. Just as Green Scarf makes another lunge for Jack, I roll the pot straight at his back and give it a hard kick to spin it faster. The pot, spraying dirt as it goes, crashes into Green Scarf's legs, sending him sprawling backward onto the grass. Those few seconds help Jack. He dives forward and seizes Green Scarf's hand still holding the knife. On the ground, they roll and clutch each other, silently struggling over the knife until they both stiffen, muscles clenched, hands gripping each other, bodies tight together.

Green Scarf gurgles and gasps. His body jerks. His hands slip away from Jack, and he slumps flat on the ground. When Jack gets to his feet, I see the knife sticking into Green Scarf's chest, blood spreading in a broad circle, soaking his shirt. Another gurgle comes from his throat. His breath exhales in a long wheeze, half inhales, and stops.

Shaking, I dart a glance at the clinic windows—no sign of anyone.

Jack bends over, hands on his knees, catching his breath, then leans down and puts his fingers where Green Scarf's pulse should be. He looks at me and shakes his head, his face pale in the moonlight, blood still trickling down his cheek. I close the few feet between us and wrap my arms around his neck, feeling the shudder going through him. Slowly, he puts his hands on my shoulders and holds me an arm's-length away.

"Are you hurt?" He's still gulping air, his voice rough. "Jenny?"

Hooking my fingers in the slash in his shirt, I pull apart the fabric so I can see his wound. The cut isn't deep. Blood is already clotting along the thin red line made by the knife.

"We need hydrogen peroxide," I say automatically. Then shivers overtake me, and I have to gasp for breath.

Jack runs his fingers through my hair, murmuring it's over and we're all right. He gently touches my swollen lip, wiping away the blood at the corner of my mouth with his thumb. "Who was he?" he asks.

"I thought he was going to kill you."

"He looked like he wanted to kill you when I got out here," Jack says. "Where did he come from?"

"He's Hilda's husband."

"Hilda, the cook? Why was he attacking you?"

I sag against him. "He thought I had something of his."

"What?"

"Before Elise and I met you, he attacked me on the road, but Elise hit him in the head with a rock. She went through his pockets, and she took. . . we took his money. He had a little case with jewels—I guess they were rubies—and we took those too. We left him next to a stream; we thought he was dead."

He's silent for a long moment. "Where's the money and the rubies?"

"Elise kept the rubies—they're with her at the bottom of the well. Her share of the money must be there too. My share is in my room—it's not much. He wanted the rubies. He kept asking me for the rubies."

"When he attacked you, did he. . . ?"

"He didn't hurt me. Elise saved me." I take his hands in mine. He winces when I rub my fingers across his knuckles. "This is my fault," I whisper. "What are we going to do?"

"We can't leave him here." Jack glances around the yard. "If the Germans find him, they'll tear the clinic apart, and we'll never get to the border. What about Hilda? She probably sees her husband every day."

"I don't think so. Her light was off, so she wasn't expecting him tonight. Miss Cavell told me he often goes away on business, so he could be gone for weeks without anyone wondering about him."

Jack rakes his hand through his hair, staring at Green Scarf's body. "I'll drag him behind the shed. At least he'll be farther away than fifteen feet from the back door of the clinic."

I glance at the windows again—still dark. No one's heard us. "What about the ash pit?"

"You mean bury him in the pit?"

"Would that work?"

"Only until the collection men empty the pit, but it's a good way to hide him tonight."

We drag Green Scarf's body across the grass and along the side of the fence to the back of the shed. When we reach the pit, Jack halts and swears under his breath. The pit is nearly empty. The ashes must have been collected in the last couple of days.

"Is there enough to," I swallow hard, "cover him?"

Jack seizes the shovel leaning against the shed and pokes in the pit. "Not enough to hide him, but it's dark and some ash is better than nothing."

Grunting, pushing, we heave Green Scarf's body into the pit. Jack scrapes enough ashes together to make a light layer over him, but the outline of a man's body is plain enough.

"We have to tell Miss Cavell." Jack tosses the shovel against the fence. "We've no choice because when the sun comes up, anyone passing by will see there's a body in that pit."

28

The clinic is dark and quiet. Only one nurse is on duty, and she's at the far end of the ward, not likely to notice us as we slip through the back doors. With our hands locked together, we walk to Miss Cavell's office.

She's at her desk, writing in a notebook. When we stop in her open door, she looks up, her glance taking in Jack's bloody shirt, my swollen lip, the reddening bruises on our faces. She slowly puts the pen in a holder on the desk, closes the notebook, slides out a hollow panel on the desk, slips the notebook inside and pushes the panel back under the desktop. The seam in the wood is so tight no one would notice it.

"What is it?" she asks in a low voice.

Jack squeezes my hand, straightens, and stands at attention. "I regret to say I've just killed a man in the garden. Jenny tells me he's the cook's husband." His quiet voice is steady.

She sends a sharp glance my way before she focuses on Jack. "Hilda's husband? How did you kill him?"

"He had a knife. We struggled over it, and the knife went into him instead of into me."

She pushes her chair away from the desk and rises, hands nervously opening and closing, tense lines on her face. "Why were you fighting?" Her voice lowers into a soft whisper although no one is close enough to overhear us..

"He attacked Jenny. When I came outside, he was beating her. I had no choice."

Now her gaze locks onto me. "Jenny?"

I babble out the story of meeting Green Scarf on the road with the refugees, fighting him off, hitting him with the wine bottle, and stealing his money in one long breath. Her lips tighten as she listens, and she nods as if I've confirmed a long suspicion she had about him. What I omit from the story is Elise and everything connected to her—the rubies, the countess shooting her, and her body along with the rubies resting at the bottom of the well. The countess trusted us to keep her secrets, and revealing them won't help Miss Cavell figure out what to do now.

When I run out of words, the three of us stand silently in the dim light from the desk lamp, staring at each other. Spilling the story in one rush releases the tension in my chest. I drag in a long deep breath, fill my lungs, and slowly exhale. Jack reaches for my hand, and he squeezes my fingers. "I'm sorry." My whisper is so faint I'm not sure she hears me.

"Where is he?" Her calm voice doesn't reveal what she's thinking. If she's angry, if she's horrified, if she's desperate, she doesn't show it. Her face has the same quiet, closed expression she has when she's talking to the German officers.

"In the ash pit." Jack sounds as calm as she does. "I covered him as well as I could, but the pit was nearly empty."

She touches her hair, smoothing the few loose strands into place, and shakes out her skirt. "I'll have to see someone." As she reaches for her cape, she gestures toward Jack's bloody shirt. "Jenny, you need to dress that wound. You know where the supplies are." She puts her finger under my chin to raise my head and examine my swollen mouth. "Take care of yourself as well. I'll be out for a time." Then she slips out of the office, heels tapping down the hallway, heading for the back entrance.

In the supply room, Jack slumps against the wall and slides down until he's sitting on the floor, leaning back, eyes closed, while I search for a bottle of hydrogen peroxide, clean gauze, pads, and tape. Millicent uses saline solution first if the wound is fresh, so I hunt through another cabinet to find a bottle.

I kneel next to Jack, awkwardly fumbling with the buttons on his torn shirt. My hands shake so much I can't maneuver the buttons out of the buttonholes. Tremors take over, making my hands even more useless. After a minute, Jack opens his eyes, moves my hand away, slowly unbuttons his shirt and shrugs it off.

He touches my cheek. "Stop shaking."

"You could have been killed because of me!" I cross my arms across my chest, trying to stop shivering.

"But I wasn't killed," he says in a low voice, "and you weren't hurt."

He rests his hand above my collarbone and strokes lightly over my cheek. My breathing steadies, and my pulse settles into a normal rhythm. I sit back on my heels. "Let me bandage you." I manage a shaky smile. "I'm getting to be a good nurse." The long cut across his chest is below the leather envelope hanging around his neck and above his bullet wound, which has healed into a narrow red line. I carefully pull the leather cord over his head and hand the envelope to him.

"Hold it while I clean you." My fingers brush as lightly as I can manage over the cut. It's not deep—a red streak, dark against his pale skin.

After soaking a cloth in the saline solution, I pat it along the wound, cleaning away the dried blood. The hydrogen peroxide follows—he winces as I press the liquid into the cut. While I bend over him, positioning the gauze, putting the pieces of tape in place, he grins. "Doesn't hurt a bit. You might become a real nurse after all."

I press the ends of the last piece of tape over the bandage and draw in a long breath of relief before I sink next to him on the floor. "If it weren't for me, you wouldn't have fought him, and Miss Cavell wouldn't be out somewhere trying to find a way to hide his body. Maybe she won't find anyone to help, and the Germans will discover us." I wipe my eyes on the end of his bloody, discarded shirt and mumble again how Elise and I caused this problem.

"Give me some of that saline stuff and some gauze," he says. "You're not thinking straight."

I dampen the gauze with the saline solution, and he gently pats it on my lip, daubing at the corner of my mouth, wiping the traces of blood away from the corner of my mouth. "What happened isn't your fault. He was beating you. I had to fight him. I can't let anything bad happen to you—I love you." He dips his head and gently kisses my puffy lip.

"He's dead." I sniff and swipe at a tear dribbling down my cheek.

Jack leans against the wall and slides his arm around me, pulling me closer. He sighs. "It had to be that way."

We sit on the supply room floor, arms around each other, not talking, listening to our breathing in the quiet room. The silence is broken by a faint creak as the back door opens, and then heels tap across the wooden floor. When she finds us in the supply room, her glance takes in the bandage across Jack's chest and the way we're clinging to each other.

"It's taken care of," she says quietly. "I'll find a new shirt for you. We all need some rest before tomorrow."

"Did you—" I can't finish the question.

She nods. "He's gone. I can't say more."

In the back hallway before I go upstairs and Jack heads for the cellar, I grip the front of his brown shirt and pull him close. He kisses the top of my head and whispers, "It's only a few days now. We'll be in England together."

Only a few days to be together.

Keeping my arms tight around him, I tilt my head to reach his lips, ignoring the little jolt of pain that comes when I press my bruised mouth against his. I feel him hesitate, but then his lips are soft and gentle against mine, his arms tighten, and we cling together for another minute. Before he pulls away, he kisses my temple. I try to reach his lips again, but he whispers that we need to sleep, and sends me up the stairs to my room.

29

The next day we meet behind the clinic after the noon meal. Jack and Pete wear old floppy black hats, pulled low over their faces. With his new mustache drooping over his mouth, Pete looks like one of the workers at the chateau. My head is covered in a black square scarf folded into a triangle and tied under my chin. I feel truly ugly now.

"We're going to a café nearby," Miss Cavell says. "Your guide will meet us there. I've told my contact I'm bringing two soldiers and a cousin of one of them. The guide will take you to the border." Worry lines frame her eyes, but her voice is cool and soft. "The Belgian army is under siege at Antwerp, so you have to travel west to get around the city and avoid the fighting. Once you get past Antwerp, you can reach the border through farmland, but it's difficult because there are German sentries stationed at many points, and some fields have barbed wire. You'll need to find a clear place to get across. When you cross the border into Holland, continue north to the town of Roosendaal and from there take the train to Vlissingen—Flushing. Trains run daily. At Flushing, you can get a fishing boat to England."

Roosendaal. The name is familiar, but my adrenaline won't let me think about it. Sentries, trains, fields—all sound familiar but just beyond my consciousness, like a blurry dream in the morning. Aunt Connie's words swirl in my brain—"*The spirits can reach us because time*

*moves in overlapping circles, and we have other lives but what happened in
the other lives can never be changed."*

Miss Cavell opens the large carpet bag hooked over her arm.
"Here are your papers and passports. If you're stopped by a patrol,
you'll have to show them to prove your identity."

We leaf through the papers. None of us can read the French. My
name on the passport is Anne Demy, and my stern picture—a little
fuzzy—looks like someone I've never met. I imagine soldiers checking these papers and asking questions we can't answer, and my mind
goes numb.

"You'll need money," she continues as she takes paper money out
of her bag. We each get a few bills plus some coins. "This is enough
for food and the train tickets if you're careful with it."

"How far?" Jack asks.

"From Brussels it's about 106 kilometers to Roosendaal. That's
about 65 miles," she adds, looking at me. "The distance rather depends on the side roads you'll have to take most of the way. Once
you're across the border, follow the signs to Roosendaal and ask directions for the train." She pulls on her gloves. "We'll walk to the café.
Stay close to me but don't talk."

As we pass the ash pit, I can't resist turning to look at it. There's
no trace of Green Scarf, nothing but a thin layer of leftover ash on
the bottom of the pit. Jack sees me staring, takes my hand, and steers
me out of the gate into the alley.

The café on a narrow side street is half empty. Middle-aged men
sit at round, wooden tables, beer glasses in front of them, while they
smoke and talk in low voices. Two old women sit together at a small
table finishing their meals and sipping tea. The air is thick with
smoke and stale food smells. Miss Cavell picks a table at the rear of
the café with a direct view of the entrance, daintily brushes crumbs
off the table top, and motions for us to sit. When a boy, who looks
about twelve, wrapped in a white apron reaching to his ankles, arrives at our table, she orders in French and pays. Beers arrive for Jack
and Pete. She and I get tea and a little plate of round crackers. My

mouth is so dry I can't swallow the cracker until I take a long gulp of tea.

After a few minutes, she takes a torn playing card out of her bag and places it in the center of the table—a jagged half of a red ace of diamonds. She adjusts the teapot so it casts a shadow over the card.

The café door opens, and we look up expectantly. A group of German soldiers enter, laughing, stamping their boots on the floor. They take over two tables near the door and call for service. The boy runs to them and then runs back to the kitchen with their order. Men at the other tables mumble only a word or two to each other, keep their faces turned away, and drink their beers. When the boy returns, he's staggering under a tray loaded with beer mugs and plates of fried potatoes and thick sausages. Miss Cavell murmurs that we are not to look anxious. We should appear as if we are friends enjoying ourselves, but in spite of her advice we say almost nothing to each other. Tension hangs over the table.

Minutes seem like hours. My tea grows cold. Jack reaches for my hand under the table, and I clutch his fingers so tightly he catches his breath and winces. His knuckles are still sore from the fight. I loosen my grip, but I can't relax. The Germans finish their food, linger over their beers, call for a second round, and light cigarettes, leaning back in their chairs while two soldiers compete in blowing smoke rings. Miss Cavell orders more tea.

A Belgian sitting at a rear table with four other men, pushes his chair back, stands, and walks slowly over to our table and greets us as if we're old friends. Miss Cavell smiles and murmurs a polite response. He nods and smiles while he leans over the table and glances at the card lying in the middle. Casually, while he mumbles something in French, still smiling, he takes a torn card from his pocket, and carefully places it next to her half, his calloused, tobacco-stained fingers moving the edges until they fit together. He's our guide.

He sweeps up the torn pieces, pulls up a chair, and signals the boy to bring another beer. He's thin and looks middle-aged. A bushy beard covers the bottom half of his face, and a floppy felt hat pulled low covers the upper half. His work clothes match what Jack and Pete are wearing, but his are dirtier with ragged cuffs hanging over his mud-covered shoes. He's completely unremarkable and forgettable.

He and Miss Cavell mumble to each other in French, both smiling and nodding as if they're chatting about something amusing. He drinks his beer and shifts his attention, running his gaze slowly and thoroughly over each of us. Bending closer to her, he says something to her and points to me.

Her voice is so quiet I have to lean over the table to hear her. "Jenny, he says you'll have to pass as someone's wife. It will raise less suspicion if you're stopped. He says it's easier to explain a wife than a cousin."

Jack brings our linked hands above the table and squeezes mine. "We can do that," he says. "Newlyweds," he adds.

She taps her fingers silently on the table while she thinks. "Yes, that's best because your papers don't match, and you have no wedding ring. I'll tell him to say you've been married only a few days." She murmurs to the guide and he nods.

"Does he speak English?" Pete asks.

"Some words," the man answers.

Miss Cavell gathers her cape around her shoulders. "Your guide is Auguste. I'll leave you now. Be careful and good luck." She pauses to look directly at me. "Don't take unneeded risks, and don't be over confident." She stands, says *adieu* in a clear voice, and walks toward the door without showing the slightest trace of nerves. As she passes the soldiers, she nods politely, and two of them rise and make a little bow.

Auguste leans over the table speaking softly to us—mostly in French, mixing in a few English words. He says nothing important; most of it doesn't make sense, but to anyone in the room, we look like a table of old friends sharing beer and conversation. The German soldiers are too far from us to hear what we say. Occasionally, Auguste laughs, and Pete laughs with him. I'm too nervous to let go of Jack's hand. Long minutes tick by on my inner clock.

At last, the Germans scrape back their chairs and leave. We wait a few more minutes before Auguste gestures and leads us through the back door of the café, heading, I hope, to safety.

The streets are crowded with soldiers. Belgians hurry past the shops and offices, keeping their eyes turned away from their invaders. Aside from the daily inspections, the clinic was like an oasis, away from the real war. It's easier now to see why Louis was captured when he tried to reach the border—so many ways to make a mistake.

Auguste leads us down two narrow streets before turning into a broader intersection. "Tram," he grunts, pointing to a dark green streetcar sitting on tracks in the middle of the street. People hurry to get in line at the streetcar. We do the same, following Auguste.

My pulse pounds. I have to stay calm, but when I climb to the top of the steps in the streetcar, I'm stuck. I don't know how to pay the fare. Auguste mutters under his breath and takes out his coins to show me how many to put in. Jack and Pete follow his example. Every eye in the streetcar is fixed on us as we walk down the aisle and take seats in the rear. We're obviously not locals if we need instructions to pay the fare. Maybe the Belgians in the streetcar know what we are, but no one talks to us. After a minute, they look away and stare out of the windows or at the floor.

At the next stop, three German soldiers climb the steps, grab onto the hanging straps, and remain standing while they look over the passengers. When they fix on me, Jack puts his arm around my shoulders and kisses my temple, moving his lips down to my ear as though he's talking to me. I turn my head and fake a giggle, pressing my forehead against his. The soldiers lose interest and stare out the front windows, watching pedestrians on the sidewalk. Holding hands, Jack and I stare into each other's eyes, smiling, ignoring the soldiers. Newlyweds.

We ride the streetcar until it reaches the outskirts of the city at the last stop. The four remaining passengers rush past us, eyes averted, and hurry down the streets toward houses. Auguste leads us along a narrow path behind a row of houses to a country road. Away from other people, I rip the hideous scarf off my head and tie it around my waist. We trudge down the dusty road and then into smaller lanes until it's so dark, we can't see where to step. Leaving the path and striding over gravel and dried grass, Auguste leads us to a small house. We wait at the sagging fence gate while he knocks on the door and mumbles something when a woman answers. She glances at us, points to the shed behind the house, and slams the door.

Inside the shed, Auguste says, "Sleep." He stretches out on a thin piece of canvas, pulls some empty sacks around him, drags his hat over his eyes, and goes to sleep immediately. His gentle snore whistles in the background as we whisper to each other.

"Not very talkative, is he?" Pete says as he settles on the dirt floor.

"How close are we to the border?" I ask.

Jack shakes his head. "Can't tell."

"We'd hear guns if we were close to Antwerp," Pete says. "Probably get there tomorrow. We have two or three days yet because we can't cross the border in the daytime." He stretches out, crosses his hands over his chest, and drifts into sleep within seconds.

"How can he sleep so easily?" I whisper.

Jack slides his arm around my waist and kisses my ear. "Soldiers have to sleep wherever they can. However, I am not at all sleepy right now."

"I'm not sleepy either." I slip my arms around him and tilt my head up for a kiss.

A violent, rumbling snore, like an enraged animal, erupts from Auguste, shattering our concentration on each other, and we have to clap hands over our mouths to smother our laughter. Pete snorts in his sleep, rolls over, and curls on his side. Jack nuzzles my neck for a minute before we settle, side by side, hands clasped, the way we slept during the nights when we hid in barns.

"When we're in England," Jack whispers, "we'll have better accommodations."

I snuggle into the heat from his body. The night air is chilly, keeping me awake until Jack's deep, steady breathing soothes me. It's not

England I'm thinking of as I drift into sleep. *Roosendaal* echoes over and over in my mind.

I wake with a jerk. The morning sunlight coming through a crack in the roof shines directly in my eyes. Auguste and Pete are both gone, but Jack is still sleeping, a faint smile on his face. I lean over and kiss him awake. He grins and pulls me close for another kiss.

Footsteps crunch in the gravel outside the shed. Pete leans in the doorway and snorts. "Sorry to interrupt, but you'd best hear this news. I did some scouting, even went to the house where I can tell you the woman was not friendly. Auguste is gone."

Jack is out of my arms and on his feet so fast, I lose my balance. "Gone?" he asks.

Pete nods and strokes his mustache. "He must have decided guiding us was too dangerous. We're on our own again."

"Where are we?" I straighten my crumpled skirt, ignoring my stomach's hungry gurgle.

Pete shakes his head. "Don't know. I asked for *north,* and the woman pointed. She wasn't giving specific directions. I asked about food, and she slammed the door."

Jack shifts his pistol under his shirt. "We'd better go on. No point in staying here."

The morning sun is warm, but the daytime breeze doesn't hold summer heat anymore, and the chill creeps through my cotton blouse when the wind picks up. I tie the ugly scarf around my shoulders like a shawl to keep the wind off my neck. After a couple of hours walking along foot paths, crossing fields, staying away from the main roads, we meet a farmer loading a wagon in his field. He watches us walk toward him and stops working. He knows what we are. Jack and Pete probably aren't the first soldiers who've passed this way trying to reach the border.

"Give it a try?" Pete asks.

"Might as well," Jack says. He puts his hand under his jacket, touching his pistol. He steps closer to the farmer. "*Nord?*"

The farmer considers Jack's question and glances up and down the path we just left. Finally, he grunts and gestures to the back of his wagon. We climb in, squeeze between the bushels of squash and Brussels sprouts, and huddle against the wooden sides of the wagon while the two horses pull at a steady gait. Riding this way, dressed in the clothes we got at the clinic, we probably do look like workers the farmer is transporting. My stomach growls. I'm tempted to snatch a zucchini and gnaw on it, but I resist. I can't steal food from someone helping us—I don't even like zucchini.

When we reach a few buildings clustered at an intersection of three roads, the farmer stops the wagon, ties the horses to a post, and leads us into a small tavern with two round tables in the back where we order dark bread and soup with vegetables but no meat. Jack puts his money on the table. The farmer picks out some bills to pay for the food and pushes the rest of the money back across the table. No one drinking in the tavern pays any attention to us, or maybe they want to claim they never saw us if they're questioned. Another hour in the wagon, and we get out at a crossroads because the farmer is turning in another direction. He points north, and we set out again down a narrow road. In the distance, heavy booms reverberate in the air.

"Must be coming from Antwerp." Pete says. "Sounds like German howitzers. How long can the Belgian army hold out?"

"Not long," Jack answers. He rubs his forehead, leaving a streak of dust. "Let's hope they last another day or two because if we get caught up in a retreat or surrender, the Germans will be on their heels and close the border as tight as they can."

As darkness closes in, we find a dilapidated barn. Jack and Pete sleep the way exhausted people sleep—falling nearly unconscious the minute they close their eyes, but I can't sleep. The booming guns in the distance echo in the night, and I can't stop myself from keeping track of the pounding guns—when they start, when they pause, when they start again.

30

We're lucky.

In the morning, refugees fleeing the shelling around Antwerp fill the roads. It's easy to blend in with the lines of carts and wagons, screaming children, growling dogs, and stumbling old women. No one looks closely at us. Refugees are a daily sight in the countryside. I tie the ugly scarf over my hair, Jack and Pete pull down their hats, and we walk in the general direction of the border mixed in with crowds of Belgians.

"Can't say I'm certain where we are," Pete mumbles under his breath.

"The guns are behind us and the sun came up behind us, so we must be heading somewhat north and west," Jack says in a low voice.

He reaches for my hand and pulls me next to him as more refugees join us, and the road becomes jammed with a slow-moving mass of people. He and Pete keep one hand close to the pistols under their shirts. I look over my shoulder—refugees as far as I can see.

We tramp along steadily until we reach a crossroads where people separate, some going one direction, some another. A few refugees turn into dirt paths alongside fields and head south again. We slow our steps, not sure of our direction.

"Do we go ahead?" Pete asks.

"No point in turning down paths we don't know," Jack mutters. "It's a wide road. It must lead somewhere."

A hand pulls at my sleeve. An old woman, only as tall as my shoulder, keeps pace with me, in spite of a slight limp. She's tiny, wrinkled, worn, and helpless looking, but her eyes are sharp, black, knowing. She tilts her head in a slight gesture indicating Jack and Pete and asks, "Border?"

Her thick accent blurs the word, and it's a second before I understand her. She knows what we are. I have to be cautious. Elise was friendly at first. The countess warned me some Belgians support the German invasion, and some want rewards for turning in British soldiers. I open my mouth to start my tale about being a lost American, but Jack steps closer and bends down to speak to her.

"*Nord?*" he says in a low voice.

She nods and gestures ahead.

Pete clears his throat. "Do we trust her?"

Jack strokes his pistol under his shirt and glances at me. "We've lost our guide," he says. "We'll follow her for a while. She could be friendly. She's running from the shelling at Antwerp like the others. We have to chance it."

We trail her until she beckons us into a narrow country lane lined first with trees and bushes, then open ground, and then woods again. The lane dips and twists and suddenly ends at a river bank. A footbridge about three feet wide made of narrow boards tied together sways and dips on the surface of the water. Each end of the bridge slopes up one of the banks, stretching about six feet on land and anchored with ropes tied to slender trees that don't look strong enough to hold the bridge in place if the river turns rapid or if the water rises after a storm. The river's calm now, but ripples in the moving water lap over the boards, making the wood slick and treacherous, and the bridge skims the top of the river, so any weight will put it under the surface.

"How far under the water will the bridge drop if we get on it?" I hate sounding like a coward, but the wooden boards swaying back and forth across the river's surface don't look sturdy enough to hold us. There's no guide rope or railing on the footbridge, so we'd have to balance on the boards without anything to hang on to. I peer into the river, but it's murky, so I can't see the bottom.

"Bridge might dip only an inch or two," Pete suggests.

The old woman gestures and smiles, but we hesitate. Finally, she scowls and looks to the sky, shrugging her shoulders. She hooks the basket she's carrying over one arm, balancing it in the curve of her elbow, steps on the boards, and scampers—the only word for it—over the bridge. The water splashes around her ankles as she crosses to the other side while the entire bridge bends and sways under her feet. Standing on the opposite bank, she laughs and motions to us.

"Right then," Pete says with a forced smile. "One at a time." He looks at me. "Ladies first."

"No," Jack says. "I'll go first. Watch my feet." He doesn't scamper. It's a balancing act without the help of the long pole tightrope walkers use. I hold my breath. When he reaches the middle of the bridge, it sways roughly with the current. He staggers, boots slipping on the wet wood, until he catches his footing. When he steps on firm ground, he turns and waves at us.

It's my turn.

I step gingerly on the bridge. The boards are wet and covered in green slime in places, making every step a slippery challenge. I circle my arms in the air for balance while the water sloshes over my shoes. Pausing between each step and swaying with the movement of the bridge to keep my footing is a struggle. It would be easier to swim across, but swimming is impossible. My heavy clothes would drag me down, and I can't strip to my underwear, so keeping my balance on the creaking bridge is my only choice. At least, the current isn't fast. One step, sway, one step, bend, arms outstretched. When I reach the other side, Jack leans down, grabs my hands, and pulls me up the bank.

Pete takes a longer to cross than I did. His feet slip, and his body shakes with the swaying movement of the bridge. Sometimes he freezes before he waves his arms and regains his balance. Then he screws up his face, bites his lip, and moves again. His progress is agonizingly slow. On this bridge, we'd be perfect targets for any German soldiers who happened to come along, but the old woman doesn't seem concerned. When Pete steps on land and gives a relieved whoop, she claps her hands, and we all laugh with relief.

"Can't swim," Pete confides to me as we follow the woman down another narrow path.

I tuck my hand in his arm. "I'd have rescued you."

He laughs. "I counted on it."

We plod along the dirt path behind the old woman, tired and hot in spite of the cool breeze. Everything hurts. My feet throb—my legs ache—my toes are numb. I rip off the scarf again and tie it around my neck. When Jack leans over to ruffle my hair, I'm too tired to smile at him. Pete shuffles behind us. He's not using a sling anymore, but he's holding his arm across his chest to keep it from moving. The sun dips toward the west, and we know for sure we're heading north. That's all we know. The landscape never changes from country fields to woods and back again.

We turn into a lane, and the old woman points to a small cottage. One wall has bullet holes in the wood, and a piece of the roof is missing. The front door is splintered. We could probably kick it in, but the woman takes a key out of her basket and unlocks the door as if it's still intact against intruders. She's not rich. The wooden table in the small kitchen is scratched and slightly off balance with chipped corners. A dented bucket in one corner sits under an opening in the roof, half filled with rain water.

She smiles, points to the table, and we drop into chairs while she lights the stove and fills a tea kettle. While the water boils, she cuts thick slices of bread from a dark crusty loaf she had in her basket. A small pot of strawberry jam from a shelf goes on the table. We spoon the jam on our bread and make contented grunting sounds of appreciation. Delicious.

"Wait," she says as we sip the tea. "Border is near. Rest now."

"Thank you," I say softly.

Jack rises and stretches out his hand to her. She shakes his hand once with a quick jerk. He glances around the small room. "We're grateful for your help. Do you live here alone?"

Her eyes fill with tears, and she dabs at them with a napkin from her basket. "My two boys—at Liege."

"Are they—" I stop, not wanting to finish the question and get the answer I dread.

"Prisoners," she says. Her lips quiver. "No word, no word."

Later, while she's outside feeding two scrawny dogs and the few chickens scratching in the dirt behind the house, Pete dozes off at the table, his head in his arms. I'm too jittery to sleep. Jack pushes his chair next to mine and holds my hand under the table while we both stare at nothing. I can't imagine how we'll cross the border to Holland in the dark. Our last rush to safety seems the most dangerous.

It's close to midnight when the woman pokes Pete awake and stirs us from the table. "Time now," she says, pulling a dark shawl over her head. "We go."

I stumble in the dark, and Jack has to grip my arm to steady me. Sometimes the thick clouds shift and allow a sliver of moonlight through but only for an instant before they shift again to blot out any light. I smell rain in the air, and the wind's blowing harder than it did during the day, making whistling noises through the trees. The old woman doesn't hesitate. In spite of her limp, she hurries sure-footed along the edge of a field without staggering. We follow much more awkwardly, feet crunching over dried stalks and clumps of dirt. Without Jack's hold on my arm, I'd have fallen more than once. Only our heavy breathing and feet stumbling over the rough ground break the silence.

Far away a low rumble sounds. I can't tell if it's thunder or the guns from Antwerp, but we don't pause. I lose track of distance and time. Finally, she stops at the end of a field and points directly ahead. "Dutch," she whispers. Then she waves a hand vaguely toward the right and the left. "Soldiers," she says. "Run fast." She turns to go, but looks back at us. "Bless," she says, raising her hand. Then she's gone, disappearing into the shadows.

Jack and Pete pull their pistols as we stare into the gloom. As far as I can see whenever the clouds shift enough to uncover some moonlight, ahead of us is a long stretch of pitch-dark fields, but I can't make out anything specific.

How far?

"I'll go first," Jack whispers. "Jenny, you follow me, and Pete, you follow her."

"Right," Pete says. "Make it a fast run for as long as we can."

We start running. Jack moves ahead of me, fading into the darkness, so I can barely keep track of him. Pete stays a few steps behind me. My feet slide on the slick dirt in the field, making me stagger as if I'm drunk. Pete's breathing turns into pants and gasps. When the clouds part for an instant, I see Jack, a dim figure running far ahead. Immediately, the clouds slide over every flicker of light, and we might as well be running in a dark cave. Gasping for air. Shins burning with every step. Slipping, nearly falling. Almost there, I repeat over and over in my head. Getting close.

A figure looms out of the darkness on my right. A shout. Another shout. I see the flash of light before I hear the rifle.

I stop running, not sure which way to go. Behind me, Pete groans and drops to the ground. Turning back, I sink to my knees beside him. Ragged breaths hiss from his mouth, as he lies flat, arms flung out, his pistol in the dirt next to me.

The clouds shift again, and the faint moonlight shows the dark splotch on Pete's chest spreading wider and wider. I use the bottom of my skirt to press on his chest, but the blood seeps into the cloth as I push down.

Pete's eyelids flutter. "I'm sure hit, Jenny." He coughs and tries to smile.

"You'll be all right." I press harder, my fingers slippery now with the blood soaking my skirt.

The dark figure reaches us. *"Fraulein?"* The soldier looms over us, his mouth open, confused to see me when he probably expected two men. He fumbles with his rifle and lets the barrel sag toward the ground.

"Jenny, I'm coming!"

"Jack, stay back! Pete's hit."

The soldier spins in the direction of Jack's voice, rifle coming up, searching the darkness for his target. The moon suddenly breaks through the clouds, shining bright over the field, and clearly showing Jack running toward us. The soldier raises his rifle to his shoulder and takes aim.

I loosen my pressure on Pete's wound. I don't think. I don't plan. Seizing his pistol lying next to him, I grip it with both hands, jerk it up fast and steady, and squeeze the trigger. The force of the gunshot kicks me backward into the dirt. The German drops to his knees. His rifle slips out of his hands, and with a groan, he topples over on his side only a few feet from us.

I drop the pistol and press my skirt against Pete's chest again, my pulse thumping so hard I'm dizzy. I've shot someone. Nausea surges through me. I swallow hard and press harder on Pete's chest.

Jack reaches us and stops to check the soldier lying unmoving on the ground.

"Is he dead?" My voice cracks.

"Yes." Jack falls to his knees next to Pete. "Let me see Pete." He pushes away my skirt and inhales sharply.

I rip at the fastenings of my skirt and pull it off so we can fold it and press harder on Pete's wound. I know it's not going to do any good. Jack looks at me and barely moves his head, but I know what he means.

"Hang on, Pete," I say. "We'll get help."

There's no place we can go that will be fast enough. We've been walking and running for more than an hour and couldn't retrace our steps to the old woman's house in the dark. I peer into the distance.

Did other sentries hear the shots? Are more Germans coming to find us?

"I'm cold, Jack. I'm cold." Pete mutters.

Jack sits in the dirt and slides his leg behind Pete, raising him so he's leaning against Jack's chest. "It will be warmer in the morning," Jack says, putting his arms around Pete, one hand flat against his chest, holding my skirt in place.

Pete coughs a rasping sound deep in his throat. "You two go. I'll follow—when I get warmer."

Jack pulls Pete closer against his body, keeping his arms around him. "We're not in a hurry. We can wait for you to be warmer."

Tremors run up and down Pete's body. "Tell me mum—she'll be in a bloody snit about this—tell her it wasn't my fault that—" He stops, sucks in air and coughs. The raspy sound in Pete's throat gets louder with every breath. He tilts his head to look at the dark sky. "Jack, the bowmen are here. Do you see them in the clouds? The old English archers with their longbows?"

I scan the sky. The dark clouds spin, changing patterns, stretching into thin ribbons then clumping again, but all I see are advancing rain clouds, covering the stars as they swirl.

Pete gurgles in his throat as he drags in breath. "Longbows, Jack. Do you see them?"

"I see them," Jack says softly. "The warriors and their longbows. You're right—they're here to help us cross the border." My bloody skirt slips out of his fingers, away from Pete's chest—useless.

Pete shivers. Another cough. A long hissing exhale of breath. Silence.

Jack carefully lowers Pete to the ground. "We have to go." His voice is a faint shaky whisper. "Those shots are bound to bring more sentries."

"Pete?" My breath heaves in my chest.

Jack pulls me to my feet. "We have to leave him." His voice shakes, and he covers his eyes for a second. "Did you shoot the German, Jenny?"

"Yes." Shudders start in my chest, snaking down to my toes. The German soldier had a mother. She'll be as angry as Pete's mother when the news reaches her. Not angry—heartbroken.

Jack grips my hand. "When they find the sentry and Pete this way, they might think they shot each other. If we're lucky, they won't search for us. We have to run."

My bloody skirt is soaked. I can't bear to put it on again.

Jack pulls me forward. "Take it and drop it somewhere later."

We run. No looking back. For at least a mile, we hang on to each other, stumbling, holding each other upright, never letting our hands slip apart. Breathing hard, gasping, we stagger up a rise and down the other side, hurry unsteadily across more ground until we reach a dirt trail that merges into a country road. I toss the skirt behind a bush when we slow to a walk.

The rain starts, splattering our faces, washing over our bloody hands. Dirt on the side of the road turns to mud. When we reach a wooden post on one side of the road, I squint at the signs above us, blinking to clear the rain from my eyes.

Bergen Op Zoom—13 Kilometers

Rotterdam—66 Kilometers

Roosendaal—8 Kilometers

Antwerp—37 Kilometers

The arrow on the Antwerp sign points behind us. The other signs point ahead or to the left.

"We must be in Holland," Jack says. The rain turns into a downpour while we wrap our arms around each other, shivering, holding tight. I put my head against Jack's chest and let myself cry about Pete, the German soldier, my aching body—hot tears mixing with the cold rain. Jack's chest heaves, and I know he's crying too. We cling together next to the sign, rain soaking us.

"You saved me." Jack's lips press against my ear. "You saved my life."

31

The rain fades into a drizzle, and by the time daylight cuts into the black sky, we've trudged hand in hand, sometimes half holding each other up, to what must be the outskirts of Roosendaal where a few scattered houses sit back from the road.

My feet stumble. "I'm so thirsty."

Jack slips his arm around my waist and keeps me upright as we walk on. "It's not far now. The last sign we passed said two kilometers, and we've come at least half way."

I stop moving entirely, pain shooting from my feet to my hips and back again. Am I too tired to go on or am I afraid to reach the town? During the long, dark tramp through the night, along with concentrating on survival, I remembered Roosendaal. Dan's grandmother read Jack's entry—he lost her—me—in Roosendaal. I think—I believe deep inside I'm in a past life. Somehow, Aunt Connie's séance and maybe my concussion allowed Jack to find me. Aunt Connie would be thrilled to know one of her séances finally paid off.

It's like starting a book in the middle. I only know the portion I've lived in Belgium. We're nearly at the end of Belgium, close to getting Jack on his way back to England. What happens after that? Do I die here? If I return to Aunt Connie, how exactly do I manage it? Kissing Jack doesn't have the same effect in 1914 as it did in my twenty-first century life. Questions drum through my brain, but no answers come.

"We're close to Roosendaal now. See some houses up ahead of us?" Jack groans and stops walking. He bends over, then straightens and stretches his arms, cautiously looking around. The morning sun dissolves the night shadows, but it's so early not even a dog is outside. "I'm thirsty too." He points to a small house not too far up the road. "There's probably a well in the back. We might get water before any-one's awake."

I gape at the house, trying to focus my eyes in the uneven light. White scalloped trim around the edge of the steep orange-brown sloped roof, deep green walls with neat white shutters framing win-dows showing white gauzy curtains inside, and trimmed low bushes along both sides of the path to the front door. "Very tidy people live there," I mutter. "We look like we've been drowned at sea and washed up on shore."

"It's early," Jack says. "They're still sleeping. We'll get some water, and we'll be gone before they're stirring. They won't know we drank from their well."

I'm too thirsty to question him or care if someone sees us. Yanking my dirty, shredded petticoat up to my knees, I half run, half walk to-ward the house, leaving Jack to follow. We slip past the clipped hedg-es along the side of the house as silently as we can, but as we turn the corner, the back door opens and a woman steps out. Her brown hair, streaked with gray, hangs over her shoulder in a long, partially undone braid. She's wearing a long robe with a faded blue apron tied loosely around her, and she's gripping a black cast-iron frying pan. We freeze in place. She stares at us, her mouth open. I pray she won't scream. The rain washed Pete's blood from our hands and clothes, but we don't look respectable. I'd certainly scream if I met two people outside my back door looking like we do.

Jack moves a step ahead of me, makes a little bow, points toward the well, and makes a drinking gesture. "Water?"

She stares at us, lingering on my muddy petticoat and on our tired faces. "*Ja,*" she says.

I gulp the cold water, swallowing fast to get as much as I can, letting it splash down my chin and throat. Next to me, Jack does the same. By the time we finish drinking and turn back to the house, a man stands next to the woman in the doorway. He's wearing woolen pants held up by suspenders, but he's shirtless, his hairy chest merging into a round bulging stomach sagging over his pants.

Jack wipes his face and slips his hand under the edge of his shirt where his pistol is looped inside his belt.

The man sends a searching glance over the yard, followed by a long look at houses in the distance. With a side step, he motions us to the doorway and mutters to the woman. She holds the door open for us.

"Railway? Roosendaal?" Jack asks as he follows me into the kitchen.

"*Ja,* close." The man flings a hand in the general direction we're been walking.

"Papers? No papers—prison—Belgians, soldiers, all to prison."

Jack nods. "We have papers."

"*Ja, goed.*" The man takes another look outside and closes the door. He picks a gray shirt off a wall hook and slips it on, buttoning it over his suspenders.

The kitchen is spotless. White plates rimmed in tiny blue flowers with matching cups sit on the polished wooden table. Water boils in a cast-iron kettle on the stove. The woman gives us a thick bar of strong-smelling soap, soft towels and sends us outside to a pump at the back of the house.

How incredibly fantastic soap is. I roll my sleeves over my elbows and slide the bar over my skin, working up a thin lather. Jack sticks his head under the pump and when he stands up, I push him out of the way and duck my head under. When I come up gasping, he grins and ruffles my hair, sending sprays of water into the air. It's the first time he's smiled since Pete died, and it's brief, but real.

In the kitchen, I sink gratefully into a chair at the table. The woman puts plates and cups on the table in front of us. Hot coffee and thick slices of bread with butter come first. Sausages sizzle in the frying pan, the fat spurting up as she turns them. The spicy aroma makes me jumpy with hunger until a thick, round sausage appears on my plate, and I devour it in four bites. Jack eats more slowly—he's savoring the taste. A grateful sigh escapes me when the woman drops a second sausage on my plate. I hope they can afford to give us this food, but I'm too hungry to refuse it.

The woman points to my torn petticoat, and I make a lot of gestures indicating I lost my skirt in the woods. She looks unconvinced but leaves the kitchen and returns with a faded cotton skirt for me. It's blue, a little too big, but I turn over the waistband a couple of times into a lumpy roll around my middle to make it shorter. I've given up all hope of looking attractive or even properly groomed.

We don't exchange names. The man draws a little map, so we can find the train station. The woman pours more coffee and cuts more bread for us. I blink a teary declaration of gratitude. My emotions are churning in conflict. Roosendaal is a short distance down the road, and Jack is nearly on his way to England.

And me? I have no idea.

When we finish eating, the man steps out of the house and checks the road before he beckons us outside. No one is in sight. He points in the direction we should walk and thumps Jack's shoulder, grunting something I can't understand. Jack shakes his hand, and we both say thank you several times. Impulsively, I put my arms around the woman and hug her.

The walk to the train station seems short and easy, possibly because I'm dry and well fed. The walk for me is also how I imagine a prisoner feels going to his execution. I'm going to leave Jack here. I feel it so strongly, it's no longer a question. We hold hands, my fingers linked with his, hanging on tight.

A train schedule hangs on the wall next to a huge round clock inside the railway ticket office. A train leaves for Vlissingen in four hours. Jack steps to the ticket window and says *Vlissingen* in a low voice, holding up two fingers. His pronunciation probably isn't right, but I couldn't have said it any better. The ticket agent stares at us for a long minute, running his gaze over our mismatched clothes.

"Identificatie," the agent growls and holds out his hand.

Jack jerks the leather envelope over his head, slides out our papers and passports, and pushes them through the opening in the ticket window. The agent slowly thumbs through each page, reading, then looking up at one of us and down at the page, then licking his thumb again and reading the next page the same way. My pulse speeds up, and my muscles tense as if I'm getting ready to run, which is ridiculous since I have no idea where to run. After what seems like a thousand years, the agent stops flipping the pages but his searching gaze goes on for more endless minutes until he returns our papers to Jack and punches out two tickets.

The ticket office has benches, but I drag Jack out to the platform, away from the agent who still has a suspicious look on his face. The platform is damp from the rain last night with shallow puddles in spots the morning sun hasn't yet reached. We sit on a wooden bench and stare at the empty tracks. I desperately want to say something significant, something terribly wise and memorable, so Jack never forgets it, but nothing comes to my brain.

When the train comes, am I going to get on with Jack? Or am I going to die in some strange way? According to Aunt Connie, I can't change what's already happened. I'm reliving a past life, but I don't know what happened every minute in that past. I don't want to leave Jack, but I don't want to stay without him. I especially don't want to die.

"Remember what Miss Cavell said. The train—then a fishing boat—and you'll be back in England." I keep my voice low and full of confidence.

"Pete won't be going back," Jack says.

I clutch his hand. "You couldn't do anything. Nobody could do anything. It all happened in a second."

"I shouldn't have gone across the field ahead of you two. I thought that was the best way. It was stupid."

"Why would it have been better for you to die?" I shiver. "The soldier was going to shoot whoever he saw. It happened to be Pete."

"Pete let me take the lead since Mons. He relied on me to get us through. We were so close. I made a mistake, and Pete caught the bullet."

"It wasn't a mistake." His eyes look so dark and miserable, I can't stand it. The platform starts filling with travelers waiting for the next train to Rotterdam. I lower my voice. "You know I'm right." My throat tightens when I think of Pete lying on the muddy ground in the dark. "There was nothing we could do. I tried to stop the blood, but there was so much." I choke on the words.

The train to Rotterdam roars into the station, grinding to a stop, steam pouring from under the cars, filling the platform with a smoky gray haze that quickly fades. Departing passengers wait politely in lines while the conductors bring out portable steps, so arriving passengers can climb down to the platform. The arrivals clutch their suitcases and quickly leave, while departing passengers climb into the cars, settle into seats, and wave from the train windows to those left behind. The conductors collect the portable steps and shout orders as they jump onto the train already slowly moving out of the station. It's all so efficient—as if there were no war going on only a few miles away.

Jack pulls me into his arms and rests his head on the top of mine while we sit teary, clinging to each other, ignoring the morning travelers. Looking over Jack's shoulder, I see a policeman step out of the ticket office onto the platform. He glances over the waiting passengers and catches my eye for a second, but I bury my face in Jack's shoulder and grip his arm, digging my nails into him. Jack's muscles tense, responding to my signal.

We're supposed to be newlyweds. Jack shifts on the bench and turns my face to his, kissing me softly on my cheek. The policeman watches us. Is this my moment? I squeeze my eyes shut and picture Aunt Connie's garden, but when I open my eyes, I'm looking up at Jack. The policeman has walked to the other end of the platform, and I'm still sitting on the bench at the Roosendaal train station.

"Jack," I whisper against his lips. "Don't ever tell anyone about me."

"Why not?"

I shake my head. "Don't tell anyone about me."

"Why should I keep you a secret?"

"We know what happened to us, but no one else needs to know what we've done." I tilt my head and kiss his jaw, his chin rough with stubble under my lips. "It will be our secret."

"Without you—I'd never have gotten this far without you," he whispers in my ear. "Sometimes I think you're a mirage—someone I made up because I needed you."

"Maybe that's right—a mirage."

"No, you're real." He strokes my cheek.

The station is crowded with travelers again. A mother with a small boy sits at the other end of our bench—too close.

"Come here." Jack pulls me around the corner, and we wedge ourselves into a narrow space between the station wall and a wagon stacked high with crates, out of sight of anyone on the platform. "I mean it. You kept me going, but that's not all. Having you with me. . . ." His voice is rough, and he fumbles in his pocket. "I found this in the library at the chateau, and I copied it for you." He slips a piece of paper out of his pocket, handing it to me. "I want you to have it now. It says how I think about you all the time."

I unfold the creased paper and read the first few words. It's the poem the ghost recited before he kissed me. For one mad second I'm tempted to crumple the paper, pretend I don't know what it means, and get on the train with Jack. Instead, I draw in a long breath and hold out the paper.

"Read it to me."

He smiles and closes my fingers over the paper. "I know it by heart. It makes me think about being with you always." Taking my other hand, he holds it against his chest. His heart thuds under my palm as he recites the lines softly.

Jenny kiss'd me when we met,
Jumping from the chair she sat in;
Time, you thief, who love to get
Sweets into your list, put that in!
Say I'm weary, say I'm sad,
Say that health and wealth have miss'd me,
Say I'm growing old, but add,
Jenny kiss'd me.

"I love you, Jack." I rise on tiptoe and fling my arms around his neck, kissing him, softly and then harder, kissing him for all the times I never will again. His arms tighten around me, his hands slide up my back to hold me against him.

Whirling darkness, soft empty blackness takes me.

32

Something wet and rough rasps across my cheek—little delicate strokes against my skin. I'm lying flat on what feels like grass. Groaning, I exhale in a long whoosh before opening one eye at a time. Snowball stops licking my face, raises his head to look intently into my eyes, and then crouches next to me, a dull purr rumbling in his chest. I let my lids drift shut again, listening to his steady, comforting, vibrating murmur close to my ear.

"Jenny!"

When I open my eyes this time, I'm looking into dark brown eyes with amber glints. Thick black hair falls over his forehead.

"Jack?"

He kneels next to me, his hand on my shoulder. "Who? Jenny, it's Dan. What happened? Did you fall?"

"Umm." I groan again. I rub my temple, sensing the traces of a headache—coming or going, I can't tell.

"It's your head, isn't it? Your concussion made you black out, or you tripped and hit your head again." Dan sits back on his heels. "Stay still. I'll call 911."

"No." I struggle to sit but only manage to lean on my elbows. "Don't call." I look around still dizzy. We're in Aunt Connie's garden, and I'm wearing the same shorts and tee shirt I had on when Jack kissed me. "What day is it?"

Dan frowns. "What day is it? That's enough. I'm calling 911."

"No." I grab his arm and pull myself to a sitting position. "I'm not hurt. Just a little—" I search for an explanation to satisfy him. "I think I slipped on the grass. Don't leave me. Help me up."

He grips me under my arms and lifts me, holding me upright until I get my feet in place. I hang on his arm for a minute and wait for my head to stop whirling. "Ah, that's better. I'm fine, just had my breath knocked out of me." Whatever I'm clutching in one hand is a crumpled wad, so I shove it in my pocket. "Sorry I scared you." I manage a smile.

"Why are you in the garden this early?" Suspicion flashes in his eyes. "Did you come out here last night to meet that ghost figure you thought you saw?"

"Of course not." I muster an expression of what I hope looks like complete innocence and load my voice with sincerity. "I had a little headache this morning, and I thought the fresh air would help, and I wanted to cut some flowers, but I forgot the clippers, and when I turned to go to the tool shed, I slipped on the grass, and you found me after about two minutes." I paste a smile on my lips and shrug. "I'm fine now, really I am."

I have to look directly at Dan to establish my honesty, even though gazing into those dark brown eyes—Jack's eyes—is like stabbing myself with a sharp knife, a kind of torture. But these eyes are Dan's, I remind myself. I'm back in my present time, very far away from Jack.

Dan keeps his hand under my elbow and stares suspiciously at me. "Okay. I'll help you into the house. Aunt Connie told me to come early for breakfast before I cut the lawn."

"If she sees you helping me, she'll be all over me and want to call a doctor. I'm fine, really." I hold my hand balanced in mid-air to show him how steady it is. "You go in first, and I'll follow so she doesn't get suspicious."

He mumbles another protest, but I'm winning the argument, and after I insist one more time I'm not hurt and don't need help, he gives in and heads toward the kitchen door.

I wait for him to disappear inside before I take the crumpled paper out of my pocket and smooth it out. It's the poem. I run my fingertip across the pen strokes. Every minute in another time with Jack was real—I stepped into a war and survived.

I close my eyes, trying to understand how time can shift from past to present and back again, but I can't. Instead, I concentrate on keeping Jack's face in my brain, storing memories of easy smiles, dark shining eyes, silky black hair, and every kiss we had, so I'll never lose him because I'll remember everything—because we loved each other.

I hold the poem against my heart for a moment, then carefully fold the paper and put it in my pocket before I walk across the patio to the kitchen. When I open the door, Aunt Connie stands at the stove, flipping pancakes, while Dan sits on a stool at the breakfast bar. They're laughing. With an expert twist of the spatula, Aunt Connie slides three pancakes on a plate and sets it in front of Dan.

"Sweetie," she turns to me. "How many pancakes do you want?"

"Two." I slide onto a stool next to Dan. We grin at each other.

When Aunt Connie puts the pancakes in front of me, I glance up at her. The tiniest smile curves her lips. Her eyes spark with excitement. "Were you in the garden last night?"

"For a while," I murmur, dribbling syrup on my pancakes.

"And this morning so early." Her smile broadens. "How marvelous. One day you must tell me everything."

"I promise I will. Someday." I touch the poem folded stiff in my pocket, and I smile at her. Jack's voice echoes in my head—*Jenny kiss'd me.*

I'm waiting, Jack.

The End

HISTORY NOTE

Most of the characters in this novel are fictional, but **Edith Cavell** was a real British nurse working in Belgium before World War I broke out. She was on vacation in England when it became obvious war was beginning, and she decided to return to her hospital in Brussels. The German invasion of Belgium was so rapid many Allied soldiers like Jack and Pete were caught behind the lines, and their only possible escape lay in reaching neutral Holland. Edith became an important figure in the Belgium underground and helped many Allied soldiers evade capture and reach safety. Estimates are that about 200 soldiers evaded German capture because of her. The Germans discovered her activities in August 1915 and arrested her for treason. At her trial, she readily confessed her activities, saying she felt a moral duty to save lives. She was executed by firing squad on October 12, 1915. Her death made her a heroic symbol for the Allied cause in World War I, and she appeared on posters designed to rally the English public. She remains a heroine of the war.

The papers Jack carried in the story represent the efforts to develop military tanks early in the war. The first versions of tank-like vehicles typically were tractors with weapons attached. The British produced the Mark I tank in January 1916, and it was used in battle in September 1916. Improvements in design continued, and by March 1917, the Mark IV tank was ready for combat. Because tanks could travel over difficult landscapes, they helped bring an end to the war's stalemate with troops on each side trapped in trenches, unable to advance. The United States entered the war in 1917, and American forces ensured the Allied victory.

The poem Jack recites is titled "Jenny Kissed Me," written by James Henry Leigh Hunt and published in 1838.

Pete's story about seeing Medieval warriors with longbows aiding the British at Mons reflects a popular legend repeated by many soldiers during and after the war. The tale appears to have developed from a short story, "The Bowmen," by Arthur Mechen, published in September 1914. The fantasy evolved into a legend many believed during the following decades.

World War I began with the assassination of Archduke Franz Ferdinand of Austria, June 28, 1914, and ended November 11, 1918. The exact number of casualties in the war is not known, but estimates indicate nearly 40 million people, military and civilians, were killed or wounded.

Keep reading for an excerpt from
THE DANGEROUS SUMMER OF JESSE TURNER
By D. C. Reep and E. A. Allen
Available now

HEADLINES

The Liberty, Missouri News-Gazette
February 16, 1898
U.S.S. MAINE BLOWN UP IN HAVANA, CUBA!
Explosion yesterday sinks our battleship in Havana harbor
and kills over 250 sailors. Spanish treachery is suspected.

The Liberty, Missouri News-Gazette
April 22, 1898
CONGRESS DECLARES WAR ON SPAIN!
President McKinley issues call for 125,000 volunteers to free Cuba
from Spanish oppression and avenge the attack on the *Maine*!

1

Everybody knew I was an outlaw's kid.

Aunt Livia always warned me to keep quiet about my pa riding with Jesse James and the Younger boys while they robbed banks and shot up the countryside, but in a small town like Liberty, Missouri, everybody knew everything. I was Hank Turner's son, and that meant I was *Turner Trash.*

I reckon my pa felt fine about riding with the James gang. I never knew him, so I couldn't ask. He named me after Jesse James and lit out when I was a baby. My ma died before I could talk. Aunt Livia raised me like I was her own although she was a maiden lady of forty when I came along.

"You've got to rise above what people think, Jesse," Aunt Livia would say when I was little and came home bloody and crying from being beaten up. "Turners can be decent folk. You do the right thing and you'll get respect."

Finding a way to blot out my pa's reputation was not an easy thing, but then war came. Most people in Liberty didn't know where Cuba was, but once they heard about our ship and the fallen sailors, they got worked up about the attack, and by the time Congress declared war on Spain, people were ready for a fight. When I heard the call for volunteers to go to Cuba with Lieutenant Colonel Theodore Roosevelt,

I knew my chance to prove a Turner could amount to something had come.

To join the First U.S. Volunteer Cavalry Regiment, I had to swear I was seventeen, but what the heck, six more months wasn't so very far away, and I reckoned I could be just as good a soldier as any other fellow.

When the time came for me to leave, Aunt Livia got weepy at the train station. "You're going so far away!" She let out a wail and hugged me in a fierce grip. Her tears made my shoulder wet where she pressed her forehead. "Be careful!"

"I will," I muttered. I wanted to sound tough, but my throat felt tight, and my voice came out like a gasp. "Don't worry about me."

The train whistle sounded, and the conductor yelled "All aboard!"

Aunt Livia's fingers pressed into my arm. "Don't get hurt," she said. "Promise me."

"Fighting might be over before I get there," I said.

By the time I got to Camp Wood outside San Antonio, a thousand volunteers were there, and more coming in from every state and the western territories. The place was dusty and rowdy, but I felt good because I was one of the crowd, and nobody knew about my pa and his robberies. In camp, I was like everybody else.

Uniforms hadn't arrived at Camp Wood yet, so the volunteers didn't look like much of a regiment. Rich New Yorkers—Fifth Avenue Boys somebody called them—still wore their city suits, white shirts and straw hats with wide hatbands—boaters. Cowboys carried ropes and had leather fringe on their jackets. Some of them were real bron-cobusters. Indians from the territories arrived the day after I got to camp. We weren't much alike, but we were all fixed on being Colonel Roosevelt's Rough Riders.

The third day in camp, I was in line waiting to get into the mess hall when the fight started.

A cowboy pushed in front of one of the New Yorkers standing in front of me. "Git to the back of the line, la-de-dah boy. Real men go first, not a boy in silk undies he'll dirty up as soon as he hears any guns."

The New Yorker started out polite enough. "I beg your pardon. The end of the line is well back there."

"Then you better git back there. This is my spot now." The cowboy looked about twenty. He had a long thin scar on his cheek and when he smiled, his whole face went lopsided. Gave him a real evil slant.

The New Yorker stood his ground. "I don't intend to move," he said. "You cannot push your way in wherever you want to. You'll have to go to the rear."

"A la-de-dah boy telling me what to do—that's ripe." The cowboy sneered, slapped the boater off the New Yorker's head, shoved him out of line, and sent him reeling backwards.

We all got quiet. The cowboy shifted his weight to the balls of his feet, grinning, getting ready for a fight. The New Yorker took a step and slowly bent over toward the ground. I thought he was going to pick up his hat, but instead he came up quick and hard with a punch that caught the cowboy on his jaw and knocked him back on his heels.

"Fight! Fight!"

The orderly line of fellows turned into a pushing crowd. I was up front from the start. In spite of taking the cowboy by surprise, the New Yorker started getting the worst of it pretty quick. The cowboy knocked him down, and his head hit the ground hard. I could tell he was dizzy when he stood up. His eyes weren't focused, and he didn't keep his hands high enough to avoid the punches landing on his chin. The cowboy bashed him in the stomach next and tripped him when he tried to straighten up.

The crowd started tossing in advice. "Hit him hard! Step back! Move around!"

I couldn't tell who the advice was aimed at, but it wasn't helping the New Yorker because he doubled over with the blows he was taking from the cowboy. Every time he tried to fight back, the cowboy landed another sickening body punch.

Aunt Livia had always warned me, "Jesse Turner, don't meddle in other people's business."

Mostly, I'd followed her advice, but I didn't think it was right the way the cowboy was bearing down on the New Yorker with a murderous look. I'd seen that look in fights back in Liberty. Blood ran down the New Yorker's chin and dribbled on his white shirt. Another punch and he was back on the ground. The cowboy kicked him in his side.

"Give it up," I shouted. "He's down. Just let him be."

The cowboy picked me out of the crowd, and his lopsided grin told me I was in for it next. I set myself to handle the blow coming my way, when he pulled a knife from his back pocket. The blade was short—thick—shiny.

"Don't mix in this, kid." The cowboy moved toward me.

I'm plenty quick on my feet, so I dodged his first swipe at me. The crowd was too close to let me back up much. He got the knife near my chest, and I danced away again.

Now the crowd started giving me advice. "Watch out! Keep back! Dodge him!"

The cowboy had dark eyes—almost black—and he was getting near enough for me to see the sparks in them. He was excited about the chance to cut me up. For sure, I was going to get that knife in me before too long.

Something flashed past my face, and I spun around. One of the Indians in the crowd had flicked a leather strap and took the blade right out of the cowboy's hand—sent it flying some twenty feet.

"What in hell is going on here?"

I'd seen Colonel Roosevelt earlier, looking just like an officer should—all polished up. Now he glared down at us and shook his fist while his horse reared up, snorting and pawing the air. I jumped back to avoid the bay's hooves.

"You three there, step apart!" Colonel Roosevelt roared. "Captain Capron! Get control here!"

An officer pushed through the crowd. I'd seen him earlier too. Captain Allyn Capron came to Camp Wood from the Seventh U. S.

Cavalry. He was the commander of the Indian volunteers. He frowned at the Indian. "Ben Hatchet, what's going on?"

The crowd suddenly got interested in reforming the mess line.

The Indian slowly wrapped his leather strap around his wrist. "It's over now, Captain Capron."

The captain glanced at the New Yorker still doubled up on the ground and pointed to the knife. "Whose knife is that?"

The cowboy grunted. "It's mine, Sir. Slipped away from me." He made a motion to pick up the knife but then stopped and left it where it was.

The New Yorker rolled over on his side and slowly got to his feet. He wiped his bloody chin on his sleeve and spit some blood on the ground.

"I won't tolerate fighting in this camp!" Colonel Roosevelt got his horse under a tight rein. He leaned over and glared directly at me. "We're here to fight the Spanish, not each other. Now you all pay attention to the captain, and I don't want to hear about fighting among the men in this camp." He pulled his horse around and trotted away.

"Listen to the colonel," Captain Capron said. "We have to stick together in this war. Stay where you are for a minute." He walked over to some fellows in the mess line. I couldn't hear what they were saying, but judging from the gestures, some fellows had a lot to say.

"You little bastard," the cowboy hissed at me. "Keep your mouth shut."

I didn't look at him and kept my breathing steady to show him I didn't care what he said.

Captain Capron walked back to us. "What's your name and where are you from?" he asked the cowboy.

"Ike Dillon, Santa Fe, New Mexico, Sir."

"And you two?"

"William Arthur Lockridge, New York City, Sir."

"Jesse Turner, Liberty, Missouri, Sir."

The cowboy sucked in his breath and whipped his head around to look me over. I couldn't help a shiver going through me.

The captain's mouth twitched in a half-smile. "Well, boys, I know military life is new to you. Keep yourselves in order. Is that understood?"

We all said "Yes, Sir" at the same time.

The captain frowned at Dillon. "I hear you're ready to take on anything, Dillon. I've got something for you to tackle. You can use some of your energy right now in a cleanup detail. Follow me and step lively." He walked away and didn't look back. He had that confidence officers have, knowing when they give an order, the rest of us will obey it.

Dillon glared at us, snatched his knife from the ground and hooked it on his belt under his jacket. "It might be a long war," he muttered. He flushed dark red while he looked me over again. "Turner from Liberty, Missouri, you say? I used to have folks around Liberty. I'll be seeing you again. And, hey, la-de-dah boy, I ain't finished with you. Hell, I ain't finished with any of you. You can bet I'll make sure there's no officer around to save you next time."

He walked away and then looked back over his shoulder. "Watch out for me, boys."

ABOUT THE AUTHORS

D. C. Reep—A former university professor, Reep taught American literature, film studies, the King Arthur Legend, and business and technical writing. Publications include novels, a technical writing textbook in its 8ᵗʰ edition, a writing handbook for educators, short fiction, and over 30 articles focused on business communication or popular culture topics. Fiction interests focus on the Gilded Age, the Civil War, early 20ᵗʰ Century, and the early movie industry. Reep and Allen's YA novel, *The Dangerous Summer of Jesse Turner,* follows three young men who volunteer to join Colonel Theodore Roosevelt's Rough Riders in the Spanish-American War of 1898.

   E. A. Allen—A former middle school and high school teacher, Allen enjoys researching history. With an intense interest in interior design, and as a regular visitor to antique stores, Allen is thrilled when discovering long-forgotten sports trophies to add to a growing collection. A lover of all things Italian, including Italy's food and Cinque Terre, Allen enjoys country life in the Midwest during the warm months but flees to the Southwest when winter strikes.

Made in the USA
San Bernardino, CA
26 March 2017